JAYNE FAITH

Rise of the Stone Court

First published by Andara Publishers 2020

This novel is entirely a work of fiction. The names, characters and incidents portrayed in it are the work of the author's imagination. Any resemblance to actual persons, living or dead, events or localities is entirely coincidental.

First edition

ISBN: 978-1-952156-04-5

Cover art by Deranged Doctor Design

This book was professionally typeset on Reedsy.
Find out more at reedsy.com

Contents

Chapter 1

SWEAT DRIPPED DOWN my temples as I launched into a flying lunge. At the moment I landed, my broadsword punched against my opponent's leather-bound shield. My feet barely hit the ground before he parried and swung in a counter-attack.

He shifted too much focus to the motion of his sword, letting his shield droop. Seeing the opening, I changed to a two-hand grip, pushed magic into my arms, and swung hard.

My opponent's eyes popped wide as he realized his mistake. He started to bring up his shield arm, but he was too slow. My blade collided with the side of his shoulder with a bone-cracking blow, hard enough to force his grip to release. The shield went tumbling to the ground.

I danced closer and held the blade edge of my sword an inch from the side of his neck. He went down to one knee, as if in surrender, but out of the corner of my eye I saw his hand tighten around his sword.

Lightning quick, I switched my grip again and knocked his blade aside just as he raised it for a sneak attack. The point hit the ground. I stomped my boot on the flat of his blade, holding it down. He let go.

A smattering of applause confirmed my victory. Still breathing heavily, I backed up, turned to my audience, and inclined my head in acknowledgement.

King Periclase let out a delighted chortle from his throne. "Isn't she marvelous?"

My expression remained stony. I was exhausted, heartsick, and just wanted this little exhibition to end. The Duergar King Periclase—my blood father—had granted asylum to me and my twin sister Nicole only hours ago, and though it had been very late by the time we arrived to the Duergar palace, he'd insisted on showing me off by arranging this impromptu sword match. Even the nobles he'd gathered to watch looked as if they'd prefer to retire to their rooms.

I would have refused the match if I'd thought I could get away with it, but I was at Periclase's mercy for the moment.

I nearly wilted in gratitude when Periclase rose, indicating the show was over. I reached up to slip Mortimer, my shadowsteel spellblade, into my back scabbard. My escort of half a dozen armed military men surrounded me and took me back to the quarters Nicole and I had been assigned. The rooms were dark, and I closed and locked the door quietly, trying not to wake my sister.

I went to my bedroom, but my pulse was still thumping too hard and swiftly for me to fall asleep, even though it was well past midnight. Periclase had been my last hope for safety after Marisol Lothlorien had sent assassins after me and Nicole, and his offer of protection had literally saved our lives. But the relief of it had worn off all too quickly. I paced the dark sitting room, and my mind spun around the confines of my predicament.

I was caught between three Faerie rulers. Marisol, my sworn sovereign and monarch of the New Gargoyle Stone Order, who wanted me and Nicole dead. King Periclase, who'd been vying to take control of the Order, and whose protection was sure to have a dreadful price. And Sebastian, the Spriggan king who'd loaned his soldiers to help me reclaim the stone fortress not long ago. For that favor, I'd been forced to swear an oath to Sebastian, promising he could absorb me and the Stone Order into his kingdom and submit to his rule.

It was a hell of a bind.

The sting of Marisol's attempt on my life was still fresh, but I couldn't afford to get emotional. I was safe from her for the moment, but I probably had only hours before Periclase discovered that I'd been cornered into promising the Stone Order to Sebastian. When the Duergar king found out that his two New Garg blood daughters wouldn't gain him the Stone Order as he'd so desperately desired, there was no telling how he'd react.

I didn't think he'd kill me or Nicole—a pair of princesses was too valuable to him—but my twin and I were his prisoners now, and he could certainly make our lives miserable.

"What's going to happen in the morning, Petra?" came a soft voice from the darkness of one of the bedrooms.

I stiffened and spun around, nearly reaching for my broadsword. Nicole shuffled out into the sitting room where I'd been walking circles around the furniture.

"Sorry, did I wake you up?" I whispered.

There was no one else in our quarters who might have been disturbed by our conversation, but we were in Unseelie territory, which meant there were probably at least three spies trying to listen through the walls or ceiling at any given moment. Hence the whispering.

"I couldn't sleep," she said. She went to the loveseat and sat down, pulling her feet up and hugging her knees to her chest.

"Yeah, me neither," I said. I shoved my fingers into my hair and then let my arms drop to my sides. My hands moved reflexively, pulsing into fists a few times. I'd developed some serious twitches and fidgets recently, little muscle movements that took effort to control. I chalked them up to stress. "As for what happens next, I'm sure Periclase will want to speak to us. He may want a binding promise in return for letting us hide out here."

"He thinks he can use us to take control of the Stone Order, doesn't he?" Nicole knew about my oath to Sebastian.

I forced my hands flat against my thighs. Damn twitches. "Probably. Still think you want to stay in Faerie?" I asked wryly.

She was a changeling, a Fae who'd been placed with humans in the Earthly realm as a baby. Until Periclase had kidnapped her not long ago, she'd spent her whole life believing she was human. I'd rescued her from Periclase, and she'd been living in the stone fortress, learning about Faerie and working on bringing forth her magic. It was part of the homecoming process, the induction of changelings into their true Fae heritage.

But something else had happened during the time she'd spent in Faerie, and whether or not she would admit it, it had a lot to do with her desire to embrace her Fae roots. She'd fallen in love with Maxen, Marisol's son and only child. Apparently, he'd fallen in love with her, too, and his mother had decided that wasn't acceptable. Marisol had sent an assassin to kill me, and Nicole had been next on the hit list.

"I don't think I have a choice at this point," Nicole said. "I'm fully embroiled in Faerie, whether I want to be or not."

Embroiled was a good word. Nicole and I were both so deeply entrenched in Faerie affairs, I could hardly imagine a future in the Earthly realm for either of us. Far cry from the days when I thought I'd sworn off Faerie forever. My former life of vamp hunting and sharing an apartment with Lochlyn in Boise, Idaho, seemed like a distant dream. Again, I pulled in my focus. Longings for things to be different wouldn't get me anywhere.

I planted my hands on my hips and blew out a long breath. "Maybe we can find a way to use Periclase," I said.

"How?"

"I'll have to feel it out and see what he's willing to do to gain the Stone Order. But I'll figure out something."

My confidence was somewhat forced. I wasn't a politician. I preferred settling things with my broadsword. Battles would likely come later, but for the moment I needed to summon up every shred of social finesse I could muster.

I continued to pace until dawn, and shortly after, servants came with breakfast. I tried to put on a serene face as I watched them wheel in a cart that contained plates of steaming eggs and sausage, bowls of fruit, pastries, and coffee and tea service. The spread would rival that of a luxury hotel in the Earthly realm. One might even look at the quarters and the food and guess that Nicole and I were honored guests of the Duergar. But guests wouldn't get locked into their rooms. And servants wouldn't have come with their own armed guards.

Our two female attendants from the night before, the women who'd brought us here after we'd surrendered to Periclase, arrived on the heels of our breakfast. They, too, were accompanied by a couple of Duergar soldiers bearing short swords and holding magi-zappers.

Did Periclase really think I would attack his people? If so, he should have taken my weapons. But I knew why he hadn't. He was trying to walk the line between welcoming his daughters into his palace and ensuring we didn't try anything—attack, escape, otherwise make trouble. Well, the locked doors and armed guards told me he didn't trust us for a second. That was fine. I didn't trust him either.

Ah, family.

"Your clothing will arrive shortly," said Darla, the spindly, sharp-eyed woman who'd identified herself as my attendant. "We will return to help you dress for audience with the king. Is there anything else you require in the meantime?"

The juxtaposition between her seemingly gracious offer and the guards who stood there poised to zap us was almost absurd. But I didn't laugh. I tried to channel Maxen and his decades of training in diplomacy.

"I believe I have what I need, though I appreciate your concern," I said. I turned to my sister. "Nicole?"

5

She just shook her head.

It was a relief when we were once again left alone.

I wasn't particularly in the mood to eat, but I forced down some toast and two cups of coffee with generous doses of sugar and heavy cream. Nicole made an admirable effort, eating a plate of fruit, two croissants, and then starting in on a bowl of oatmeal.

When she caught me watching her, she stopped chewing. "What?"

I shook my head. "I'm just impressed you can eat like that. My stomach's too knotted."

She swallowed and gave me a sheepish look. "I've been a ballerina since I was six years old. I was about eleven when I realized I needed to restrict my calories if I wanted to stay competitive. For years, I've dreamt of being able to eat whatever I wanted. Now I can!"

I let out a short laugh. "Hey, at least you've found an upside. Your metabolism should be able to accommodate more calories anyway, now that your magic has come in. It takes a lot of energy to generate stone armor."

"Even better," she said around a giant bite of a jam-laden croissant.

Our amusement was short-lived, as our attendants returned just as Nicole was scraping the last of the oatmeal from her bowl.

I expected Periclase's people to try to force us to wear ridiculous, frilly frocks. He'd all but threatened to use us as pawns, marrying us off to men of his choosing to increase his standing, and I figured he'd want us on proper display from the start. But instead, Darla presented me with a tight-fitting pair of black jeans, a gray camisole to go under a sheer white pullover peasant-style blouse, a black leather belt, and black calf-high Doc Martens. Darla also offered an optional moto-style leather jacket, which I declined, as it was of course pleasantly warm in Faerie.

Looking in the mirror, I couldn't find any fault with the clothes. It was an outfit very much aligned with my personal style, if I'd had the money for nicer things.

It made me suspicious. Periclase was trying to butter us up. Or something. Annoyed that he'd so perfectly hit the mark, I turned away from my reflection and went out into the sitting room.

Nicole's getup was similarly tailored to what I assumed was her taste. She emerged from her bedroom wearing a pretty floral skirt with a hem that hit just below her knees, a top and cardigan in pale green, a cropped jean jacket, and low-heeled brown booties.

We both raised our brows at each other but didn't comment.

Damelle, Nicole's attendant stepped forward with a little case in her arms. "Hair and makeup?" she offered.

I declined, and neither attendant pressed me. Nicole asked for light makeup but twisted her hair up into a loose bun herself.

I slung Mort's scabbard over my head and settled the strap diagonally across my chest, and then I leaned against the wall and eyed the attendants while Nicole got her face done.

When my sister and I declared ourselves ready, Darla folded her hands at her waist.

"His majesty will speak with you alone," my attendant said to me.

I frowned. "And Nicole?"

"She'll be introduced to our team of magic tutors," Damelle said. "His majesty is committed to continuing her homecoming with as little disruption as possible."

I traded a glance with Nicole, and in her wide eyes saw that she wasn't particularly pleased with the idea of being taken off on her own. But our attendants were herding us toward the exit, and outside two pairs of guards waited, clearly ready to escort my sister and me in different directions. I gave her a quick hug.

"You'll be fine," I whispered in her ear. "I'm sure they truly do want to help you with your magic. Keep your eyes open."

My words seemed to calm her.

Damelle guided her to the pair of guards on the right. The four of them took off down the corridor.

When I turned to my armed escort, my brows lifted in surprise as my eyes met the golden gaze of Periclase's bastard son, Jasper. My heart bumped my ribs as his golden eyes landed on me.

He gave me a subtle nod, and his lips twitched with a ghost of a smile. It couldn't be coincidence that he was there. I felt comforted, even though I knew this time there would be no dramatic escape from the Duergar palace on the back of one of Jasper's Grand Ravens.

There was an intensity in Jasper's tri-colored eyes that I'd only seen a few times before. Once when he'd kissed me until my knees turned to jelly in Melusine's barn, and the handful of occasions when he'd spoken about the looming threat of the Tuatha De Danann, the Fae gods who'd faded into the mists of legend—or so we'd all thought. As my armed escort led me away from my quarters, it struck me that carefree moments were likely long behind us.

Us.

I had indeed begun to think of Jasper and myself as "us." I could admit that I enjoyed the thought very much. But I couldn't dwell on romance.

I drew my focus inward as we strode through the hallways of the palace toward wherever King Periclase waited, working out possible strategies in my mind. It was impossible to ignore Jasper's presence at my side, though, and I sensed his attention attuned on me as well.

When we arrived at a pair of enormous oak double doors carved with significant scenes from Duergar history, I inhaled a slow, deep breath.

The guards pulled open the doors, revealing Periclase alone on his throne. Jasper, the other man, and Darla all stood back, indicating that I was to proceed to the audience alone.

I stepped through the doorway and heard the faint whine of brass hinges as the doors were closed behind me. A curious sense of battle readiness descended over me as I strode down the long gold-threaded runner that led to the throne.

I stopped before King Periclase and sank into a curtsy.

"Hello, Father," I said as I raised my eyes to the Duergar king.

I braced myself for whatever was coming next, my stomach tightening with the certainty that things were going to start happening quickly from now on.

Chapter 2

PERICLASE'S STONE FACE remained rigid, but I caught the gleam in his eyes when I addressed him as "Father." It had pleased him.

"Petra," he said, articulating my name as if it were an announcement.

He was in full regal dress, with his crown settled on his head of thick, dark hair and one of his signature capes—this one navy velvet—around his shoulders. A handsome, if stern man, he looked every bit a king, even as he leaned one elbow on the arm of his throne and shifted his weight to that side. It was a deceptive posture, meant to look casual. But if he wanted this to be a casual encounter, he'd have picked a much different setting. No, he wanted to remind me exactly who he was. Impress upon me exactly who I'd begged for help.

As I waited for him to speak, my right hand twisted in a twitchy movement. I subtly moved behind my hip, hiding the spasms until they passed.

"I trust you've found your quarters amenable and the palace services satisfactory?" he asked.

"Yes, your majesty. Your staff has been most accommodating."

"Well, it's not every day they get to wait upon two newly-found Duergar princesses," he said.

There it was. He would take every possible opportunity, it seemed, to remind me that I was not only his blood daughter but a Duergar royal. Technically, anyway. I certainly didn't consider myself a princess.

And I hadn't sworn allegiance to him. Marisol Lothlorien was still my sovereign.

I held my neutral expression as a pleased smile spread over the half of his face that wasn't encased in stone. My entire body was tensed as if readying for a duel.

"You said you wanted to discuss terms?" I prompted, wanting to move the discussion along before I became too irritated at repeatedly being called a Duergar princess.

He waved a hand. "Oh," he scoffed. "No need to rush into business so quickly."

My jaw stiffened. "Apologies, your majesty, but my situation is too dire for me to focus on pleasantries," I said. It was the truth.

He gave a slight inclination of his head, looking at me from under his brows. "There's something you wish to tell me?"

"Um, yes," I said, surprised he'd picked up on that so specifically.

I paused, taking a second to gather myself, knowing I needed to pick my words carefully from then on.

"I feel the need to confess something up front," I said, deciding it would be better not to beat around the bush. "You're . . . not going to like it."

"Oh?" His chin lifted. "Please, go on."

I shifted my weight and pressed my palms into the sides of my thighs. Here we go.

"I have a binding oath with King Sebastian that promises him the Stone Order," I said. "The Spriggan kingdom will absorb the Order. We'll be Sebastian's subjects."

Periclase went perfectly still. His stone-gray eyes tightened.

"How did this come about?" he asked, his voice so quiet it caused a cold shiver to spill over my scalp and down my spine.

Here came the really awkward part.

"When you and the Undine tried to take the stone fortress, I asked

11

King Sebastian for help. We struck a bargain, and that was the price."

Haha, yeah. Remember that, Dad? When you breached the fortress and attacked us with the fish people, and I had to fight off the Undine with the Spriggan and their ironwood shields? Good times.

His eyes narrowed, and several seconds ticked by as he considered my confession.

"A desperate move you felt you had no choice but to take, I'm sure," he said finally, stating it as a not-quite question.

I swallowed hard and nodded. I could see the gloating glint in his eye, the little spark that meant he believed he'd won, in the end, because there I was, and I'd just told him something that could very well be the key to getting what he wanted.

"But how were you able to promise the Order?" he asked. "You were not its leader."

I lifted a shoulder and let it drop. "Sebastian didn't seem bothered by that when I made the offer. I certainly wasn't going to point it out."

He gave me a shrewd look. "But he must have had something in mind."

Again, I fought the urge to fidget under his gaze.

"Well, there is a logical train of thought," I said reluctantly. I paused, but I knew Periclase had already realized what I was about to say, so it wasn't as if I could keep an ace up my sleeve by refusing to speak. "If he ousted Marisol and put me in her place, he could then call in the oath."

"Yes," he said. A smug look came over his face, and he leaned forward slightly. "But he can't very well do that with you here, protected by me, now can he?"

I gave him a chilly smile. "No, he can't."

"Very well played, Petra Maguire."

He meant it as praise, but it didn't give me warm fuzzies.

"What would you do in my place?" he asked.

I peered up at him, trying to read his expression. I knew he was angry about my oath to Sebastian, but Periclase was doing a bang-up job of keeping his cool. He seemed genuinely curious about my response.

"You have several choices," I said carefully. "You could release me and allow Sebastian to play out what we assume is his plan to get rid of Marisol and install me as Stone Order leader. But, of course, you run the risk that your assumptions about his next moves are wrong. There's also the very real possibility that Marisol will have me killed before anyone can do anything else. Then you'd be out a daughter, and Marisol would still be in charge."

He nodded. "Go on."

"You could have Marisol deposed yourself and use Nicole and me as leverage to take the Stone Order." I'd purposely not said "have Marisol killed," but we both knew that was implied. You couldn't take a kingdom or an Order and leave the leader standing. Especially not one as tenacious as Marisol Lothlorien.

Periclase lifted his index finger. "But I tried to take the fortress once before and failed."

Yep. Thanks to me and Sebastian's forces. I bit down on the inside of my cheek to kill the satisfied little smile that threatened to stretch across my lips.

"Or," I continued. "You could wait to see if Finvarra takes the High Court and then appeal to him to assume control of the Stone Order. You're Unseelie, so he'd likely grant your petition. Then there'd be no bloodshed."

"Many dependencies there, but yes, an option," he said.

I licked my dry lips. There were other possibilities, but I hoped I'd said enough to satisfy him.

His brows knitted together as if he were in deep thought. "Hm, I think I like the idea of allowing Sebastian to get rid of Marisol and put you in her place. It saves me the trouble of unseating her. Then I could have him killed and take the Spriggan realm by force," he said in a leisurely tone, with all the casualness of a man discussing the wine selection at dinner. "I would gain two new realms, the Stone Order and the Spriggan, in one fell swoop."

I swallowed back the bile that threatened to rise up my throat. This was all so calculating and unsavory, and somehow I'd put myself at the epicenter of the tension.

"But what would you want with the Spriggans?" I asked. "They'd surely rebel. And no doubt the New Gargoyles would team up with them in that effort."

"Yes, that would be a lot of trouble," he said. "Which is why that route isn't the most desirable one. But, I do believe that no matter what, Marisol Lothlorien must go."

Before, when Periclase had briefly stormed the stone fortress, I'd watched him and Marisol exchange heated, defiant words, and I'd realized there was something—some old rivalry, perhaps—between the two of them. There was history there. And apparently it was bitter enough that Periclase wanted to teach her a lesson.

It stung to admit it, but I was on his side in one thing, at least. As Periclase said, Marisol had to go. If she didn't, Nicole and I were as good as dead. It might take her time to hunt us down and finish the job, but Marisol would never give up on her dream of raising the Stone Order to full kingdomhood. And according to her prophecy, that couldn't happen unless Nicole and I died.

I would end Marisol with my own hand, if necessary, but I didn't want the New Gargoyles to lose everything. The thought of the New Gargs becoming Unseelie subjects, forced to do the bidding of a king we didn't want, made my sick to my stomach. And a future where Nicole and I would be subjugated and married off to men of Periclase's choosing was unacceptable.

Mentally, I tried to take a step back to view all possible routes. Sebastian appeared to be the lesser of the evils, if I had to choose between him, Marisol, and Periclase to rule the Stone Order. Sebastian had even agreed to allow the fortress and its ruler to stay intact as a sort of lord of the realm, though he hadn't specifically said that ruler would be Marisol. I could always find a way to beat Sebastian later, if I had to. I didn't yet know how, but he seemed the least formidable foe. I needed the Duergar king to decide to not assassinate Sebastian, at least for the time being.

"By your reasoning, it wouldn't make sense to eliminate the Spriggan king, either," I said. "It would have a similar effect of turning his people against you. You could, of course, exile him later. That would soften the blow."

"True," he said.

"May I ask something?"

"Please do."

I lifted my chin and looked him in the eyes. "Why do you care so much about assuming control of the New Gargoyles? You rule a powerful realm. One of the largest Unseelie kingdoms in population, land mass, and military size. In the big picture, you don't stand to gain all that much by taking the Stone Order. If the Duergar kingdom were smaller or weaker, the addition of the Order would make a real difference. But the kingdom you rule is already so formidable."

It wasn't completely true. Anyone who could absorb the Stone Order would automatically acquire a ready-made specialty army of some of the fiercest and most skilled fighters in Faerie. But I still had a point. The Duergar were unbeatable due to the size of their realm and population. They had the largest armed force this side of the hedge, and only a mad ruler would try to challenge it. The Duergar kingdom was as safe from foreign challenge as they came.

He took a slow breath in through his nose. "I'll let you in on something, Petra. I don't like Marisol Lothlorien much. It would greatly please me to see her fall. I tell you this now only because I presume any love you had for her fled the moment you realized she wanted you and your sister dead."

I clenched my jaw for a moment before I spoke. "It was the gravest possible betrayal," I said quietly. I let a second or two go by before I asked, "You really want to crush her out of . . . spite?" I wasn't sure I'd chosen the right word, not knowing the details of the history between Periclase and Marisol, but it seemed to work for him.

"Something like that." He gave a little laugh. "But that sounds terribly petty, so I wouldn't cite it as my primary reason. There are other reasons. I have a kinship with the New Gargoyles. After all, I'm part New Garg myself. And a wise king would never turn down the chance to strengthen his military."

"But how would you gain their loyalty?" I asked. "New Gargs are an extremely independent-minded people. Damn stubborn, too, when pushed."

"Ah, yes. Therein lies a problem. It would be difficult, dangerous even, to bring a group of resentful, angry fighters into my realm," he said, his voice low. A slow smile began to touch his lips, and intensity sparked in his eyes. "But I believe that's where you'll come in."

He squinted, and his focus seemed cast at some faraway point over my shoulder. I shifted my weight, waiting for him to say more.

"Your majesty?" I said finally, after an uncomfortable number of silent seconds had ticked by.

He looked me in the face, and for a split second, his expression was so blank I wasn't sure he even remembered who I was.

"You're dismissed," he said faintly.

He rose, stepped down the few steps to the floor, and swiftly strode toward a side door.

"But King Periclase." I took a few steps after him. "What will you do?"

"You will know soon enough," he said without turning.

16

Periclase disappeared through a curtained doorway, leaving me alone.

I stood there in the grand throne room, looking at the elaborate wall tapestries woven in the Duergar colors of forest green and soft orange. The place was cavernous and steeped with the history of a kingdom that had existed in Faerie for eons. This was just one room in a palace so large I might never completely learn my way around it. So different from the New Garg fortress, the only territory my people claimed, built in the interior of an old Earthly prison that had been transmuted into Faerie.

I couldn't be certain whether I'd nudged Periclase in a direction that would help me toward my goal or given him a suggestion that sealed my own doom. I sorely wished Maxen were there. He knew how to talk to kings. He understood the give and take, push and pull, of courtly dealings. But who the hell was I? Just a Fae mercenary who wanted to hunt vamps on the Earthly side of the hedge. A fighter who'd come to the rescue of her people by way of her sword, but who wasn't fit to be holding their fate in her palm.

I puffed my cheeks and let out a long breath. Then I turned and trudged toward the double doors, wondering how the hell I was going to navigate my way through all of this.

Chapter 3

NOW THAT NICOLE and I were safe from Marisol, Periclase was my biggest problem, that much had become clear.

When I pushed open the doors leading out of the throne room, I'd sunk so far into my thoughts I nearly shouted in surprise when I found half a dozen Duergar military men waiting for me.

Jasper stepped forward. "In light of the threat to your life, you'll be under full guard whenever you leave your quarters," he said. "By the order of the king."

I swallowed back a groan. No doubt Periclase legitimately wanted to make sure I stayed alive. But that wasn't his only purpose in keeping me under such close watch. I'd escaped the palace three times before with his soldiers hot on my heels.

Jasper's lips twitched, and I saw a flicker of amusement in his eyes. Of course he would know how a constant contingent of guards would grate on my nerves. He came to stand next to me.

"You find this funny?" I asked. I was irritated, but I kept my tone mild, almost bored.

"You're asking whether I'm amused that the Champion of the Summer Court and one of the finest blade warriors in Faerie needs an armed guard?"

I shot him a glare.

"Yes," he said. He leaned over to speak softly near my ear. "But probably not for the reasons you think. If we actually got attacked, you'd be protecting at least a couple of these men, not the other way around."

I snorted a laugh, my irritation dissolving for a moment, but my own amusement was quickly replaced with the tension I'd felt as I'd left the grand royal room.

Jasper straightened. "Give her room. No need to smother the princess," he barked at the other men. My eyes widened. I hadn't realized he was in charge of this contingent. The other men backed up a foot or two at his command. "You two, lead. You other three, rear guard."

The men shifted around with sharp, quick movements into the formation Jasper had ordered. He remained by my side.

"Now, give us *space*," he said, looking each man briefly in the eye. "The princess isn't a prisoner. Don't crowd her. Understood?"

"Yes, sir," they answered in unison. The formation left a good bubble of space for me and Jasper, enough that a very quiet conversation wouldn't be overheard. Our eyes locked for a second, and I sent him a silent thanks for making sure we had a little breathing room.

"Can we speak privately?" I whispered.

Jasper's brows rose. "A private conversation in Unseelie territory while you're under guard round the clock? Oh sure, not a problem at all."

"You don't have to respond to everything with a question, you know," I said. "A simple yes or no would do in a lot of cases."

It was his turn to chuckle.

"I'm glad you're alive, Petra Maguire," he said. "And I can't say I'm disappointed you're here."

I peered up at him, and just as I saw a flicker of heat in his tri-colored eyes, the same heat I'd glimpsed when he'd kissed me, my group of guards halted. My pulse bumped at the memory. Part of me wanted to warn him to be careful. Periclase surely wouldn't allow Jasper to lead my armed escort if the king caught wind of Jasper looking at me that way.

At the same time, it struck me with renewed force just how badly I needed an ally in the palace. Jasper had come to my aid before when I'd gotten cornered in the Duergar palace, once calling in a Great Raven to fly me to safety and another time showing me a secret passage out. I needed something different this time. I was still formulating exactly what that was, but I was surprised to find how comforted I was by his presence.

"I'm glad to be alive and to see you here," I said, allowing myself to flash him a brief, sincere smile. But any pleasant feelings quickly dissolved in the urgency of the situation. "But do you think you can manage to get us a few moments alone?"

He gave me a slight nod. "I'll work on it."

Neither Jasper nor the other guards asked me where I wanted to go but escorted me straight back to the quarters I shared with my twin. Not that I expected to get a tour of the palace or anything, but getting deposited back into my rooms, knowing there were always armed guards outside the door, made me feel that much more hemmed in.

The shared sitting room was empty. I found Nicole on her bed with a slip of paper in her hand and tears on her cheeks.

"What happened?" I asked, going to sit next to her.

She held out the note.

I will not let you waste away with the Duergar, I promise. Be brave, and we'll see each other soon.

It wasn't signed. The paper was curled, having been rolled up, and there'd been a wax seal on it. I glanced at the plain white wax and saw there was no insignia—it was just a generic seal.

"Maxen?" I whispered.

She nodded.

"Did it have any identifier?"

Her brow furrowed. That was a no. He might have deliberately left off all identifying things to protect himself and Nicole. Or the note might have been a forgery.

"You need to destroy it," I said.

She nodded again, and we moved to the main sitting room where there were a few lit logs in the fireplace. I watched as she tossed the paper in. We waited for it to burn up, and then she moved close to me to speak in my ear.

"He didn't say anything about his mother, though," she said. She'd stopped crying and wiped her cheeks. "You'd think he would have acknowledged that she tried to murder us. He knows, right?"

"Yes," I whispered. "I sent him a note through Lochlyn."

"Do you think he didn't believe it?"

"No, I think he's just being very careful." If the note actually was from Maxen.

My stomach tightened as I thought about what Maxen had been contending with as I'd been arranging asylum for myself and Nicole. His own mother had tried to murder the woman he was in love with. I couldn't imagine the series of emotions he must have been feeling. And how was he with Marisol? Had he confronted her, or was he playing dumb?

His note seemed to indicate that he intended to fight for Nicole. I didn't know what that meant, though. I couldn't say for sure what level of action he was willing to take against his mother. But things seemed to have grown serious between Maxen and Nicole in the short time they'd known each other.

Nicole and I passed a restless couple of hours. I alternately tried napping, stepping through some calisthenics, and attempting to find secret passages out of our quarters, but without any real satisfaction. When a late lunch was delivered on a linen-covered cart, I was relieved to have something else to focus on even though I wasn't hungry.

"They can't just keep us cooped up in here twenty-four seven," Nicole said as she tore a roll into smaller and smaller pieces.

"No, I don't think they will. Periclase is going to want us on display eventually."

"His new princesses," she said with sarcasm and a wrinkled nose.

"Yeah," I said with equal distaste.

My neck tensed involuntarily, making my right shoulder jump. Nicole's brows rose.

"You okay?" she asked.

I frowned, rolling my shoulder. "Just muscle spasms, I think."

Part of me was starting to regret my choice to turn to Periclase for safety, if for no other reason than the discomfort of the anxious boredom I was experiencing. But I'd had no other viable options, and Nicole and I were still alive—that was the important part.

Along with our dinner a few hours later, our two attendants came with tablets.

"There are books and movies loaded for your entertainment," Darla said and handed me a device. As she peered around the room, her beady eyes and sharp, thin nose reminding me of a curious bird who might be up to no good. She was probably looking for anything at all about the twin Duergar princesses that might provide her a bit of currency in the palace gossip mill.

"In the morning, we'll have you fitted for wardrobes," Damelle said with a smile that obviously said it was something we should be excited about. But all I could think of was Periclase dressing us up like dolls to present to potential husbands.

Neither Nicole nor I tried to make conversation with our attendants, and the two women quickly got the message and departed.

My sister settled onto a sofa with her tablet, and a minute later I heard the sounds of a movie playing. But after thoroughly scouring my own tablet for anything useful and coming up empty, I tossed it on a chair and went to a window that overlooked one of the palace gardens.

I didn't know every detail of our surroundings, but I wasn't a stranger to the Duergar palace or its grounds. The rows of vegetables below and the pastures beyond likely meant one of the larger kitchens was located somewhere under us. If I remembered correctly, the soldier training grounds were around the corner to the left, and the butchery buildings and meat-smoking houses were out of sight off to the right somewhere. Beyond were some trees and then the wall that partially surrounded the palace grounds.

My mind kept reaching for escape plans, and I had to keep reminding myself that there was nowhere to escape *to*.

Feeling restless, I paced from one window to the next, watching the activity outside. After a few passes, I realized there was a fairly steady line of birds angling in from the right and disappearing overhead. Messenger ravens.

I turned to Nicole. "Who brought you that message?"

She shrugged. "A random errand runner. Some young guy. No one I'd seen before."

"Huh."

"Why do you ask?"

I sucked in a slow breath. "I don't know. There was just something a little odd about it." I paused and moved closer so I could drop my voice to a whisper. "Odd that Maxen would risk it."

She squinted up at me. "You think someone else wrote it?"

"I don't know."

"Could I send a message back to—"

"Shh," I hissed, cutting her off. I whipped around to face one of the doorways. There'd been a soft thump and rustle.

"What?"

I placed the side of my index finger against my lips and she zipped it, her eyes going wide. I pointed toward my bedroom and then started tiptoeing that way. I silently pulled Mort from my back and drew magic. There was more rustling, and it wasn't particularly subtle. If one of the palace spies was trying to eavesdrop, he or she didn't seem to understand the importance of stealthiness.

The noise was coming from the general vicinity of an oak armoire. I stole quietly across the carpet, grasped the knob on the mirrored door, and jerked it open.

Someone was inside, and she was holding her hands over her face in a protective gesture. "Don't cut my head off," she said irritably.

I knew that voice. I lowered Mort.

"Hey, sis," I said drily as a lithe woman with long platinum blond hair stepped the rest of the way through the open panel in the back of the armoire.

She blew her bangs off her forehead and brushed dust from her sleeves.

"Bryna?" Nicole said, peeking through the doorway. Realizing it was safe to join us, she hurried into the room to stare at our half-sister.

"What's up?" Bryna said, her voice flat.

"You could have just come in the front door," I said, reaching up to re-sheath Mort on my back in a smooth, practiced motion.

Bryna rolled her eyes. "That would have been stupid."

"Why?" Nicole asked.

"Because I'm here to take her to a super-secret meeting with her boyfriend-slash-half-brother." Bryna jabbed her index finger in my direction. She tipped her head toward the armoire and then gave me an impatient look. "You coming, or what?"

Stifling a grumble, I followed my half-sister into the big oak wardrobe and the darkness of the hidden passage beyond.

Chapter 4

THE CRANKY BLOND girl bore no resemblance to me, but as I followed her through an uncomfortably tight passage, I realized Bryna and Nicole actually looked a bit alike. Bryna was a bastard daughter of Periclase. It was common knowledge that she was his blood daughter, but he'd never officially claimed her, and so her name wasn't on the Duergar royal family registry.

Nicole and I had been confused about why Periclase hadn't publicly recognized Bryna as his daughter. After all, our current situation proved just how highly he valued his blood children. But I'd recently discovered that Bryna's mother was human. Human-Fae halflings were a source of shame in Faerie because the Fae traditionally considered dalliances with humans to be extremely distasteful. It wasn't that the Fae hated humans. It was more a cultural desire to keep Fae blood and loyalties pure.

So, long story short, Periclase had apparently multiple affairs, some of which had produced offspring—including me. No wonder his wife, Queen Courtney, always looked so sour. I felt bad for her, knowing how much her husband must get around to produce the number of bastard offspring he had. Fae fertility was much lower than that of humans, so to have even produced a handful of illegitimate children, he must have had, well . . . a lot more liaisons than I really wanted to think about. Not that he was the only ruler who had affairs—it was practically expected when it came to Fae kings—but it was still a shitty thing to do to his wife.

The Duergar king certainly didn't strike me as the romantic type, but clearly there was a seductive side to him that most didn't see.

I cringed at the thought. "Blech."

"Quiet!" Bryna whisper-yelled at me over her shoulder.

I nearly made a face at the back of her head but then remembered we weren't seven years old. This wasn't new, though. In our few encounters, Bryna and I had managed to push each other's buttons multiple times. I'd even had to knock her out and carry her through a doorway once. But that was nothing. She'd nearly killed me with a wraith.

Ah, family.

"Why'd Jasper send you?" I asked. "You're obviously not too stoked to be doing this."

She glared at me again over her shoulder.

I didn't expect an answer, but I was still curious. Jasper clearly had something on her, because this wasn't the first time Bryna had reluctantly aided him.

As far as she was concerned, she and he were half-siblings. But Jasper, unlike Bryna, was an official bastard of the Duergar king. Ironically, Jasper wasn't actually Periclase's son. I was one of the only people who knew the truth, that Jasper was the offspring of the Unseelie High King Finvarra, who'd been banished from the High Court and Faerie in general ages ago. But in Oberon's recent absence, Finvarra had returned to try to claim the highest seat in the realm.

All of the family ties—legitimate and otherwise—meant for some crazy criss-crossed lines connecting people in Faerie. It was a lot to keep track of.

And since I'd been outed as a daughter of Periclase, it appeared as if I had the hots for my half-brother, which of course Bryna delighted in reminding me.

I squirmed inwardly, and a faint wash of heat spilled over my face. Only a few people were aware of the romantic interest that had sprung up between me and Jasper, but even a few felt like way too many. I couldn't reveal Jasper's secret about his true lineage but keeping it sure was inconvenient.

Bryna led me through a series of turns through the secret passages in the walls, and though I tried to keep track, after a while I was fairly sure I'd lost all sense of direction. There was a tiny bit of light from a series of tiny holes in the walls, as if someone had gone along with a hammer and punched a needle through at random intervals.

As we walked, it struck me just how urgently I needed to get in touch with Maxen. I'd been so focused on the three Fae rulers who were vying for my life one way or another, but Maxen was the crucial piece. He was the only one who might be able to help us—the only one who'd be willing, if his feelings for Nicole were stronger than his loyalty to his mother. I needed to be able to communicate with him without having my message intercepted by Duergar spies, Marisol, or anyone working for the New Garg leader.

When Bryna finally stopped at a seemingly random spot, stuck her finger in a notch in the wall, and slid a pocket panel to the side, I let out a relieved breath. It made me edgy to have to trust her, and even more so in spaces so tight I probably couldn't even draw Mort, let alone effectively wield my broadsword.

We stepped from the passage into an uncomfortably small compart-ment, with barely enough room for both of us. Bryna slid a pocket door closed behind us, blocking off the passage. That seemed to activate the next door, as there was a soft click of a latch unlocking. She jabbed her elbow into my ribs as she maneuvered around to get to the next secret door, and I let out a soft grunt.

"Seriously, you need to learn how to be quiet," she whispered irritably.

"You're never going to survive here if you can't stop gallumping around in those boots and talking and making noises every three seconds."

"Skulking in the shadows isn't my style, and I have no intention of perfecting the skill," I shot back.

Her head whipped around, and even in the semi-dark I saw her eyes flashing.

"Then you'll suffer for your stupidity," she said. She slid another panel aside, and a blessedly fresh waft of air hit my face. "Maybe your sister will be wiser. At least she knows when to shut the hell up."

I looked past her, refusing to engage further. Instead, I focused on the sudden muscle twitches in my forearms and rolled my wrists around, trying to calm the spasms. The involuntary movements were annoying, but I was starting to get concerned that an ill-timed twitch—say, in the heat of battle—could cause me some serious problems. I prided myself on the fact that I hadn't seen a doctor or healer in years, but perhaps I needed to consider it.

We stepped out into cool night air, and it felt like freedom. My eyes watered a little at the relief of it. Bryna had brought me to a broad balcony patio. It appeared to be a private area connected to living quarters.

The rooms within were dark except for soft yellow candlelight that flickered through the windows.

"I'll be back in thirty minutes," Bryna said and disappeared into the secret passage, pulling the panel closed behind her.

The secret door was impressively disguised, as the exterior of the palace appeared to be solid stonework.

The curtains slid aside a couple of feet, revealing Jasper standing behind the glass door. The latch released with a soft click, and he stepped out.

He was dressed in jeans, a plain dark t-shirt, and running shoes, and I realized I'd never seen him in anything but a military uniform. I caught a waft of soap from his skin, and the ends of his still-damp hair curled in Cs over his ears and across his forehead.

I expected his usual mild demeanor, so when he moved into me, spun me half around, and forced my back against the palace wall, I lost my breath for a moment.

His lips, warm and firm, pressed into mine. My heart jumped, and my pulse sped as warmth flooded through me. I snaked an arm up to curl around his neck, the dampness of his hair soaking into my sleeve. For the space of a breath or two, I sank into the kiss, the surprise of his strength, the smell of his freshly-washed skin, and the feel of his tongue brushing against mine.

When he finally pulled back, I was breathless.

"Welcome to the Duergar kingdom," he said, his voice low and casual.

"Thanks," I panted.

His hand began to sneak to my wrist, and his eyes gleamed mischievously. A couple of times before, he'd tried to catch me off guard with playful wrestling moves. Fortunately for me, he had a couple of tells. Sensing he was going to try for a standing arm lock, I reacted.

With movements automatic and swift from years of practice, I spun out of his grasp and drew Mort. In the space of a blink, I stood with the tip of my broadsword an inch from Jasper's Adam's apple.

"But I don't intend to stay long," I finished, grinning wickedly.

As unconcerned as if my weapon were a lollipop instead of a sword, he arched a brow and gave me a crooked grin, showing a dimple.

"That so?" He cocked his head to one side.

His arm came up in a blur, the permanent stone armor that covered one forearm knocking against Mort's blade hard enough to throw me off balance. As I shuffled to right myself, Jasper grabbed my sword arm, forcing it down. In his other hand, a glinting dagger appeared. He'd drawn it so fast, I wasn't sure exactly where it'd been sheathed.

He'd pulled us close together again, his chest against mine and the dagger poised as if to slice my neck.

"I like your style, Petra Maguire. I like the way you fight. In fact, I like damn near everything about you," he said, his eyes intense.

"Near everything?"

"Okay, everything," he relented. "You are the most sexy, fierce, intriguing woman on either side of the hedge."

My pulse sped at his words. "Then how about you take that blade away from my throat?"

He relaxed, stepped back with a chuckle, and tossed the dagger up, catching the handle without taking his eyes off me. He tucked the knife away into a sheath that had been hidden on the back of his belt. Then he held up his hands. "Truce?"

"For now," I agreed, reaching over my shoulder for Mort's scabbard. With my broadsword safely stowed, I crossed my arms and leaned against the balcony's railing, trying to ignore the little flutter-dance my heart was doing. "As much as I'd like to continue our . . . *banter*, Bryna said she'd be back in a half hour."

He flicked a hand. "She'll give us however much time we need."

I peered at him, again wondering what he held over her.

His demeanor turned serious. "You know I can't help you escape this time."

"I don't expect that. It'd be stupid of me to leave. This is the safest place for us at the moment." I pushed my fingers into my hair and then let my arms drop. "But I need to be able to communicate with Maxen. I've got to know what his intentions are."

It was Jasper's turn to peer at me. "Maxen?"

"He knows his mother tried to have me and Nicole killed," I said. "I need to know where he stands."

His mouth tightened, and he didn't respond.

I watched him for a moment and then shook my head vehemently. "I didn't mean those kinds of intentions. Not with me, anyway." I let out a laugh. "Trust me, Maxen has no interest in me. He's ass over teakettle in love with Nicole."

Jasper's brows lifted, and relief relaxed his features, though he tried to hide it as he turned and placed both hands on the railing and surveyed the view.

"Ah," he said. "You're hoping his romantic convictions will drive him to help you overthrow Marisol?"

"No. Yes. Well, not help me, exactly. I'm not really in a position to maneuver." I paused to take a deep breath and let it out. Jasper's kiss had unsettled me more than I'd realized. "I need him to help me understand what's going on in the fortress. Because I think—"

I snapped my mouth closed and scrubbed one hand down the side of my face, unsure about whether I should divulge what I suspected Periclase had in mind, his intention to let Sebastian install me at the head of the Stone Order.

"You really think Marisol is going to trust him?" Jasper asked, seemingly to mistake my hesitation for frustration. "She obviously knows his heart if she tried to have Nicole killed to remove her as an option for her son."

"That's a good point," I said. I lifted my palms and then let my arms drop. "I'm honestly not sure what to do or who to go to. All I know is that I can't just wait around and sit on my ass while everyone else acts."

"Do you trust me to help you figure it out?"

He'd moved closer, leaving one hand on the railing and turning to look down at me.

"Yeah," I said, my voice faint as I looked into his tri-colored eyes. I couldn't make out the hues in the dark of the balcony, but they were so vivid in my mind I didn't need to. "What do you have in mind?"

"I need a binding oath," he said.

I frowned. "You already bound me in a promise. Why do you need another one?"

"Because this time I need your full trust. That last one was under duress. You needed me to help you escape, and that was the only reason you were willing to do it."

I gave a little shake of my head. Jasper and his need for sincerity. He'd been trying to persuade me to work with him to mend the relationship between our two realms, seeming convinced that I was the only New Garg who could help him do it in spite of my protests. He could have called in our existing promise any time, but he'd held it because he didn't want to force me unwillingly into an alliance with him.

A tiny smile played across my lips. "You want a fresh oath, a deeper one."

He nodded. "But only if you trust me."

I went silent for a moment, tipping my gaze up to look at the Faerie sky. Stars winked here and there in between the clouds. It was the night sky of my childhood, but I'd left the fortress as soon as I could, seeking a life on the other side of the hedge in the Earthly realm. But I'd been drawn back into Faerie. Oberon's *balls*, oh how I'd been drawn back in.

"I trust you," I said.

"A blood oath, then," he said, reaching for his knife again.

I drew an involuntary breath, but not because of the weapon. A blood oath between Fae was an open-ended promise that could go either way—from me to him or him to me, to provide some equity to both parties—and could exact nearly anything short of death.

"That's extreme," I said, my voice a wisp.

"We're living in a time that calls for extreme measures," he said evenly. "But you don't have to do it, Petra."

"I know."

Trying to focus on what I knew to be true, rather than on my attraction to the mild-mannered Duergar soldier, I recalled the handful of times he'd come to my aid. The long journey to Melusine and the things we'd each discovered about our bloodlines. The battles we'd fought together.

He'd never shown himself to be anything but trustworthy, and he'd never tried to manipulate me, even when he easily could have by way of the oath that already existed between us.

With a blood oath, he could ask something momentous of me, but I could do the same of him. We had equal power in this type of promise.

"I'll do it," I said.

Chapter 5

JASPER INSERTED THE tip of the knife in between our clasped hands, the blade biting into his palm on one side and mine on the other. It wasn't much more than a nick, but I sucked in through my teeth as oath magic began to glitter the air.

He withdrew the blade, but our hands remained locked together.

"As our blood and magic mingle, we swear an unbreakable oath," we said together. "You to me and me to you."

That was it. It felt as though there should have been more to say with such a deeply binding promise, but blood oaths were very old, a relic from an earlier time in Faerie that had been much more vicious and violent, a time when bloodshed meant far more than words.

The faint sparkle of magic began to fade, and I shivered. Jasper released my hand, and I swiped my palm across my pants to wipe off the residual blood. Being a New Garg meant the minor wound would heal itself in a matter of seconds.

I blinked up at him. "What in the name of Maeve did we just do?"

He grinned. "Having regrets?"

I wasn't sure how to respond. But then I lifted my chin. "No. You may be Unseelie, but I don't believe you've ever meant me any harm."

He chuckled. "Ah, the age-old Faerie prejudice," he said, referencing the traditional distrust between Seelie and Unseelie.

"Would you be able to get a message safely to Maxen?" I asked, my earlier concerns returning to the forefront of my thoughts.

"Aye, I can." He went to the door and beckoned me to follow him inside.

We stepped into a sitting room with the usual features—sofas, a fireplace, lamps, but in this case the only sources of illumination were candles.

He caught me looking at the lit pillars and tapers around the room.

"I'm not a big fan of artificial light," he said.

He picked up a silver candelabra with three stubby candles and led me toward a doorway to another room, a small office.

"I'm guessing this is a lot nicer than the typical soldier's quarters," I said as I took in just how extensive the rooms were. It appeared he had as much space as Nicole and I shared.

He placed the candles on the desk.

"It is," he said. "I may be a bastard, but I'm on the royal registry as a son of Periclase. It does afford me some privileges."

We exchanged a glance, both of us probably thinking the same thing—that Jasper wasn't actually the offspring of the Duergar king. But that little fact was a dangerous thing to voice.

He gestured to the desk chair. "Compose a note and seal it with the black wax and stamp. I'll make sure it reaches Maxen."

I sat down and pulled a note card from the pile and then picked up a pen from a shallow box of writing utensils. My fingers spasmed, and I dropped the pen. I couldn't help a wince.

"Is it the cut?" Jasper asked.

I showed him my smooth palm. "Nah, it's healed. Just a twitch."

Jasper moved off to give me some privacy, pulling a book from a shelf and settling with it in a leather chair.

I tapped the pen against my lower lip, considering what to write.

We are safe for the moment. I need information about where things stand there. I also need to know where you stand in your own mind and in relation to the future and the leadership. What do you see as the way forward?

Damn, but it was inconvenient to be so vague.

Best, 9/10

No way in hell was I going to sign my own name, though someone savvy enough might guess that I'd authored the note. "Best, 9/10" would be enough to tell Maxen that it was me writing. It was an inside joke between us—over the history of our lives and training, I'd bested him in nine out of ten times we'd faced each other with swords on the practice fields. I loved to rub it in.

I folded the notecard a couple of times and then used Jasper's generic wax and seal, infusing it with magic that would allow the note to be read only by the intended recipient. It would self-destruct in the hands of anyone else. Most of the time, anyway. Nothing was a hundred percent foolproof. There were ways around all magical "rules."

I printed Maxen's name and realm, the New Gargoyle Stone Order, on the outside.

Jasper looked up from his book. "All done?"

"Yeah," I said but stayed where I was. "What's happened in the Summerlands? Where do things stand with Finvarra?"

Jasper's jaw tightened at my mention of his blood father.

When I'd been leading Sebastian's Spriggan soldiers to fight off Periclase and the Undine in the fortress, the rest of the New Garg forces had been in the Summerlands, trying to fend off Finvarra, the banished High King of the Unseelie. Oberon, High King of the Seelie, had ousted Finvarra generations ago. But in Oberon's absence, Finvarra had returned and was trying to take the High Court. I'd been too busy with my own problems to follow what was happening in the Summerlands. But the battle there would affect every kingdom and every Fae.

"The fighting has stopped," Jasper said. "Titania still occupies the castle, but Finvarra has her surrounded."

"Surely he's not stopping at a stalemate, though."

He shook his head. "No, he definitely isn't giving up."

Titania and Oberon were Old Ones, Fae who'd existed in Faerie for many hundreds of years, so long they were living legends. Not quite immortal and not quite gods, but the closest to either that we had. The Tuatha De Danann, the actual gods who'd created Faerie, had left the Old Ones in charge of this world when the Tuatha had faded from existence.

Finvarra wasn't an Old One, but he was old and powerful. Long before I was born, he'd united the wild and warring Unseelie realms and briefly taken the High Court. Under his influence, the Unseelie kingdoms had become more civilized and organized, feats that many had thought impossible. The Duergar were a good example of the progress—Periclase's kingdom was almost indistinguishable from Seelie kingdoms in terms of being modern, refined, and fully engaged in courtly life and inter-realm politics. But many of the Unseelie realms had preserved some of the more primitive aspects of their cultures. A few were still so rooted in their former wild ways, it was all but impossible to engage them in modern negotiations and inter-kingdom relationships.

But generally speaking, the Unseelie kingdoms all had one thing in common: they viewed Finvarra as their savior, the one who had empowered them in a world dominated by the Seelie's Summer Court. The one who might someday take the High Court again.

Oberon had disappeared from the Summerlands only weeks ago, but Finvarra had wasted little time trying to seize the Seelie High King's place. Oberon's queen, Titania, had been left alone to defend the High Court.

"Did Melusine come to Titania's aid?" I asked.

"I've not heard of Melusine's presence in the Summerlands," Jasper said.

Jasper and I had had the rare and dubious honor of meeting Melusine, a Fae-witch who possessed both Fae and human magic. We'd sought

Melusine to divine Nicole's true parentage in an attempt to settle a dispute between the Stone Order and the King Periclase, who'd been claiming that Nicole was his daughter and demanding she swear to the Duergar. Melusine was the only one in Faerie with the magical talent to tell a Fae's specific blood parents. Jasper and I had both learned our true lineages from Melusine, too.

"Marisol told me that Melusine and Titania were tight when they were young, but their friendship ended over some disagreement."

"Apparently the threat to the Summerlands wasn't enough to draw Melusine out. Not yet, anyway. Titania is working on trying to bring in other allies."

"You think Titania can hold off Finvarra for a while longer?" I asked.

He shrugged. "Your guess is as good as mine. Either way, we need Oberon back."

I let out a heavy sigh. "Yeah."

Jasper's golden eyes sparked in the candlelight. "Would you be up for a journey to find him?" he asked softly.

My brows shot up. "You know where Oberon is?" My voice had dropped to a whisper.

"I may know something."

I realized I was breathing quicker through parted lips, and my pulse had sped up. Many in Faerie believed the High Court would fall to Finvarra, even with Titania and a few other Old Ones defending it. Oberon had more allies than his long-time, querulous queen.

"I can't leave, though," I said, keeping my voice at the barest murmur for fear of spies in the walls.

"You could leave for short intervals, helping me with the search, and then return."

"Great Ravens?"

He nodded. Jasper was a Grand Raven Master, one of a very select organization of Fae who could commune with the giant black birds.

He'd enlisted Great Ravens to save my ass and transport me around Faerie on a few occasions. And apparently, he'd managed to keep his skill secret from King Periclase.

A little bolt of adrenaline spilled into my veins as I relished the thought of a jail break—even a temporary one—and setting off with a vital purpose. It didn't hurt that Jasper would be my companion. Didn't hurt one bit.

"Count me in," I said.

A zing of energy shot diagonally across my back as Mort also seemed to perk up at the idea of a quest.

In spite of the seriousness of the errand, a slow grin spread over Jasper's face. I felt my own expression echoing his.

He came to me and took my face between his hands. "Your sense of adventure is part of your beauty, Petra Maguire."

He kissed me, but we didn't have a chance to take things any further. Bryna arrived a moment later to take me back to my own quarters.

It wasn't until I was following my half-sister through the hidden corridors that some of the rush of being with Jasper began to wear off and other thoughts crept in. I'd entered into a blood oath with the son of the Unseelie High King. But that wasn't even what worried me the most. My heart and emotions seemed to be slipping away from me, and I wasn't accustomed to that.

I lay awake that night, trying to sort out my feelings into neat compartments and telling myself that my attraction to Jasper didn't have to mean anything world-shattering, that it was probably just a passing thing. He was Unseelie, and that was inconvenient—or it should have been. But it'd never bothered me much. What else . . . He seemed to have a lot of secrets. Again, that didn't dissuade me in the least. I tried to think of more reasons to discredit him. But for every argument against Jasper that I could come up with, something much stronger in his favor muscled in. And underlying all of my attempts at applying logic to the situation were warmth, emotions, and attraction that I couldn't deny.

When the pale light of dawn finally crept through the curtains, I'd not managed to make much progress in talking myself out of Jasper Glasgow.

Chapter 6

I'D PASSED A restless night with Jasper in my thoughts, and perhaps because he was at the front of mind, I'd half expected him to summon me to fly off to the far reaches of Faerie in search of Oberon. But it wasn't Jasper who sent for me. It was King Periclase.

Nicole and I had just finished breakfast when our two lady attendants showed up.

Darla, with her sharp elbows and sharper gaze, bustled over to me with a stack of folded clothing in her arms.

"His majesty wishes for you to be ready for royal audience within the hour," she said, clearly flustered at having so little time to prepare me.

"Audience with whom?" I asked.

"The king wouldn't make one such as me privy to those details," she said, already focused on shooing me into my bedroom.

I suspected she had more information but just didn't want to give it to me. Information was currency in Unseelie kingdoms, and it was second-nature to many Unseelie Fae to covet even the smallest tidbits.

A glance over my shoulder revealed Nicole being ushered into her own room by her attendant, Damelle, who pushed a large garment bag that hung from a rolling wardrobe bar. Nicole's eyes met mine, and I shrugged. It wasn't like we could refuse.

I peered at Darla's bundle, and my curiosity turned to suspicion when I spotted a lacy edge of a garment.

My attendant did indeed intend to put me into a dress. It wasn't so bad, though—no stays in the bodice or hoops in the skirt—and the low-heeled brown leather ankle boots were actually pretty cool. The frock had bell sleeves that flared at my elbows but left my hands unencumbered, and the gold tone of the fabric accentuated the tawny flecks in my eyes and deepened the light tan of my skin. The skirt fell straight from my hips, and the lace I'd seen edged the hem, neckline, and sleeves.

Darla wrestled my hair into an attractive topknot and thankfully didn't try to put makeup on me. She didn't even say anything when I slung Mort's scabbard over my head and pulled the strap into place across my chest.

When I walked out into the living room and found Nicole waiting, I saw just how much worse I could have fared. My twin stood in a turquoise dress with a big bell-shaped skirt made up of several cascading layers of fabric. The thing was hideous, and it looked like it weighed about fifty pounds.

Nicole pulled a face when she saw me. She pinched the fabric of her skirt between her thumb and forefinger, lifting it as if it were the tail of a dead rat. Her nose wrinkled, and one side of her mouth turned down in distaste. I couldn't help snorting a laugh, which I covered with a cough when Darla turned a sharp look in my direction.

"I have a feeling we're not going to the same party," Nicole said flatly.

"Your armed escort is waiting," Darla said, herding me toward the door. Damelle was doing the same with Nicole.

Outside our quarters, two groups of guards waited. Jasper was once again heading my escort. His golden eyes lingered on mine for a bit longer than was probably wise. My mouth twitched as I resisted the smile trying to tug at my lips.

Realizing that Nicole and I were being taken in different directions, my mood sobered considerably.

"Where are they taking her?" I asked Jasper.

"She's attending a brunch reception of nobles, my lady," he said, his voice tightening slightly with subtle disapproval.

Reception of nobles? My stomach tightened. She was being presented to potential suitors. Men of Periclase's choosing. Well, the Duergar king wasn't wasting any time. At this rate, he seemed to be planning to have Nicole married off by the next week. Not that I had any intention of allowing that.

I couldn't help wondering what my blood father intended for me.

"If you please, we will take you to your royal audience," Jasper said formally.

I peered at him, trying to read in his expression what might be awaiting me. I didn't see the hint of disapproval he'd conveyed about where Nicole was headed, so chances were good that I wasn't going to be put on display at one of Periclase's dog-and-pony shows. But there was a shadow in Jasper's gaze.

We strode through hallways populated by Duergar nobles and staff going about their daily business. Many of them side-eyed me, or stared outright, as I passed. Maybe they were thinking about how I'd nearly killed Darion, brother of their king, as I'd bested him in the Battle of Champion. Or maybe they were noticing how trapped I appeared. Eventually we ended up in smaller corridors that were richly decorated with thick carpets, textured walls, and luxurious gold fixtures. There, we only occasionally encountered a palace employee or well-dressed official of the palace.

The men took me to an unmarked, gilded door. Jasper opened it for me and gave me a slight nod as I passed him to go in.

I paused just beyond the doorway, and Jasper came in.

"I present the princess Petra Maguire," he said in a voice loud enough to carry to the people seated on the sofas at the far end of the room.

Heads turned, and my breath stilled as I recognized King Sebastian sitting near Periclase. The Spriggan ruler had brought a contingent of his own officials who were all in formal dress and sporting the royal purple and medium brown colors of their kingdom.

Realizing that all eyes were expectantly trained on me, I bent into a deep curtsy. Jasper turned and retreated, and I heard the door close. I straightened, leveled my shoulders and chin, and strode toward the group that awaited me.

Stopping at the edge of the furniture arrangement, I curtsied again.

"Your majesties," I said. I tried not to flick my gaze around too rapidly.

It appeared to be a typical gathering of officials, except for one person. There was a man in simple gray riding pants and a plain, loose white shirt, weaponless and well apart from the group. His hands were clasped in front of him, and he stood stock still. Only his eyes moved, and for a second or two they were unblinkingly rested on me.

"Ah, Princess Petra," Periclase said, rising and greeting me with a broad smile. "So pleased you could join us."

As if I'd had any other option.

"You know King Sebastian," he said.

"Yes," I said. "We've become recently acquainted."

I tried not to smirk at my own understatement. Sebastian and I had defeated Periclase and the Undine in the Stone Order. It would be uncouth to refer to those events, but everyone in the room had to be thinking about the recent battle. I wondered how many also knew of the oath I'd had to swear to Sebastian to secure his aid.

Sebastian was dressed in a business suit, differentiating him from the other Fae in the room who wore more traditional courtly dress. But he did sport the Spriggan crown nestled atop his fashionably spiked hair.

He rose. "I must extend my congratulations on the recent revelation of your royal parentage."

Sebastian said the words smoothly in that carefully cultured voice of his, but his eyes darted warily to Periclase before meeting my gaze again. The Spriggan king was on edge. As well he should be. For all his posturing, he was the ruler of a relatively small kingdom, one that couldn't realistically stand up to the Duergar alone. Sebastian and I had defeated Periclase at the stone fortress only because we hadn't faced the full force of the Duergar military at the time.

I inclined my head, acknowledging Sebastian's congratulations, but didn't bother trying to fake any happiness over the fact that Periclase was my blood father.

For a moment I could almost swear I felt the tingle of the oath that bound me to King Sebastian. There was no actual physical sensation—that would come only when it was time to make good on the promise—but the oath still seemed to hang in the air like a live wire.

When I looked up, my attention slipped back to the man at the wall, the one who didn't seem to be part of either the Spriggan party or the contingent of Periclase's people. The stranger would have been quite ordinary-looking, except for his long, sheet-white hair that hung straight and thick to his elbows. It was an odd contrast to his tanned face, which didn't appear much older than my own. His features told me almost nothing about his possible bloodlines. If anything, he looked more human than Fae, just by the sheer absence of any distinct Fae features, but I could sense very strong Faerie magic in him.

Periclase swept a hand through the air in a graceful arc, indicating the seat next to his was meant for me.

I sat down on the ornate chair, taking a moment to smooth my skirt over my legs. I had to perch on the edge of the seat so as not to rest uncomfortably against the scabbard on my back.

My blood father looked pointedly around the group, setting off a shuffle of movement. Everyone except me and the two kings quietly rose and exited the room. The man at the back remained where he was, and Periclase appeared to have no problem with the stranger staying.

"Now." Periclase crossed one ankle over the other knee and leaned back. "We are alone. We can just be ourselves, yes?"

Sebastian didn't even bother to try to fake a smile. He sat rigidly, one hand on each thigh, his nostrils slightly flared. His entire demeanor said he knew he was in deep shit. I figured that meant things weren't much better for me.

I found myself holding my breath as I waited for Periclase to drop the hammer.

"I believe the three of us agree that we'd be best served by removing Marisol Lothlorien from her position in the Stone Order," my blood father said.

"Yes, your majesty," I said.

I didn't feel remiss in agreeing with him because he hadn't said anything about murdering her. Yet.

"As we know," Periclase continued. "That sets us up to place Petra as the leader of the Stone Order."

I shifted on my seat. "That assumes the New Gargs would accept me."

"No," he said sharply. "That's irrelevant." He looked pointedly at Sebastian.

"Uh, yes," King Sebastian said. He cleared his throat. "Irrelevant."

"And why is that?" I prompted, my brows raised. Sebastian's reluctance to continue speaking was almost painful to watch.

"Because you're going to take the Stone Fortress high seat by force," the Spriggan king finally said.

I looked back and forth between them. "Me? What do you mean exactly?"

"You're going to stage a coup," Periclase said. "You'll defeat Marisol and then assume her place."

"You want me to murder her?"

Periclase's lips pursed in a little twist of distaste. "Well, yes, if you must put it that way. Disposing of the current leader is typically the best way to carry out a coup."

I thought I'd been prepared for the idea of Marisol's death. She was too ruthless, and given the chance, she'd murder me and Nicole in a heartbeat to ensure her goal of a Stone Court. But the thought of killing her myself sent a sharp dart of discomfort through my chest.

"As her conqueror, you'll be in the position of installing yourself as leader," Sebastian said. "And then, we'll, ah . . . well, you know."

"Carry out the oath so the Stone Order falls under Spriggan rule," I finished flatly.

I was going to be the biggest pawn in Faerie. My stomach clenched into a hard little stone.

Periclase leaned back with a satisfied gleam in his eyes. Sebastian looked like he wanted to vomit. I didn't blame him. The minute the Stone Order fell under his rule, Periclase would no doubt make his move to take the Spriggan kingdom. Silence crept into the room like a fog that settled over the three of us.

"Aside from the oath I swore to King Sebastian, which itself has certain dependencies, you can't force me to do any of the rest. What if I refuse to go along?" I asked.

Periclase leaned forward, propping his elbows on his knees and drilling me with his eyes.

"If you don't want to do it the easy way, we'll have to do it the hard way," he said softly. "If you refuse to cooperate, we could simply murder the Lothloriens and everyone who has served under Marisol. *All* of her most loyal supporters."

He said the last slowly and then paused to let it sink in.

Oliver. He was talking about my father. The one I'd grown up with. The one who'd raised me, trained me, and protected me.

"You could try," I said. My voice held steady, but inside I was shaking with anger. "But if you think my father would fall so easily, you don't know him at all."

Periclase peered at me for a long moment and then his eyes tightened. Without a word, he rose and walked to a side door to my left. I'd assumed it led to a food prep area or a closet. He rapped sharply on it twice with the knuckle of his index finger. All the while, he kept his gaze on me.

The door latch clicked, and Periclase stepped back as the door swung inward.

A hunched figure with a bloodied face, thanks to a large cut across the scalp, stumbled out. A guard followed and roughly grabbed the arm of the bloody man, whose own hands were cuffed behind his back.

When the prisoner straightened, my blood froze.

It was Oliver.

I opened my mouth to cry out, but no sound came.

He wasn't just bleeding from his head. One of his eye sockets was a gory mess. Horror rushed through me like a nauseating storm.

Oliver caught sight of me and made a sound that was half pain and half despair.

"Petra, don't swear any oaths to—" he choked out.

But before he could finish, I was on my feet, my hand whipping back for Mort. I only managed to draw my broadsword before something thick and viscous swirled around me. Within a fraction of a second, I felt encased in an invisible blob of rubber. It plugged my open mouth and blocked my nostrils. The tingle of strong magic pressed into my skin, turning into an uncomfortable prickle as it tightened around me.

Unable to pull air into my lungs, my heart bucked and raced. I couldn't turn my head, but my eyes flicked to Periclase. He watched with his arms folded, in a stance of cool detachment.

The seconds ticked by, each one more agonizing as the air in my lungs expired, and as I ran out of breath, time seemed to elongate.

My temples pounded, and black spots danced in my eyes.

When I reached the verge of passing out, the encasement suddenly vanished. I collapsed forward, landing hard on my kneecaps and the heels of my hands. My head hung as I sucked air.

Mort had clattered to the floor. I stretched out a hand for the hilt, but the broadsword slid away, stopping a few feet out of reach.

Knowing that going after my sword would only bring more torture, I pushed back to sit on my heels, still panting.

Oliver was gone, apparently taken back through the side door in the few seconds that I'd been sucking wind. Periclase still stood impassive, and Sebastian hadn't moved from his spot on the sofa, though his brow was visibly slicked with sweat.

The man who'd been standing quietly at the wall had moved forward a few feet. Magic glittered around his outstretched hand. The sparkles thinned into a filament that stretched from him to Mort. He flicked his hand, and my broadsword clattered a few more inches farther away, a metal puppet on a string. My jaw muscles clamped as my entire body tightened with anger. I couldn't stand it when someone else touched my spellblade without permission.

I slowly reached for the skirt of my dress, shifting the fabric so I wouldn't trip on it as I rose to my feet.

My fingers tightened into fists at my sides, and my chest rose and fell rapidly, now from anger rather than breathlessness.

"What do you say now, Princess?" Periclase asked.

I glared murder at him and bit the inside of my cheek until I tasted blood, the pain the only thing that kept my lips from trembling. The image of Oliver's bent, bloody head was flashing through my mind's eye so vividly it was almost as if he still stood in the room with us.

My gaze fell on the door through which they'd presumably removed my father, and my chest clenched.

"I'll do as you wish," I said finally, the words grating up my throat and seeming to scrape against my entire being.

My blood father and I locked eyes for several long seconds, and then the corners of his lips widened slightly in acknowledgement.

I glanced at my broadsword and then at Periclase, and he gave a small nod. He was allowing me to keep Mort, which in some ways felt worse than if he'd confiscated my prized weapon. The Duergar king was using it to send me a message, which was that he didn't consider me and my sword a serious threat.

I moved to retrieve my weapon. Even with Mort strapped to my back, I'd never felt so powerless in my life.

"Wonderful," Periclase said, spreading his arms in a gesture that seemed to say, *See that wasn't so hard, was it?*

I opened my mouth, ready to tell him that I would go along only if he promised not to hurt Oliver any more. But then I pressed my lips together and swallowed hard. My father had begun to say something to me, he'd started to warn me not to swear any oaths, but I'd cut him off before he could finish the sentence.

Periclase would surely want a binding oath for the promise I'd nearly asked for. But Oliver was right. I shouldn't do it. I couldn't put myself in that position.

With an aching heart, I ground my teeth to keep myself from begging for Oliver's safety. He wouldn't want me to do such a thing.

King Periclase strode back to the sofas and resumed his position. He gave me an expectant look and a slight lift of his brows.

Realizing he was waiting for me to rejoin him and the Spriggan king, I trudged over to the seating area, sat, and braced myself for whatever was next.

Chapter 7

I TRIED TO imagine how Periclase might have captured Oliver and kept circling back to his greatest weakness in the world: his love for me. The Duergar king must have faked a message from me or otherwise invoked my name to draw Oliver out. Otherwise, he never would have been stupid enough to fall prey to a trap. With those thoughts came a sickening mix of guilt, fear, and anger that I had to swallow back as I tried to focus on Periclase.

The Duergar king didn't have a whole lot more to say to me. I think he mostly just wanted to dive home how completely I was at his mercy.

"The coup will happen as quickly as possible," Periclase said. "We will ensure that. We don't want to harm anyone who doesn't deserve it, and we certainly don't want to kill innocents. We only want to oust Marisol Lothlorien. Of course, our soldiers will know they have the option of taking things in a much uglier direction, if you decide not to cooperate fully. We wouldn't want that, would we?"

"No," I said tightly. "We wouldn't."

"So, all you need to do now is wait until King Sebastian and I have things in place. It shouldn't be long. In the meantime, I have suitors in mind for you."

I squinted at him, trying to process the sudden change in subjects.

"Suitors?"

"You and your sister are quite old for unmarried Fae princesses. We'll want to remedy that very soon."

Annoyance sliced through me. I wanted to tell Periclase exactly where he could shove his suitors and then slice him through with Mort for good measure. My right arm spasmed, the unexpected twitch distracting me as my shoulder jumped and my elbow tried to lock out at my side. I tried to mask the movement by pulling both hands into my lap and tightly lacing my fingers.

I was suddenly once again aware of the man with the long white hair standing at the back wall, but a glance at him showed only an impassive face and eyes that seemed focused on a point at the far wall, as if he couldn't be more disinterested in the discussion.

I turned my attention to Sebastian. He looked downright miserable. He'd realized by now that the binding promise he had from me had utterly backfired. If only I could get the Spriggan king alone for a moment, I was fairly sure I could convince him to let me out of the oath. But Periclase wouldn't sit back and allow that.

My chest ached and my head hurt as I tried to think of other ways to maneuver. What a mess. A fricking mess of Fae politics and greed. Perhaps the Tuatha de Danann had the right idea in their plan to return to Faerie to punish us for straying from their ideals.

The impending threat of the Fae gods turned my thoughts to our missing High King, and Jasper's proposal that we go looking for Oberon. But after what'd transpired the last half hour, I wasn't sure I could do that. I had to think about Oliver and what I'd have to do to keep Periclase from dishing out any more harm to the only real father I'd ever known.

I squeezed my eyes closed for the briefest of seconds, trying to block out the mental image of Oliver's mangled eye socket. My stomach knotted, and bile threatened to rise up my throat.

"Do you have a headache, Princess?" Periclase asked, all sincere concern.

Yeah, asshole. I had the king of all headaches, and my blood father was holding the hammer that pounded against my temples.

I smoothed my expression. "No, just taking in everything that must be done."

There was no point in acting openly snide to Periclase's face. But I would kill him. After Oliver was out of danger, I would find a way.

"Perhaps you could use some rest," he said.

He rose, and Sebastian did the same. I stood, my face tight with the effort of holding back the tide of hatred, and then stiffly about-faced and headed toward the main doors. Courtly protocol called for me to wait for Periclase to dismiss me and then give him a deep curtsy, but I just didn't give a damn about etiquette.

At the door, I looked over my shoulder. My gaze was drawn past the kings to the white-haired man. As I watched, he lifted a palm, curled his fingers and moved them as if doing some rapid sign language, and then the air around him seemed to darken.

My mouth fell open as shadows crept from nowhere to surround him. I squinted as if peering into a dark wood, trying to make out a creature who stood in the protection of a thick forest, where little light was able to penetrate. The shadows darkened until I couldn't see the man at all, and then the darkness began to dissipate like smoke.

The white-haired man was gone.

It all happened within a second or two, and then guards were surrounding me. Before, the soldiers had seemed protective and vigilant. Now, they all carried magi-zappers with little green lights indicating they were fully charged and ready to jolt me into oblivion if I misbehaved.

Jasper was there, also holding one of the magical stun guns. He was the only one who held it casually at his side instead of in a more brandishing grip. The sorrow in his golden eyes spoke to me silently. He knew what had happened to my father—my *real* father—and what I'd just seen. I had to look away.

We marched silently through the palace to my quarters. Jasper stayed at my side. His presence gave me some small reassurance but did nothing to lift the weight on my heart. At my door, his eyes lingered on mine, but I knew he wasn't in a position to say anything of consequence to me while we were surrounded by Periclase's men.

Once I confirmed that Nicole was still away and I was alone, I carefully took off my scabbard and propped Mort against the wall. Then I went to my bedroom and the window there and gripped the decorative bars installed across it, squeezing so hard my fists soon trembled and ached. Unfamiliar, high-pitched sounds of misery escaped from my clenched teeth as a few hot tears leaked from my closed eyelids.

I allowed myself five minutes to stand there and try to punish the metal bars for what Periclase had done to my father. Then I loosened my fingers, stepped back, wiped my face, and drew a deep breath.

When Nicole returned, I didn't tell her about Oliver. I reasoned that I was protecting her from something awful, but the truth was, I couldn't handle describing it out loud.

She recounted the series of forced "introductions" she'd been subjected to, a parade of seven men who were apparently in the running for her hand in marriage.

"They were all awful," she said, nearly gagging. "Every one of them. The only one who wasn't abhorrent I'm pretty sure isn't into women."

"Maybe you should choose him, then," I said, deadpan.

She stared at me, horrified, and then burst out laughing. "Actually, he probably is the best choice, if I had to pick one. Which I refuse to do." The smile quickly faded from her face. "Where did they take you?"

"To Periclase," I said. I looked away. "He wanted to talk business."

"No introductions?"

"Not yet, but he indicated it's just a matter of time."

"You haven't heard from Maxen, have you?" Nicole asked, dropping her voice to a whisper.

I shook my head. "I'm hoping to soon, though."

She'd removed the most egregiously poofy parts of her dress's skirts so she could sit cross-legged on one of the loveseats while we talked. She looked down at her hands, but not before I saw the worry in her eyes.

"There was gossip in the stone fortress," she said quietly. "Apparently some people believed he was only paying attention to me because his mother told him to."

I winced. I'd been one of those people who'd suspected Maxen's interest in Nicole wasn't completely genuine, though I'd never said so to anyone else.

"But you never thought so?" I asked, carefully neutral.

She tilted her head, her gaze slanting up at an angle. "Maybe the first couple of times he came to speak with me. I could tell that he was there as the son of the monarch, not as a guy who wanted to get to know me. But after that . . ."

Her cheeks pinked, and she looked at me and then down at her hands again.

"When did you find out that Maxen doesn't have much freedom as far as romantic relationships go?" I asked.

"Pretty early on." She gave a small sigh. "We talked about that, and it was . . . yeah. Early on."

My brows lifted the tiniest bit. I was beginning to get the idea that things had heated up between Nicole and Maxen much more and much faster than I'd suspected.

We were interrupted from further conversation by the arrival of our attendants. The two ladies insisted on helping us out of our nice clothes, and Darla tsked over the faint smudges of dirt on the front of my dress from when I'd fallen to the floor. There was also a sizeable rip on the hem that left a piece of lace dangling.

Soon after our attendants departed, dinner service came. I stifled a sigh, wondering if we were going to be confined to our quarters forever. After what'd happened earlier that day, the answer was obviously yes. The memory of Bryna sneaking into our rooms surfaced in my mind. I knew where at least one secret exit was. But surely Periclase wouldn't have left such an easy means for us to escape in a palace that everyone knew was riddled with secret passages. I mentally smacked myself for not asking Bryna how she'd managed to get me out and back in undetected. Bribing guards? Likely.

I closed my eyes and pressed my fingers into my brow.

"What happened?" Nicole asked.

I looked up at my twin. "What do you mean?"

"I can tell something bad happened today. While you were with Periclase. Something worse than what he did with me."

I bit my lip for a second. "It wasn't good," I admitted finally.

"You can't tell me?"

I took the out she'd given me and shook my head. "I can't. I'll just say that he's pulled in Sebastian."

"Oh, the oath you have with the Spriggan king is already coming into play."

"Yep," I said, my voice flat.

One side of her mouth turned down. Her expression mirrored mine, but she didn't probe for more information.

I forced down some of the venison stew, crusty rolls, and roasted root vegetables we'd been served. The food was top-notch, but it was hard to focus on things as mundane as meals. After eating as much as I could manage to get into my knotted stomach, I went to my suite, showered, and changed into my usual jeans and t-shirt. Then I sprawled on my bed, ignoring the movie that played on the tablet next to me.

After about a half hour, I slid off the bed, tiptoed to the wardrobe with the secret panel in the back, and opened the door. Trying to remember how the mechanism had worked, I slid my fingers around the inner seams between pieces of wood. I methodically pressed and tapped along the surface. When one edge of the panel popped inward and it swung on a hinge, a little bolt of triumph burst through me.

But when I fully opened the secret door, I found the bulk of a Duergar soldier filling the space beyond. He ducked and peered at me with dark eyes.

"Back inside," he said sternly. "For your own safety, your highness."

My mouth twisted in disappointment and irritation, and I pushed the panel back into place and shut the wardrobe.

Standing there with my hands on my hips, I cursed long and colorfully under my breath. Irritation sent me stomping around in a circle. After about a minute of pacing and swearing, I started to calm down. I had to hand it to Bryna. She was crafty when it came to getting around the palace.

There was a rustling within the wardrobe. With an exasperated exhalation, I strode forward and jerked the door open.

"I heard you the first time, there's no need—" My words broke off mid-chastising when I realized who was there.

Jasper pressed the side of his index finger to his lips, silently shushing me. I blinked at him, watching with open-mouthed surprise as he stepped into my bedroom.

Chapter 8

I LEANED TO the side and looked past Jasper. "How'd you get rid of the other guy?" I asked.

"Shift change," he whispered and winked.

"Nice," I said approvingly. "Hey, if you're here about us going off to hunt down Oberon—"

He swiftly covered the few feet between us, and suddenly his arms were around me and my face was in his chest.

"I'm so sorry," he said.

I stiffened and tried to push away, but he tightened his embrace, not allowing my hands to work in between us.

"I'll be okay," I said, still moving, trying to loosen his hold.

His scent—a mix of the metal and leather of his light armor, the still-lingering smell of soap, and that indescribably masculine *Jasper* scent—filled my nose, and I started to weaken. I squeezed my eyes closed and tried to fortify my emotions.

He kept his arms around me, one hand moving up to the back of my head and lightly stroking my hair.

I thought I'd let out enough of the pain and anger before, when I'd gripped the window bars until my arms ached, but apparently I hadn't.

Wordlessly, I shook my head against his chest. My eyes began to tear, and I squeezed my lids closed again. I wasn't going to cry. I would let him comfort me for a moment, but I was not going to cry.

When the tightness in my chest had loosened enough that I thought I could speak without my voice hitching or cracking, I tipped my head up.

I intended to tell Jasper that I planned to kill Periclase the first chance I got. But before I could utter a word, Jasper tipped his head down, and his lips found mine.

For a split second, I thought about resisting. We didn't have time for the luxury of this. But then I gave in. I kissed him back, reaching up to circle one arm around his neck. The kiss deepened, the pressure of my lips against his increasing. Heat began to well up inside me, nudging aside some of my grief.

He broke away from me, his chest rising and falling rapidly. The only light in the room came from the tablet on the end of the bed still playing some movie, but even with only that, I could see the hot desire in his golden eyes.

He came for me again, bending his knees slightly so he could circle his arms around my waist and lift me up. Our lips crushed together with urgent passion, and I wrapped my legs around him. My entire body pulsed with heat.

He turned and found the bed and tossed me backward onto it with a gesture that was nearly rough-edged. The surprise of it further fueled my desire.

He shed his light armor in what seemed like a second flat, and pulled my shirt up and over my head swiftly enough to rip fabric. I stripped off my bra, and his clothes continued to fly off.

I pushed him away so I could go to shut and lock the bedroom door, and when I returned to the bed, he was wearing next to nothing, the flickering light of the tablet highlighting the muscled contours of his body. A moment later we were tangled together, and I lost myself in our hunger for each other.

And for a while, the sadness and pain of the day receded.

Later, with his arm around me and my head on his chest, I listened to the sound of his breath. I could tell he was still awake, but we both seemed content to keep company in silence.

Eventually I shifted to my side and propped my head on my hand.

"So, was that the intention of your visit, or did you come here for other reasons?" I lightly traced a finger down the center of his chest, a tiny smile playing across my mouth.

He tilted his head so he could peer at me fully, and his smile echoed mine. He tucked a stray strand of my hair behind my ear.

"I was going to see if I could steal you away on an Oberon hunt in the wee hours of the morning," he said, his faint brogue surfacing a bit more strongly than usual. He raised his head to look past me before resettling on the pillow. "Right about now, actually."

I arched a brow. "That was a fine way to pass the time in between, I suppose."

"You suppose?"

"Okay, it was more than fine. Much more."

He started to reach for me but then caught himself. "As much as I'd like to stay here, we really should be off."

I sat up and ran a hand over my tangled hair. "I don't think I can."

He'd swung his legs over the side of the bed and started to reach for his clothes, but then he paused and twisted to look at me.

"I know it's a risk, but I can get you out and back in without worry," he said.

I wasn't sure how he could possibly guarantee that. If we were really going to venture out into the far reaches of Faerie, a hundred different things could come up and delay us or keep us from returning at all. I couldn't risk that. Not with Oliver in Periclase's hands. If I left and didn't return, there was no telling what would happen to my father.

"Jasper, I can't," I said. "What if I didn't make it back? Periclase would torture Oliver. Maybe even kill him to teach me a lesson."

"Periclase won't kill him. I know after what you saw it's difficult to take my word for it, but I honestly don't believe he would go that far."

Under the sheet, I pulled my knees up to my chest and wrapped my arms around my shins.

"After what I saw, I disagree," I said quietly. "And even if you're right, I can't take the chance that my actions will cause more pain for my father."

Some part of me knew that my remaining in the palace was no guarantee of protection for Oliver, but all the same, I couldn't stand the thought of leaving.

A couple of seconds of silence ticked by.

"I understand," Jasper finally said. He wasn't angry or resentful, just sad.

He slowly rose and dressed, and I got up and searched for my own discarded clothing. I followed him to the wardrobe, where he bent and planted his lips on mine for a long, sweet moment. Then he slipped through the false back and was gone.

I stood there as an uncomfortable tugging sensation took root in the center of my chest. I hated inaction. Despised waiting. Yet that was what I'd chosen. I felt pulled in two different directions. Jasper's mission to find Oberon was a vital one for my people and for the continued peace of the Summer Court's reign in Faerie. I wanted to be part of it. But if I left and something happened to Oliver because of my absence, I couldn't live with myself.

I slept for a few hours, but there was no refreshment in it. The arrival of morning felt nothing but bitter. Somehow, even when I thought I'd made the right decision, it still felt wrong.

When I joined Nicole in our common rooms for breakfast, there was a mischievous spark in her eye, and a sly smile playing over her lips.

"Soo, how was your night?" she asked, her words heavy with implication.

But then she saw my expression. Her face fell.

"What's wrong?" she asked, alarmed. "I thought you were, well, having a good time."

I gave a sharp little laugh. "Oh, that part was definitely good."

"But?" she prompted. She'd stopped stirring milk into her tea and set the spoon down, intent on me.

My chest loosened a little when I took in how sincerely concerned she was. My twin and I barely knew each other. Even after the trials we'd been through together, we were still practically strangers. But she cared, and that meant something.

I told her about the mission to find Oberon, and without going into too much descriptive detail also what had happened to Oliver and why I didn't feel as if I could leave.

Her lips parted, and she blinked rapidly.

"That's horrible," she whispered, her eyes misting. "Poor Oliver."

I looked down at my plate, still empty as I hadn't taken any food yet. I nodded.

"But there must be some way," Nicole said. "We just need to figure out how to allow you to go without endangering Oliver."

"A body double. I need a clone to stand in for me." I snorted at the far-fetched idea and reached for a raspberry muffin.

"We should ask Bryna," Nicole said.

I shot her a confused look. Our bastard half-sister was the last person who'd want to voluntarily help me.

"Remember that invisibility bubble she used to get us out of here? That was impressive," my twin said. "She can use human magicked charms. I bet she's got something that would work."

"Yeah, she probably does. But how would I get her to use it to help me?"

"Jasper," Nicole said. "He's clearly got something on her."

"Jasper's gone, though," I said.

"Did he tell you where he was going?"

I shook my head.

"Well, maybe you could set something up for next time. He said the hunt for Oberon would most likely happen in segments, right?"

"You're right," I said, somewhat lifted by the thought of figuring out a way to help Jasper.

We'd been speaking in hushed tones, barely even whispering for fear of Duergar spies listening in the walls. There'd been some faint bumps and voices coming from the other side of the door to our quarters, and the noises had grown louder. We both went silent and looked toward the entrance, expecting our attendants or someone else to arrive.

But the noises intensified. The voices grew to shouts.

I shot from my chair and drew Mort. Nicole followed me as I hurried to the door. Pressing my ear to the wood, I tried to make out was happening in the hallway.

Several sets of boots pounded heavily past. Voices were hollering orders, but I could only make out a word here or there.

I was just about to crack the door open to take a look into the corridor when a banging noise came from the direction of my bedroom. Nicole shrieked as we both whirled around.

"Stay here," I said.

I ran past her, drawing magic and flowing it over my skin to form a thin layer of protective stone. I pushed more magic to my shadowsteel spellblade, and Mort ignited with violet flames of power.

The door to the armoire burst open. I gripped Mort in both hands, ready to charge, but then lowered my weapon in confusion as Jasper emerged.

"I thought you'd gone," I said.

"I was just about to leave when I heard the commotion," he said hurriedly.

He pulled out his short sword, walked over to my nightstand. He raised his weapon over his head in both hands, and then brought it down like a sledgehammer, smashing the small piece of furniture.

"Have you lost your fricking mind?" I hissed, my voice pitched high in alarm.

I lifted Mort again, seriously wondering if Jasper was having some sort of mental break. Nicole appeared in the doorway, and when she caught sight of Jasper, she screamed and then slapped her hands over her mouth.

Jasper had gone back to the armoire and was trying to rip the door off the hinges.

"It's a servitor attack," he said, speaking rapidly. "We can make it look like the servitors got in here through the passage. Use it as cover to get you out for a spell."

Grunting, he leaned back, his biceps bunching as he pulled. Metallic popping noises from breaking hinges announced that he'd managed to relieve the wardrobe of its door.

He looked at my twin. "Go lock yourself in your bathroom. When they come for you, say you hid in there." He turned to me. "Let's wreck a wee bit more havoc and then get the hell out of here."

I hesitated a split second, gripping my broadsword tightly and staring dumbly at Jasper. Then I dipped my chin once in a nod.

"Let's do it," I said.

The three of us piled out of my bedroom and into the main living rooms.

"Be careful, you two," Nicole said over her shoulder as she scooted into her own quarters. She shut her bedroom door, and then I heard her bathroom door slam as well.

Jasper and I turned to each other, wearing identical little half-grins. Then we started smashing things. We only spent maybe half a minute on our destruction but managed to do an admirable amount of damage in that short time. The breakfast cart had received the brunt of the abuse. It was just too easy a target, with all those delicate white dishes and baskets of fruit and pastries.

"C'mon," he said, grabbing my hand.

He towed me through the wreckage, back into my room, and into the armoire.

Chapter 9

AS I HURRIED after Jasper in the secret passage, I listened to the chaos through the walls. Jasper had said that servitors were attacking the palace, and I knew first-hand how sudden and violent they could be.

Servitors were conjured beings. They had solid forms and could hurt and kill just like any Fae, but they weren't real. Nearly every kingdom in Faerie had suffered servitor attacks in the past few months, and though a few deaths had resulted, the most alarming thing underlying the attacks was that the conjured creatures could seemingly pop into existence from nowhere. That meant an attack could come anytime, anywhere.

"We're going to have to pop out there soon," Jasper said to me over his shoulder. "We need to get to a different part of the palace, and it would take much too long if we have to stay in the passages. We need to make our getaway while the chaos is high."

"But someone will spot me."

"I'll pick a place that should be fairly clear of prying eyes."

I groaned under my breath. I didn't really have much choice but to go along with his plan. Still, fears about what Periclase would do to Oliver wound my insides tight. I supposed I could have backed out but decided to take the servitor attack as a sign that I was supposed to go with Jasper. Besides, I wasn't the type to sit on my hands. Oliver wouldn't want me to, either, even if it meant putting him in danger. I'd just have to make doubly sure my outing with Jasper was worth it.

From the shouts, crashes, and clangs heard through the walls, the servitor attack on the palace was still in full swing. Each attack throughout Faerie had sent increasingly stronger and more menacing creatures. It took very strong magic to create servitors. At first, no one had known who was sending the attackers. Then Jasper and I had paid a visit to Finvarra, the banished Unseelie High King, who'd recently begun hiding out in the seaside Undine kingdom.

Finvarra, who also happened to be Jasper's real blood father, had admitted to sending the servitors. We didn't know for sure that the Unseelie High King had created them himself, but he was chillingly unrepentant about it. He'd said the servitors were being used to weaken the Faerie kingdoms in preparation for the return of the Tuatha De Danann. The Tuatha were the true gods who'd created Faerie and then left it in the hands of the Old Ones. Oberon was the most recent Old One to take charge of Faerie, and he'd been at the helm for many generations, except for a brief time before I was born when Finvarra had taken over.

The Tuatha had been gone so long they'd faded into legend centuries back. Many modern Fae assumed they'd faded into the mists of times, if they'd ever lived at all. But apparently the Tuatha weren't legends and they weren't dead. They'd just been elsewhere. And, it was whispered, the gods were pretty pissed about the direction Faerie had taken in their absence.

Finvarra seemed to believe that if he helped weaken the kingdoms of Faerie, and Oberon's High Court in particular, the Tuatha would instate him as the new High King after they cleaned house. Perhaps he had actually struck a deal with the Tuatha.

Jasper and I had reached a dead end in the stifling secret passage we'd been following for the past few minutes. Smells of cooking meat, with undertones of apple pie, indicated we were likely near one of the kitchens.

He ran his fingers along the wall until he found what he was looking for. He pressed with his fingertips. There was a soft click and then a formerly invisible panel slid to the side.

"Wait here a second while I grab something for you to conceal yourself," he whispered and then cautiously tipped his head to peer out with one eye.

Apparently deciding it was safe to emerge, he stepped out and let the panel close behind him.

I fidgeted while I waited for him, trying not to worry about how Oliver was faring and telling myself that the quest for Oberon was worth the risk. If we were to have any hope of fighting back against the angry Tuatha De Danann, we needed the Seelie High King. If Finvarra took the High Court, it would be the end of Faerie as we knew it. He was already aiding the Tuatha. Oberon was our only chance.

I might have been able to brush off the rumors about the Tuatha and Dullahan, except for a strange encounter I'd had. Not long ago, when I'd ridden on the back of one of Jasper's Great Ravens, the bird took me to a mountain top where a blizzard blustered and the land was covered with snow as far as I could see. Maybe not a strange sight on the Earthly side of the hedge, but in Faerie, Oberon and Titania's Summer Court had reigned for literally ages. I'd never so much as seen a fall-colored leaf in Faerie. It was eternal warm sun and gentle breezes. The fact that there was snow somewhere in Faerie meant that the Seelie Summer Court was losing power. Somewhere, somehow, the Unseelie were gaining ground.

It was no coincidence that snow had begun to appear in Faerie and the banished High King Finvarra had returned and started stirring up trouble with the servitors.

Everything was intertwined in Faerie.

There was a rustling on the other side of the wall, and the panel cracked open far enough for Jasper to poke his head in.

"Looks as if the cooks have taken cover for the attack," he said. He opened the secret door wider. "Come on out and put this on."

I ducked through the small doorway and blinked in the light. There were huge steaming pots merrily boiling on the industrial stoves, glinting butcher knives next to raw meat left partially-chopped on a wide wooden block, and all manner of other evidence of abruptly-abandoned food preparations.

Jasper stuffed a wad of fabric into my hands. "Hurry, put this on your head."

I hastily unfurled it and found it was one of those awful frilly bonnets the palace staff women wore to keep their hair from falling in the food. I pulled it on and tied the two strings loosely under my chin while he stepped closer to me and threw something white and billowy around my shoulders.

"This'll cover up your clothing and broadsword a bit," he said and then turned. "Let's go."

I didn't have time to get a good look at what he'd wrapped around me, but as I dashed after him, I guessed it was a linen tablecloth.

Jasper was heading toward swinging double doors. I held two corners of my makeshift cape tightly in my left hand, and the tablecloth flapped around my heels as I ran after him.

Hearing the clangs and hollers in the corridor, I drew magic and formed stone armor. My right hand reflexively tried to go for Mort's hilt, but I resisted drawing my sword. If there were soldiers out there, they'd recognize my weapon.

The hallway was filled with the noisy, chaotic dance of close-quarters battle. Adrenaline surged through me, and I felt Mort respond with a delicious zing across my back.

Then I caught sight of the servitors.

"Oh, *damn*," I breathed. I started to say something to Jasper, but I was cut off by the roar of one of the creatures.

These servitors were frost giants, and true to their name, they were huge. I elbowed the tablecloth aside, drew Mort, and then let the fabric fall back over my arm to hide my broadsword.

I'd never seen frost giants in person—since the rule of the Summer Court began centuries before, Faerie had been an inhospitable place for cold and ice-loving creatures.

Two of the servitors were battling about ten Duergar soldiers. The ice-blue fur on top of the frost giants' heads brushed the vaulted ceiling, and I estimated they stood at least twenty feet tall.

"This way," Jasper said, grabbing my arm and pulling me in the opposite direction of the fight.

He was trying to run full speed, but I was having a hard time keeping up, thanks to the tablecloth. I stumbled, and he hauled me back to my feet before I went sprawling. But one edge of the fabric had wrapped around my boot and caught on the buckle, and I was struggling to stay upright.

"Lemme just untangle—" I started to say, pulling back to indicate I needed to stop.

But then a pair of huge, pale-blue furred legs appeared in front of us, blocking our way.

Jasper skidded to a halt to avoid crashing into the frost giant, but I couldn't stop my momentum. I pitched into Jasper, my shoulder driving into the elbow of his sword arm. His short sword flipped from his hand and stuck neatly into the top of giant's foot.

"Oh, shit," I said, my words completely drowned out in the enraged roar of the huge servitor.

I threw off the tablecloth and grasped Mort with both hands.

"Where're we headed?" I hollered at Jasper once the giant's roar had died down enough that I might be heard.

"We have to get past the frosty," Jasper said. "Next right turn and we're there."

"Great," I muttered.

The frost giant, having finished expressing how pissed-off he was, raised his ice-studded club and took a slow-motion lunge at us, telegraphing the coming swing by a mile.

"I'll deal with the club, you get your sword," I said quickly.

My eyes widened, and my senses seemed to heighten as I quickly calculated the arc the club was going to trace through the air. Frost giants were known for a leathery hide that was nearly impossible to pierce, but their cold blood made them slow.

Knowing it would be difficult to injure the creature, I held Mort in a hard grip and kept my eye on the huge head of the club. Damn, the ball end of it was as big as one of those yoga balls I'd seen in the Earthly realm, probably twenty-five inches across.

Gritting my teeth in anticipation of the impact, out of the corner of my eye I saw Jasper duck low and sprint forward with his short sword in his sights.

I swung Mort like a batter whiffing at a high pitch. The shadowsteel spellblade collided with the club's head. Pain burst up my arms from the force of the hit, and the blow buffeted me hard to my left. I let out a grunt as my shoulder slammed into the wall. Ice chips rained down everywhere, the unnaturally extreme cold burning the backs of my hands and the areas of exposed skin on my face.

At least I was still on my feet.

"Run!" Jasper shouted at me.

Seeing he'd already grabbed his short sword and darted through the giant's legs, I caught my balance, pushed off the wall, and charged forward with a yell.

The giant servitor was too big and slow to react but managed to hammer the club straight down, nearly clipping my heel.

I sprinted under the frost giant and angled to the right, following Jasper. Arms pumping, we ran side-by-side for about twenty feet.

"There," he said, pointing with his sword to an inconspicuous door ahead and to the right.

We skidded to a stop, he grasped the knob, and jerked the door open. It was a service closet with clean-up supplies. With a sweep of one arm, he knocked stacks of towels off a large shelf and then crawled onto it. There was a little hook and nail latch, which he flipped over. The door he opened was so narrow he had to squeeze through it awkwardly, first one shoulder and then the other. His boots disappeared as he seemed to fall off a ledge. I quickly sheathed Mort and dove in after him.

My limbs flailed as I fell, and I tensed, bracing for an impact.

Chapter 10

IT WAS A short fall from the hidden door in the closet to the pad placed directly below. So short, I didn't have a chance to twist around and pretty much landed on my face. The thin pad didn't do much to soften the impact.

My nose crunched, my lips smashed against my teeth, and stars of pain danced in my eyes. Anywhere else on my body, my stone armor would have made the impact painless, but the protection only extended in thin wisps over my cheekbones. My mouth, nose, and forehead were completely exposed.

I rolled over to my side, groaning and cursing and clutching at my smashed nose and lips.

"What?" Jasper said. "I can't understand a word you're saying."

I removed my hands from my face. "That's because I just used my face as landing gear." My mangled lips couldn't quite form the words clearly.

"Oh, damn," Jasper said, chuckling and reaching to help me up.

"It's really *not* that funny."

I tried to hit him with a death glare, but my face didn't respond the way it should have, and the stars hadn't cleared from my vision yet, so I couldn't really tell if it had any effect.

"Can you walk?" he asked.

"Of course I can," I groused. I made shooing motions. "Go, I'm right behind you."

The fall had hurt like hell, but New Gargoyles were blessed with exceptionally rapid healing, which was no doubt why Jasper had felt at liberty to laugh at me. My nose and split lips were already tingling with my body's effort to repair the damage.

I sucked in a sharp breath, gave my head a shake, and took off after Jasper. The passage was larger than the ones we'd squeezed through before, which allowed us to move a lot faster. We ran through turns until I'd completely lost my sense of direction, and then we started going up.

It was like a video game—turn, turn, up a ladder, run some more, turn, up a ladder, turn a few times, up another ladder. I honestly had no idea how Jasper was keeping track of where we were in the palace.

Occasionally we heard sounds of the fight with the frost giants. The roars of the creatures and the shouts of the Duergar soldiers didn't betray much about which way the battle was going, but the fact that it was still raging was a bad sign. Previous servitor attacks had mostly been short, though increasingly more violent.

It struck me suddenly that the frost giant attack was the first one where I'd not managed to "kill" a servitor. They weren't truly living, and so couldn't be killed in the literal sense, but they fought like living creatures. When they were defeated, they disappeared into thin air. I wondered if the Duergar had managed to kill any frost giants at all.

I also wondered if anyone would believe Nicole's story about a servitor breaking into our quarters. If a frost giant had actually gotten in, it would have done a lot more than smash some dishes and wreck some furniture. Not to mention the creatures were too big to fit through the passage that let out through my armoire. Hopefully in the stress of the attack no one would question Nicole to closely.

But it underscored the fact that it would be bad for me to stay away for long. The image of Oliver's bloody face danced into my mind's eye, and it almost weakened my resolve.

"Where are we going?" I whispered loudly, so Jasper would hear me over our footfalls.

"We'll take Ravens," was all he said.

We finally reached a door that let out onto a small terrace. It was nothing but a platform, really, lacking even a railing. I sucked in a deep breath of fresh air, grateful to be out of the stuffy passages.

We'd climbed up a handful of stories, and while I panted and used the sleeve of my light jacket to wipe blood from my face, Jasper pulled a wooden whistle from behind his breastplate and blew into it. The sound it made wasn't impressive to a Fae's ear, but there was a trickle of magic that emanated from the whistle and darted outward.

Jasper's eyes were glued to the horizon. After half a minute, he pointed. There were two tiny black birds in the distance.

Only, they weren't tiny. As they approached, their true size grew apparent. I'd ridden Great Ravens a number of times before, but their stature would never fail to impress me. With thirty-foot wingspans, they made me feel as small as a mouse and almost as vulnerable.

"We're gonna have to jump," he said, backing up on the tiny terrace. "There's no place for them to land here."

My pulse bumped with nerves and excitement.

"Watch me, and then follow suit," he said.

He waited until the lead bird began to bank directly in front of us, then ran forward with powerful strides and hurled himself off the edge. He disappeared below and the great bird swooped, and then it appeared off to the right, pumping its powerful wings with Jasper perched behind its head. Then Jasper and the Great Raven disappeared.

I didn't have time to process my alarm at their sudden disappearance.

I flattened my back to the wall, watched my bird as it approached, and then ran forward. It took all of my will to leap off and keep my eyes open, but I managed not to panic in the air. I had a brief moment of terrifying exhilaration as I hung in the air. The bird gracefully swooped down, and I landed hard. Adjusting my legs and grasping the shiny black feathers, I held on for dear life as the great bird arrowed away.

Then we plunged into the familiar cold void of the netherwhere, the non-place that existed between the doorways. Normal Fae doorways were in permanent locations scattered throughout Faerie and the Earthly realm. But the Great Raven I'd been riding seemed to have passed through a doorway in mid-air that was undetectable to me.

Just as suddenly as we'd disappeared into the void, we were back in the world. I caught sight of the other great bird up ahead. The sky was different here, cloudier and with a strange greenish-gray cast to it. I guessed we'd passed into another kingdom.

Tears streamed from the outer corners of my eyes as the Great Raven worked to catch up to Jasper's bird. A grin spread over my face at the sheer thrill of flying, momentarily drowning my worries about Oliver, Nicole, and just where the hell we were, exactly.

When I happened to look to the distance and spotted white mountain peaks, my face tensed into a frown. Snow in Faerie. We'd likely come to some place very remote.

The air was noticeably cooler, too, and it wasn't just because of the wind of flight rushing over my skin. I slid a glance over at Jasper, wondering if he saw the snow in the distance. His attention was trained ahead, but not on the mountains. There was a wide valley in the near distance with small structures scattered on the hills overlooking the V that had been carved by eons of water streaming from the mountain range. Smoke traced lazy lines from chimneys.

That was where we were headed. The closer we drew, the more apparent it became that the little settlement had been recently and perhaps hastily erected. The houses were tiny and made of rough-hewn logs. There were small areas of land scraped down to dark soil nearby, where gardens had recently been planted.

It looked like some sort of outpost. And I still had no idea what kingdom we were in.

By the time our birds landed, I was practically bursting with questions. But as I climbed down from my Great Raven, I watched quietly as a handful of men and women emerged from the little houses. They greeted Jasper like people who'd known him a very long time.

The last to come forward was a tall man, at least six and a half feet. When he got close enough for me to see his eyes, my breath stilled. His eyeballs were pure black orbs—no whites, no irises. His hair was so black it glinted blue where the weak sunlight caught it. He peered at me with an unblinking directness that was almost animal-like. The others stepped away, allowing the black-eyed man to approach Jasper. The two of them began to converse in low tones, and I got the impression they were talking about me.

I stayed where I was, shifting my weight and trying to assess whether the group was more curious or surprised that I was there. The more I watched, the more I got the impression that it was neither curiosity nor surprise. They seemed agitated.

Jasper came back to me after a minute or so, which seemed much longer while I was standing awkwardly away from the rest.

"Are you sure it's okay that I've come?" I asked in a low tone. My gaze flicked to the black-eyed man, who'd turned to go back toward the houses. "The Great Raven could take me back. Maybe that would be better, anyway, with Oliver and the servitor attack."

"It's okay," he said.

"Where are we?" I asked.

"We're in one of the uninhabited territories," he said.

There were areas of Faerie that didn't belong to any kingdom. There was usually a good reason for the chunks of land to remain unaffiliated. Some had mysteriously barren soil. Probably not the case with this one, in light of the garden rows I'd spotted. Other territories were left alone because they were overrun with dangerous, wild beasts. There were a few that had belonged to Faerie tribes long gone. And, some kingdoms held land that their rulers simply chose not to inhabit for one reason or another.

"Is this place affiliated with any kingdom?" I asked.

He shook his head.

That made me a little edgy. If no one wanted the land, there must be something wrong with it. I cast a look up at the white-topped mountains in the distance.

"There's snow here," I said quietly.

His gaze followed mine, but he only gave the peaks a quick glance, and he didn't comment. His face grew grim, though, and his jaw muscles worked.

Jasper was taking me through the settlement. The residents had mostly retreated back into their little rustic houses, and when I glimpsed through some of the windows, I realized they had no panes. At first I assumed it wasn't worth the effort and expense of putting in glass. But then I saw messenger ravens—the smaller birds that looked like the ravens found on the Earthly side of the hedge—flitting in and out of the houses.

Lots of messenger ravens, actually. The people of the settlement were rather quiet, but there was plenty of activity, I realized as I watched the birds dart around.

"Oberon's not here, if you're wondering," Jasper said.

"We're here for information, then."

"Aye."

We'd walked through the makeshift town to where the land began to slope upward. I'd thought the black-eyed man had disappeared into one of the houses, but he was up ahead, making his way through brush and conifers.

Jasper glanced at me. "That's Drifte up there. He's going to show us what he's learned of Oberon."

My brows lifted a fraction of an inch, and vague unease stirred deep in my gut.

"Who is he, exactly?" I whispered.

"My mentor. He took me into the Society of Grand Raven Masters and taught me most of what I know about working with the great birds."

I didn't want to be rude, but the guy's eyes were spooky. There was something decidedly inhuman about how his head turned this way and that. I opened my mouth, but hesitated. I wasn't quite sure how to phrase my curiosity about Drifte.

Jasper flicked a look down at me, faint amusement playing across his face. "He's a raven shifter."

"Ah," I said, relieved to know. "Daoine Sidhe?"

"Aye."

I watched Drifte up ahead of us. It all made a lot more sense. He was clearly a raven shifter, one who had spent so much time in raven form he'd permanently taken on some of the characteristics of his animal form—the glossy, feather-like hair, black eyes, and sharp birdlike movements.

A shiver snaked up my spine and over my scalp. A Daoine had to spend a lot of time in animal form for the characteristics to cross over that way. I didn't know a lot about their ways, but there were rites and tests one had to endure in order to achieve such an integration of their Fae and animal forms. Most modern Daoine didn't bother to pursue the ancient practices, as many saw them as too strange.

I glanced sharply at Jasper as something occurred to me. "*You're* part Daoine. On your father's side."

"I can't shift, though. At least, not that I know of," Jasper said.

He and I were possibly the only two people, aside from his mother, who knew that Jasper's blood father was the Unseelie High King Finvarra, who was himself part Daoine. Finvarra was one of the ilk

79

who believed shifting to animal form was a primitive practice that was beneath them. It made sense. He'd made his mark on history by "civilizing" the Unseelie tribes into proper kingdoms long ago, so being a modern man was a large part of his image.

"Jasper, I believe you're a good man," I said. "But really, why do you, an Unseelie, want to save Oberon? He's the Seelie High King. It could be argued that not bringing him back to the Summerlands would help your standing in Faerie. At least, it would help your kingdom's standing if Finvarra stole the High Court from Oberon. I know you've said before that this is all bigger than Seelie and Unseelie, but . . ."

I glanced up ahead at the strange man leading us, unsure if he could hear our conversation. Either way, I had to ask the question. I trusted Jasper, but on paper it made no sense for an Unseelie to be so passionate about saving the Seelie High King.

Jasper cast a quick look down at me, and I saw a flash of intensity in his golden eyes. "I love Faerie, Petra. Even with all its flaws and stupidity and nonsense, I *love* this place. I disagree with the Tuatha and their estimation that we've ruined their creation. They left it to us. They retreated into the mists and allowed Faerie to evolve without their hands to guide the evolution. It's not a perfect world, but it's beautiful. It's ours. I don't want to see it razed. But that's exactly what will happen if we don't bring Oberon back. Finvarra will take the High Court, the Tuatha will destroy all that we are, and winter will reign in Faerie."

His voice had broken with emotion more than once as he spoke, and when he finished, I didn't know what to say. I'd rarely met a Fae whose passion was so deep and convictions so pure. Marisol came to mind. Her passion for raising the Stone Order to kingdomhood was about as single-minded as they came. But her goal wasn't for the good of all. It was for the benefit of the New Gargoyles only.

"Can you understand that, Petra?" Jasper asked, apparently taking my silence to mean that I didn't agree with his sentiments.

"I understand," I said, my voice low. "And I admire your passion. You make me want to fight for you, to sacrifice for your ideals. Honestly, that's probably the best compliment I could pay a person."

He looked in my eyes, his face aglow with pride and gratitude. And suddenly I got it. *Really* got it. This was exactly why he'd never forced me into joining his cause, though he could have by way of our binding oath. He wanted me to feel it and believe it. He wanted me to want to fight for Faerie. And I did. I took a slow, deep breath, feeling recharged with purpose and energy.

Drifte had angled off to the right around a thicker stand of evergreens, and when we caught up, he was standing at the mouth of a cave.

My previous sense of unease rose again, pacing within me like a wary animal.

"If you're game, we're going to take part in a ceremony," Jasper said quietly to me.

I shot him a quick glance, but it was hard to take my eyes off Drifte.

"How long will this take?" I asked, worrying about what Periclase could be doing to Oliver back in the Duergar palace.

"I have people keeping watch," Jasper said. "If there's any move at all against your father, either I'll hear about it or someone else who can take action on my behalf will try to intercede Oliver."

I wasn't sure how that could be, but once again, I found myself trusting him.

"Okay," I said, but the trepidation was clear in my voice, this time directed at the cave.

"This is, uh, likely a bit different than anything you've encountered." My boots scuffed to a halt on the dark soil. "How so?"

We were still about twenty feet away from the raven shifter.

Jasper stopped, too, and scratched the back of his neck. "It requires an altered state of mind, so—"

"What, drugs?" I asked. I didn't like to do things that messed with my senses. I'd never even been too big on alcohol, though many Fae drank like fish.

"Kind of." He licked his lips. "We also need to be nude."

I snorted a laugh and arched a brow at him. "Well, good thing we already got that out of the way last night, or this might be awkward."

I moved past him as his eyes glinted with an echo of the passion I'd seen in my bedroom, and the corners of his mouth curled up. Leading the way, I hiked the rest of the short distance to the Daoine man and the cave. There was a faint scent of something burnt, like incense mixed with an old campfire, on the current of cooler air drifting from the dark space carved into the hillside.

Drifte peered at me as I stopped before him. I stood still, letting him look to his satisfaction. I kept my gaze steady but non-challenging.

"Here, you must leave your worldly things behind," he intoned.

The raven shifter turned to the mouth of the cave and walked a couple of feet into it. There, he stopped and began shedding his clothes.

With a steadying breath, I went in, too, and lifted Mort's scabbard over my head. Carefully tipping the pommel of my broadsword against the rocky surface of the cave's wall, I cast one more look at Jasper and then pulled my shirt up over my head.

Chapter 11

IT WAS COLD as a frost giant's ass in the cave. Drifte had led us deeper into the darkness, and the temperature dropped so rapidly I clamped my jaw to keep my teeth from rattling together.

The floor of the cave was like walking on dirty ice. I had to concentrate to resist drawing magic to cover myself with stone armor just to feel a little less exposed to the chill. But Jasper wasn't forming armor, so I wouldn't do it either.

"Halt," came a voice ahead. Drifte, I assumed, though I could no longer make out his form in front of me.

I stopped, and I could hear the soft sound of Jasper's breath behind me.

There was a rustling noise and then a sharp grating. Sparks jumped over the floor, and in the brief light, I caught a glimpse of the raven shifter crouched with a flint. Again, the scraping noise.

This time, the sparks caught on some tinder. The tiny flames grew and began licking at the logs that had been arranged within a stone ring.

I automatically moved toward the fire and the promise of warmth.

"Sit," Drifte said. He'd moved to a cross-legged position next to the fire. He indicated with two open palms that Jasper and I should join him around the ring.

I wasn't self-conscious about my body, but I did feel uncomfortably naked without Mort. Our magical connection reassured me that my broadsword was right where I'd left it.

Smoke was already beginning to fill the cavern as I lowered myself to the floor with my legs folded under me and my hands on my thighs. The shock of my bare skin against the cold cave floor stiffened my spine. I tried to stifle a cough, but my eyes were starting to tear up and my throat stung. I cut a look at Jasper. He was beginning to have trouble breathing, too.

Drifte was staring into the fire, tiny twin replicas of the flames reflected on the surfaces of his black eyes. I could barely see through my streaming tears, which were made worse by the effort of trying not to fall into a hacking fit. He drew a deep breath, expanding his bare chest. For a moment he held it, and then he let it go with a loud whoosh. In that exhalation came eddying swirls of red smoke from his nose and mouth. A second after, the tingle of magic washed over my bare skin.

I couldn't combat the irritation any longer. A gagging cough exploded from my mouth. I squeezed my eyelids closed and doubled over as I struggled to pull in air that was too smoky to breathe. It was starting to smell weird, too, like burning pitch and toasted grain.

Panic began to grip me as I realized there was no oxygen in the space. We were going to die if we didn't get out. But just as I was on the edge of a decision between trying to crawl to fresh air or staying there and passing out, the air cleared.

I could breathe again. I opened my eyes to find the cave was still thick with reddish smoke, the fire crackling merrily. And then it all blurred and changed.

I inhaled sharply as adrenaline zipped through my veins. Jumping to a crouch, I spun around, ready for whatever might be waiting.

I was in a forest. And I was dressed again. My hand whipped up to find Mort's hilt.

"Petra?"

I whirled at the sound of my name. Jasper was striding toward me. He'd also somehow redressed. The sight of him gave me some relief.

I peered into the gloom of the thick woods. "Where are we? Reminds me a lot of the forest we tramped through to get to Melusine's cottage."

"Yeah," he said looking up. "It is eerily similar. But it's not real."

"Huh?"

"This is all a hallucination. It probably looks like that forest because we have a shared memory of the place."

I brushed my hands down the front of my clothes. My feet shifted, crunching pine needles under the soles of my boots. It felt real enough.

"Are we asleep?"

"Not exactly," he said.

Okay, then. "What are we supposed to do?"

He lifted a finger, pointing off to my left. "Follow that."

I squinted, at first not seeing what he meant. Then I spotted a wispy line of red smoke leading away from the small clearing where we stood. Not unlike the lanternbugs that Melusine had used to guide us to her cottage. Only, we'd been conscious for that journey.

"I don't understand this," I whispered as Jasper and I set off side-by-side. "I mean, are we having the same hallucination?"

He shrugged one shoulder. "How would we know?"

I snorted a wry laugh. "Fair enough."

"Try not to think about it too hard."

"Good advice," I muttered. "But do you, if you really are more than just a figment of my imagination, have any idea what we're trying to find?"

He started to say something but then froze, touching the side of his finger against his lips.

There was something out there in the gloomy woods. I sensed it before I heard it. Then there was movement through brush. Whoever it was, they were trying to be stealthy. But it was so pin-drop silent it was damn near impossible to move undetected.

I drew magic, formed stone armor, and reached up for Mort.

Then the forest exploded with movement, grunts, yells, and flashing weapons.

My eyes popped wide as I tried to take it in all at once. There were different creatures attacking from all sides. Bulky ogres, swift little figures in black, at least a dozen charging us.

I pushed power into my sword arm, and Mort burst into violet flames of magic.

Jasper and I turned back-to-back, and I started slashing. Within seconds, I was absorbed in the rhythm of battle. When I raised Mort in both hands to hammer down a blow on a charging ogre, something tinged off the stone armor covering my ribs. A quick glance down revealed a throwing knife. It was of a type I'd seen before.

"Servitors," I grunted at Jasper as I swung baseball-bat style at another ogre.

His short sword clanged against something metallic. "What?"

"These are all servitors who've been attacking Faerie."

The throwing knife was from one of a dozen of the small, black-clad ninja servitors I'd fought a handful of times. The ogres looked exactly like the ones who'd stormed the Duergar streets when I'd been on an assignment with Gretchen, a human witch and mercenary.

"Servitors within a hallucination," Jasper observed, his voice admirably calm amid the fighting.

The ground shook as something huge—or a few somethings—came stomping through the trees. Trunks cracked and branches snapped.

"Yep, here come the frost giants," I said.

We were managing to hold off the creatures, but they seemed to be continuing to appear just out of sight. As soon as we mowed down a couple, several more took their places.

"Stop fighting," Jasper said.

"Huh?" I was planting my feet, preparing for the lead frost giant even as I slashed at ogres and their swinging battle axes.

"Stop," he said again. "This isn't real. They're not real. They can't kill us here."

"You absolutely sure about that?"

I could see the legs of a frost giant, thicker than the tree trunks it was kicking aside, less than fifty feet away.

"It's the only way through," Jasper said. "If we keep fighting, the battle will go on forever."

I paused for a split second, panting.

"Put your sword away, Petra."

I started to lower Mort, but a ninja launched himself at me from a nearby low branch, and I reflexively jerked my weapon up to meet the attacker.

"It's the only way," he said again.

I licked my dry lips and glanced at Jasper over my shoulder. He'd stuck his short sword back into his belt. He turned to me, exposing his back to a horde of servitors, and reached out his hand.

Swallowing hard, I reached up and sheathed Mort. I did it fast, before I could reconsider. Then I grasped his hand and squeezed.

The servitors were still coming, but instead of demolishing us with their weapons, they were popping like soap bubbles just before they made contact. Even though I knew they'd disappear, it took most of my focus to stand there and try not to flinch.

"When is it going to stop?" I asked through gritted teeth.

Jasper's fingers pulsed gentle pressure around my hand. "They're already thinning."

He was right, but the frost giants were still coming. The first one arrived in our clearing and sped up, his ice-studded club drawn back for a mighty swing.

I squinted, torn between needing to watch and wanting to close my eyes. Just before the head of the club struck me, which surely would have shattered bones in spite of my stone armor, the weapon and its roaring wielder disappeared.

Five more frost giants came, started to attack, and popped out of existence.

And then the forest was still.

Jasper let go of my hand. Adrenaline still pulsed through me, and every muscle in my body was taut and ready to fight. I couldn't seem to let the tension go. I took a couple of deep breaths, and that helped a little. I still felt oddly shaken.

"I think not fighting back was one of the hardest things I've ever done," I said quietly.

"I suspect that may have been the point."

I gave him a wry look, and he crooked a sympathetic half-smile down at me.

Jasper gestured at the trail of red smoke that still hung in the air, apparently undisturbed by the fight. We started off into the gloom.

Thinking of Drifte reminded me of another mysterious figure I'd recently become acquainted with.

"What do you know about a white-haired magic wielder who works for Periclase?" I asked Jasper.

His gaze turned to me quickly, and his eyes grew serious. "That's Eldon. He doesn't work for anyone."

I gaped at him. "*The* Eldon? But he didn't look like an Old One."

All of the Old Ones I'd encountered—Oberon, Titania, and Melusine—gave off a strong larger-than-life vibe. Some of it was literal. Oberon and his queen, for instance, were quite tall and always seemed surrounded by a golden mist. Melusine was dramatically odd, with strange orange eyes and the ability to change her stature depending on her mood.

Perhaps I didn't recognize Eldon as an Old One because he, like

Melusine, was a halfling—part human, part Fae. His and Melusine's magic came from both sides of the hedge. They were rarities in that they wielded human *and* Fae magic with enormous power. Most halflings had barely a sputter of magic, and some none at all. To be able to use both types, and with such strength, made them exceedingly unique.

"He was in the room when Periclase brought in my father," I said. "The man, Eldon, used magic on me. He seemed to be doing it at the king's whim. He seemed to be able to make himself disappear at will. Is he the one torturing Oliver?"

I squinted up at Jasper, not sure which way I hoped he'd answer. I planned to kill everyone who'd hurt my father. It was damn near impossible for a regular Fae like me to end an Old One, but a girl had to do what a girl had to do.

"Honestly, I'm not sure," he said. "I have a hard time imagining someone like Eldon beholden to Periclase."

His mouth twisted when he said Periclase's name, his disdain for the Duergar king clear. It was a sentiment that Jasper normally kept hidden, presumably because Periclase was believed to be Jasper's father. The king himself didn't even know the truth, and Jasper had to keep the secret for the sake of his own safety.

My jaw tightened as I considered the implications of Eldon in the Duergar court. "It's not good, though, that Periclase seems to have an Old One on his side. Eldon must be one of the most powerful magic wielders in Faerie."

Jasper nodded gravely. "He's basically Melusine's male counterpart. A Fae sorcerer to her Fae witch. Able to use both Fae and human magic. He has unusual talents. The gloaming mist, for one, where he commands the shadows of twilight."

"That's what he uses to look as if he fades from sight?"

"Aye."

"Why in the name of Maeve would Eldon be working with Finvarra and Periclase?"

"Difficult to say," Jasper said, looking genuinely baffled. "I don't know much about the Fae sorcerer's history, other than he's been extremely reclusive for many centuries. I believe he spends time in the far reaches of Faerie, studying rare magics. Maybe he goes to the Earthly side of the hedge to hone his human magic skills, as well." He squinted, his eyes unfocused as he thought. "I think I remember someone telling me that he was banished from Faerie for a time when he was younger."

"By whom? Oberon?"

"Must have been, though I don't specifically recall."

We fell silent as we continued to follow the wisp of red smoke through the trees. The forest was no longer eerily quiet, as the departure of the servitors seemed to have prompted the return of normal sounds of the woods.

I wondered how much time had passed since we'd entered the cave with Drifte. It may have been minutes or hours. It was impossible to tell.

Just as I was about to ask Jasper how long he thought it'd been, he stopped. I looked at him questioningly, and he gestured ahead.

About twenty feet away was a dark gray wall. It was perfectly smooth and seemed to stretch infinitely up and to either side. The color of it made it blend almost perfectly with the gloom in the mid distance, which was why I hadn't spotted it.

"I believe we've reached the end of the forest," he said.

Then he strode forward with purposeful movement. I jogged to catch up.

We reached the wall, which appeared solid. But when Jasper touched it, his fingertips disappeared with no force on his part, as if dipping into water.

"We need to go through," I said, both knowing and dreading it. My pulse began to thump a little harder.

He nodded. We faced the smooth expanse, and together took a step into the gray.

Chapter 12

WALKING THROUGH THE gray wall felt like passing through a sticky film. It clung gently, sealing itself to me as I went through. I closed my eyelids to keep it from getting in my eyes. But when I opened them, there was only blackness.

My forward foot hit nothing. I flailed, my arms shooting out. I had the sensation of tumbling, but then realized that I wasn't.

I'd fallen into empty space. I wasn't aware that we'd gone through a doorway, but I floated in a nothingness that I knew—the void of the netherwhere. My alarm subsided as I focused on the familiarity of the sensation and trying to trust that the space between realms would spill me out safely somewhere.

When the dark nothing began to lighten, but I still couldn't feel my body return to me, my heart skipped a beat. Or it would have, if I'd had my physical form. Panic began to grip my mind. The netherwhere had no light. It was the magical nowhere space where nothing had form.

The memory of a wraith attacking me in the netherwhere suddenly surfaced, and alarm laced through me.

But my surroundings continued to brighten, and no threat appeared. Jasper and I had stepped through the wall together, but there was no sign of him. He must have been floating in his own void. Or perhaps he'd never really been with me in the hallucination at all.

As my worry about an unexpected attack began to subside, I started to wonder how long I would hang there in the gentle glow.

Then a flicker of a shape caught my attention. Something was appearing ahead of me. I watched as forms seemed to coalesce into a scene. The process was eerie, as if watching the unseen hand of an artist begin work on a blank canvas. But before I could make out the details, a terrible sense of dread chilled me to my core. I knew what I was sensing, and if I'd had lips, I would have whimpered.

There was sky iron nearby. A huge amount of it.

There was nothing more devastating to Fae. Sky iron was a rare substance found in meteorites, and it burned Fae like acid. Too much of it all at once would dissolve a Fae's body with horrific swiftness and unimaginable pain. But smaller amounts could be used very effectively as slow torture.

The shapes before me crystalized just as my own body regained its corporeal form. I automatically reached up to grasp Mort, while at the same time desperately trying to make sense of what I saw.

I stood behind a shimmering sheet. It was similar to the filmy gray wall I'd passed through, but this new one was transparent. Every second or so, magic pulsed over it, rolling across like an oily rainbow. I had no idea who was controlling it or what it was, exactly, but sensed that it kept me invisible to the people on the other side. I left my broadsword sheathed and stared at what I saw.

Oberon was there.

His golden-brown hair was matted with blood, his head lolled to one side, and his eyes were pinched shut in pain. His shirtless body sagged against a stained stone wall, and only the metal rings around his wrists seemed to be preventing him from collapsing.

My hand flew to my mouth when I realized how much blood had dripped down his forearms and off the points of his elbows to collect in dark twin pools on the floor. His shackles were made of sky iron, and they had corroded the skin of his wrists down to the bone. I moaned my horror against my fingers as I forced myself to watch.

Oberon was muttering something over and over that I couldn't quite make out.

I collected myself enough to try scan the rest of the room. There were others there—I could see their shapes and movements—but when I looked straight at them, I saw only swirling mist.

I shook my head, as if that would force the forms to clarify. It didn't help.

Then one of the forms began to speak. The voice seemed to come from all directions, buffeting against my eardrums with uncomfortable force.

"Speak louder, Fae son," it said. A masculine voice, I believed. The accent was odd, nothing I could place.

Oberon raised his head, but it wobbled like a newborn's, as if he hadn't the strength to keep it steady.

"I failed Faerie," the Faerie High King mumbled.

"And?" the cloud-voice boomed.

"I disobeyed my creators," Oberon said.

"And why do we torment you with pieces of the stars?"

"To show the Fae how easily our gods can break us."

There was no response for a long moment.

"Such is the message you shall carry back to Faerie." The voice of one of the mist forms almost sounded regretful. "But not until you believe it."

For a moment, Oberon looked so defeated and agonized, I thought he would beg for release. Instead, he lifted his head.

"You haven't broken me," he said, his voice clear and his gaze unblinking.

"Oh, but we will."

One of the mist-forms stepped forward, obscuring my view of Oberon. But a second later the High King threw back his head, screaming. When the mist cleared, I got a view of his bloodied chest. A symbol had been carved in his flesh. I didn't know what it meant, and I didn't really care, for I suddenly knew who was there torturing Oberon and why they were so elusive to my sight.

The gods who'd created Faerie, the Tuatha De Danann, had just used sky iron to leave a mark on Oberon. They'd clearly said they intended to let him return to Faerie, which meant he was somewhere beyond our reach. Underground, perhaps in the Old World? That was where, according to legend, the Tuatha had disappeared to so many generations ago.

The scene seemed to have come to a conclusion, and I expected to be pitched back into the void of the netherwhere. But the vision wasn't done with me quite yet. As I watched, Oberon was unshackled from the rings of sky iron. He'd lost consciousness, and his limbs drooped from his body at awkward angles as the mist people descended on him. He was jostled and then lifted by many misty hands.

I squinted, half expecting the Tuatha to subject him to some new horror, but they carried him with surprising care.

The angle of the scene changed to follow Oberon as the Tuatha continued to hoist him up. They carried him to a narrow table where they set him down. I almost expected them to tend to his wounds, but instead there was a rattle of chains. I inhaled sharply as I sensed the sky iron in the links.

No, the Tuatha weren't going to dress his wounds. They were securing him to the table with sky-iron laced chain.

I only had a moment to acknowledge my own horrified reaction before the scene changed. As if a camera were drawing back for a wide-angle shot, Oberon and the Tuatha began to shrink. Backward and upward, my viewpoint shifted until the backdrop of dungeon-like walls dissolved away, and I was suddenly outside with a view of dark rocks and the sea beyond.

I sucked in a sharp breath. I recognized that place. It was in the Earthly realm, on the northern coast of Ireland. Huge columns of basalt rock formed the Giant's Causeway.

That was where the Tuatha were torturing the High King of Faerie.

The scene abruptly shrank down to a point, and then I was plunged into freezing darkness. I floated in the netherwhere, and it began to numb me. I didn't want to surrender consciousness, but at some point, I lost the battle.

I awoke with a violent shiver, the hard ground biting into my hip and cheek. I was on my side, curled into a ball. Gasping, I pushed up to sitting and swung my gaze around wildly. Embers from the dying fire provided the only light. I'd come back to the cave. Actually, I doubted I'd ever left. Not physically, at least.

Across the fire ring, Jasper was awakening as well. He sat up abruptly with a shout, as if suddenly waking from a nightmare. I went to crouch next to him, laying a hand on his arm.

"It's okay," I said, my voice hoarse with cold. "You're back."

Drifte had apparently departed, and I had the sense that night had fallen. The glowing coals were putting off decent heat, but it wasn't enough to warm the cave.

"Did you go there, too?" Jasper asked me. By his glazed eyes, he was still reliving what he'd seen.

"If you mean Oberon and the Tuatha, then yes," I said quietly.

"And the Giants' Causeway?"

I nodded. "Let's get dressed. It's a fricking ice box in here."

He stood stiffly, and together we walked away from the small comfort of the fire toward the mouth of the cave. My instincts had been correct—darkness had fallen, and there was hardly any light in this wild territory. The night air was much chillier than any I'd experienced in Faerie in my life—except for that brief moment when a Great Raven had taken me to a blizzard on a mountain top.

Jasper and I dressed quickly at the mouth of the cave where we'd left our clothes and weapons, and for a few moments the only sounds were the rustling of clothing and our shivering breaths. When I had the chance to look around, the sliver of the crescent moon was just enough illumination to polish the tops of the conifers with pearly light. I squinted into the darkness among the trunks, though I didn't really expect another attack. It'd been a test, and we'd passed.

I adjusted Mort's scabbard across my chest and let out a small sigh of relief at having my weapon on me.

"We must go for Oberon," he said, his brogue growing a bit more distinct.

My breath snagged as I thought of my father. "How long has it been?" I asked.

He squinted at the sky. "Three or four hours, maybe?"

I pulled in my lips and bit down hard for a moment as I tried to get my emotions and worries under control. Had Periclase discovered I was gone? Was he punishing Oliver for my absence?

"Petra? What is it?"

I shook my head and kept my gaze on the ground. I couldn't face the concern in Jasper's golden eyes. "I'm thinking of Oliver."

"You don't have to go with me."

"No, I do," I said, finally looking up at him. "Where's the nearest doorway?"

He paused a moment, searching my face, and then dipped his chin in acknowledgement of my decision.

"There aren't any here, that Fae like us can use anyway," he said. "We'll get the Great Ravens to take us."

We set off at a quick pace away from the cave. The faint aroma of chimney smoke was a subtle reassurance that we weren't alone in the wilderness of Faerie.

"Do you think what we saw was real-time?" Jasper asked.

I frowned into the darkness. "Maybe not. But regardless, I believe we'll find Oberon beneath the cliff. I think we're meant to go for him."

My frown deepened as I realized what I'd just said. I was tempted to backpedal—I wasn't one to make statements smacking of fate and destiny—but I couldn't ignore the reality of recent events. At that very moment, I was hiding out from a prophecy that foretold my death, and I'd just endured a vision of the High King's torture. The universe's message was clear: I was to play a prominent role in whatever lay ahead.

Jasper and I had moved down the hill as quickly as darkness allowed, and we emerged from the woods in the little township. He pointed off to the clearing where we'd alighted on our Ravens.

"Looks like they're expecting us," he said.

Two of the great birds stood there, their heads angling our way at the sound of Jasper's voice.

I wasn't sure of the time—the windows in the houses had been mostly dark—but it didn't matter if it was just past dinnertime or four in the morning. We were going for Oberon.

Chapter 13

WHEN WE GOT close to the two Great Ravens, I let Jasper go ahead, knowing that he would need to communicate with them. The birds fanned their wings and hopped over to him, bending their heads to his with an expectant air. He approached the birds and spoke to them in a low tone. I caught a few words here and there, and it definitely wasn't a language I knew.

He half-turned to me, and I jogged forward.

"Are you ready for this?" he asked, his golden eyes glinting in the moonlight.

"Can anyone really be ready to try to steal the Faerie High King from the Tuatha De Danann?" I asked with an ironic little laugh. Seriously, we had to be insane.

I took a hesitant breath and held it.

"What?" he asked.

"Maybe we shouldn't be doing this alone," I said. "Just the two of us against the gods."

He ran a hand through his hair, which was just long enough for the ends to curl over his forehead and ears.

"We can't go in with an army," he said. "They'd see us coming from a mile away. Even with the Ravens we aren't going to be able to sneak up on them. Besides, Oberon looked half-dead. We need to get him out of there, and we can't wait. Finvarra's already banging on the door of the stronghold in the Summerlands, figuratively."

"Yeah, you're right," I said.

It wasn't that I was afraid to go in with only Jasper. I just wanted to do everything possible to ensure our success.

He let out a harsh breath and then tilted his head and regarded me. "Just out of curiosity, who'd you have in mind?"

"Honestly? Oliver would be my first pick." The words nearly stuck in my throat. I shook my head. Oliver wasn't an option. "You're right. We should go. The more time we waste, the more they'll try to break Oberon."

"Hang on," he said. He reached behind the breastplate of his light armor and pulled out the wooden whistle I'd come to know well.

He blew a few sharp breaths into it, creating a signal that was detectable to me more as a shiver through the air than an actual sound. A moment later, three small winged creatures flapped out of the forest toward us.

Messenger ravens. He held his arm out rigidly, and the birds alighted on it like pet parakeets. A few whispered words from master to birds, and then they were off.

"What'd you say?" I asked.

"I sent one each to three people I trust," he said. "It's insurance. If a message from me doesn't follow within half a day, at least someone else will know where we went."

My brows rose. "There are three other people you trust?"

I'd honestly not been aware that Jasper had friends. His manner was often mild, but I knew a fellow lone wolf when I saw one.

"Other Grand Raven masters?" I asked, curious.

"Two of them, yes," he said over his shoulder as he turned toward one of the Great Ravens. "We should get going."

He'd piqued my curiosity, and I wanted to know more about the three people he trusted so much, but we couldn't afford to devote any more time to idle conversation.

I went to the other bird, and something about the creature struck me. Even in the dark, the way its tail feathers splayed up a little more than most other Great Ravens was familiar.

"Is this bird male or female?" I called softly to Jasper.

"Female," he said.

Suddenly, I was sure this same bird had been the one to cart me around the last few times a Raven had come to my aid. Maybe it was Jasper's influence, or just more time around the great creatures, but they no longer all looked alike to me.

I hopped on her back and was just about to ask Jasper if the Raven had a name, but both birds bounced a few steps on springy legs and then we were aloft. Wings pumped, feathers ruffled against my face and bare hands, and the cold wind of flight stole my breath.

We arrowed away from the settlement, but not for long. After about a minute of hard flying, the world disappeared as my Raven plunged into the netherwhere. Almost immediately, we popped out of the void.

The smell of the sea was the first thing to hit me. We'd arrived in a coastal Faerie territory that was anchored to the Old World—Ireland, I suspected, given our intended destination. But the Giant's Causeway, where Oberon was apparently being held by the Tuatha, wasn't located in Faerie. It was across the hedge in the Earthly realm, the world of humans, vampires, and other supernaturals. Great Ravens couldn't pass to the Earthly side, so Jasper and I would need to find a doorway out of Faerie and journey the rest of the way without the birds.

My Raven circled, descending in a spiral toward a cliff below, where Jasper was about to dismount. The wind and salty water in the air were cool, but nowhere near as cold as the place we'd just left.

We landed, and I slid off the glossy feathered back. After a quick pat on my Raven's neck, I jogged over to Jasper.

"Where are we?" I asked. "Not a territory of the Undine realm, I hope."

The Undine had aided Periclase in his first attempt to take the stone fortress. Jasper and I had also found Finvarra in Undine territory. The Undine definitely weren't our friends.

"Nah, this is Kelpie land," he said.

I let out a relieved breath. Kelpies—seahorse shifters—tended to spend most of their time in the water, plus they were Seelie-aligned.

"This was as near as I could think to go within Faerie," he said. "We'll pass to the other side of the hedge and then find an Earthly doorway that might put us a bit closer to the Giants' Causeway."

"You know of a doorway that exits near there?" I asked.

The Giants' Causeway was such a remote an uninhabited place, I couldn't imagine why he would have had knowledge of a doorway near it. But I'd come to understand that there was much more to Jasper than met the eye.

"Aye, I know the sigils for a doorway near it," he said. "But I can't just go through. There is a cost."

He put an almost imperceptible emphasis on "cost," and it prompted a thread of unease to snake through me. I immediately thought of Morven and how the old Ghillie Dubh pub owner was always willing to help—but only if allowed to siphon a bit of a person's strong magic in return for information. I was pretty sure Jasper didn't have a visit to Morven's Aberdeen Inn in mind.

"Let's head that way," he said, his words clipped with a sense of urgency. "There's a doorway that'll take us close to the point where we'll leave Faerie."

Jasper gestured at a rocky mound that at first appeared to be a random pile of rubble, but as we approached I made out the subtle arch formation that indicated a portal within the chaos of the stacked rocks.

I placed my hand on his shoulder as he whispered to the doorway and drew sigils in the air with his finger. We both stepped into the rock and into the netherwhere. A moment later, we stepped back into the world, still in Faerie but down nearly at sea level. I sensed we were still in the Kelpie realm—the wind felt the same and the sea air had the same scent and quality—but the cliff where we'd landed was nowhere within view. Here, the land sloped gently down to the water, in contrast to the sharp drop-off of the area where the Great Ravens had brought us.

Jasper set off at a run on the soft sand, and I pumped my elbows to keep up with his longer strides. He seemed to be headed toward a point in the distance where a fire burned atop a narrow structure. There were no other lights, houses, or even a hint of Fae life nearby.

We reached the pyre, both of us huffing and puffing after our run. When something suddenly rose out of the water to our left, I reached for Mort.

Jasper held a hand out low at his side. "It's okay," he said, his eyes on the dripping figure sloshing toward us through the waves.

I flicked a glance at him. He hadn't drawn his weapon. I lowered Mort, but kept my grip tensed, ready to react.

The approaching figure was a woman in a white dress, and neither her hair nor her clothing appeared to be wet, though her skirt still swirled around her ankles in the small waves that lapped the shore.

"Wait here," Jasper whispered.

He walked slowly toward the woman, obviously taking care to approach cautiously.

As I watched, the identity of the woman suddenly dawned on me. She was one of several women in white known as the Lorelei. They were tribeless Fae who inhabited waterways and cliffs and delighted in using their beautiful songs to lure unsuspecting humans and Fae to their deaths. Human mythology called them sirens.

This particular Lorelei probably also used the pyre as a beacon. Perhaps there was a reef offshore to snag ships.

Jasper stopped before her, and the woman in white began to hum an unfamiliar but beautiful melody. I took half a step forward. The Lorelei songs tended to affect men much more powerfully than women. He seemed to know what he was doing, but trepidation spiked through my chest just the same.

He twisted around to look at me. "Don't come any closer, Petra," he said, his voice low with warning. "Please, stay where you are."

I licked my dry lips and fought the urge to sidle toward him, despite his warning.

Jasper began speaking to the woman, but the gentle sound of the waves prevented his words from reaching my ears with any clarity. I caught a snippet here and here, but he was talking so rapidly I couldn't make out what he was saying.

The woman in white listened until his was done, and then she tilted her head and looked up at him with a slow, wicked smile that chilled my insides.

She spoke only a few words. Jasper made a short reply, nodded once, and then turned and strode back to me.

"What did you say?" I asked. "What did she say?"

Instead of answering, he pointed at the pyre. "We're going through there. We'll land at a spot in the Earthly realm very near the Giants' Causeway. This was the best I could do. You can put your sword away."

There was an agonized edge to his voice that made my heart jump uncomfortably. He grabbed my free hand and pulled me toward the thin wooden structure. There was an arch in the design between two of the pyre's feet.

I glanced back over my shoulder at the Lorelei. She'd turned to the sea and was already up to her waist in the water.

My stomach knotted. What deal had Jasper just struck?

I sheathed Mort and kept a hold of Jasper's hand as he muttered the words and traced the sigils in the air. We stepped into the space under the pyre's arch and dissolved into the chill of the netherwhere.

When we emerged back into the world, a strong wind swept my hair to the side. I squinted. The ocean smelled different. It was richer and wilder than the sea in Faerie. The booming crash of water against land indicated much larger waves than the place we'd just left. We stood on rock, and before us stood the enormous basalt columns of the Giant's Causeway.

"Oberon is somewhere under there," Jasper said. He gestured at a vertical crevice that traced a dark, slightly uneven line between two of the columns. "And I believe that's our way in."

My mouth went dry as I peered at the tendrils of barely visible mist leaking from the crack in the wall of rock that loomed ahead.

I took a steadying breath, and Jasper and I locked gazes.

"Let's go get the High King," I said.

Chapter 14

JASPER AND I picked our way over rocky land toward the crevice in silence for the first few minutes, both of us tensed and on guard. It felt like we were on the moon, or some other place so foreign it wasn't part of Faerie or the Earthly realm. The cliffs where the Tuatha De Danann held Oberon were so huge, they'd appeared closer than they actually were. What I'd expected to be a fifteen- or twenty-minute hike stretched into a trek of over an hour.

"There's no way they don't see us coming," I finally said, breaking into the steady sounds of waves crashing against the cliffs and our rhythmic breathing.

Jasper's head tipped back as he flicked a look up at the basalt columns. "Aye. There's no sneaking up on the gods. If they wanted to stop us, they certainly could have by now. They must be waiting for us to enter their domain."

That sent a chill through me. We were walking into the unknown. Maybe a trap. But whatever awaited us, we had to press on.

"Regardless," Jasper continued. "We were right to come just the two of us. Raising an army to charge into the Causeway would not have gained us any favor."

I shook my head. "I'm not sure that's going to matter in the end."

"It will," he said.

His brogue came through a bit more thickly than usual, perhaps because of the influence of being in the Old World. I'd noticed before that Scottish Fae realms tended to bring it out. It was a delicious lilt on his words that I found myself listening for and savoring.

"How can you be so sure?" I asked. "We might be marching straight to our deaths."

I cast a furtive glance at him. I hadn't meant to state things quite so starkly.

To my surprise, he let out a short chuckle. "Then we'll die tragic heroes, and they'll write sad songs about us."

I responded with a sound that was part-laugh and part-grunt.

There was something oddly absorbing and almost pleasant about hiking across the basalt formations with Jasper, in spite of our mad little mission. The calm before the storm, perhaps.

"I never wanted to be a hero, tragic or otherwise," I said after a moment. "But you . . . you seem born to rise up. Even if most of those things haven't happened yet, you seem born to do heroic things."

His mouth quirked in a faint smile, but he didn't respond, his eyes on the ground to ensure he didn't trip.

"It's like you've been waiting, hiding out for the moment that fate taps you on the shoulder." I shook my head, knowing I was rambling but unable to stop myself. "Jasper, you're the son of the Unseelie High King, for gods' sake. You're literally a born leader by blood. Yet no one would even know any of it because you wear this disguise of a skilled but ordinary soldier, the bastard son of the Duergar king."

I trailed off, suddenly feeling a little silly for saying so much.

"You feel it, don't you?" he asked. "That tap of fate's hand, as you put it."

I tilted my head. "No, I was talking about you."

"Ah, but you're a player in all of this, too, Petra Maguire. You are the Champion of the Summer Court, wielder of Aurora. Marisol Lothlorien's prophecy about the New Gargoyles centers around you and your sister.

And I am certain this is just the start. You are vital to the future of Faerie. You can't see it as I do. You will be a hero for the ages."

I started to argue, but parts of what he said were correct. I was featured in Marisol's prophesy, and I did carry Aurora on my back. I had a part to play, whether I wanted it or not. The whole thing still made me squirm inside.

"What did you give the Lorelei in return for passage here?" I asked, happy to change the subject.

Jasper's face clouded. "Don't concern yourself with that."

"I *do* concern myself with things that endanger you," I said with vehemence that took me by surprise.

We'd reached ground that sloped upward more sharply, and we were both breathing a little harder. A light sheen of sweat gleamed across Jasper's forehead. The basalt columns loomed so tall they seemed to block out the sky. We were getting close.

He stopped and planted his hands loosely on his hips, and we faced each other.

"Is that so?" he asked, mild amusement dancing in his golden eyes.

I narrowed my eyes and lifted my chin at him as if in challenge. "Yeah. That's so."

His amusement blossomed into a grin, and I had the sudden certainty that if we weren't standing at the literal threshold of the gods, he would have taken me in his arms and kissed me until I was weak in the knees.

As we stood there staring each other down, my stomach fluttered and a curious pressure began to form in the center of my chest as it hit me again how much I'd underestimated Jasper. I was suddenly sure that the entire world had underestimated this man. Chasing that thought was the certainty that Oberon wasn't going to save Faerie—not single-handedly. He couldn't do it without Jasper Glasgow.

The air abruptly cooled, the tiny hairs on my arm picking up the sensation of a strong draft coming from the direction of the columns.

Jasper and I both turned toward the vertical crevasse. Pale mist was leaking out again, creeping toward us with curling tendrils that seemed somehow impervious to the crosswind whipping over the plateau on which we stood. The ghostly fingers of fog reached for us, curling and beckoning.

"I think they know we're here," I whispered, my blood chilling.

Jasper faced me, his mouth a grim line.

The tension in the air heightened as we both focused on the last, steeper part of the ascent to the dark crack in the columns. I reached for magic, letting it flow from my blood to my skin where it formed a thin layer of stone armor. I thought Jasper might warn me against arming myself, maybe tell me it would appear too aggressive to enter with my defenses already activated, but then I noticed that he'd formed his own armor.

My right arm gave a violent jerk, my elbow locking straight so hard it was almost painful. Another one of those damned twitches. Fortunately, Jasper was on my left, so he didn't see it. After a few seconds, the spasm eased, but the relief was only partial. The involuntary movements seemed to be getting worse, and I feared what might happen if they struck in the middle of a battle.

I told myself that my training would take over in the heat of action, that I didn't have to worry about my body betraying me. I was a New Garg, a born fighter. Oliver and my other teachers had spent years guiding me, helping me hone my skills, and giving me the confidence to rely on my training.

Dread and worry about Oliver flooded in. I shouldn't have thought of my father.

"Everything okay over there?" Jasper asked casually, as if we were out for a stroll in the woods with a picnic basket. But a glance up showed his concern in the faint lines across his forehead and the squint of the outer corners of his eyes.

I couldn't let my emotions about Oliver distract me. I needed to be fully present. Not for myself, but for Jasper.

I nodded firmly. "I have your back, no matter what."

"And you know I have yours."

The center of my chest warmed, and we exchanged brief smiles.

The chilly white mist was thicker near the crevasse, and my skin dampened with its cool condensation. I wiped my palms across the front of my pants every few seconds to keep them from getting slick with moisture that might interfere with my grip on Mort. I didn't reach for my spellblade, but I was ready to in half a heartbeat if anything seemed amiss.

We'd reached the final approach and found there were uneven natural steps worn into the steepest part leading to the dark opening between basalt columns.

The external surfaces of the columns were smooth, but I sucked in a breath when I glimpsed the sharp, jagged edges of stone that made up the interior walls. One bump up against a wall would slice through clothing—probably even my jacket—and kiss skin with stone razors. My armor would prevent accidental wounds, but I would take care nonetheless.

We paused at the opening, both of us trying to peer inside.

"Do you feel it?" Jasper whispered. "The sky iron in there somewhere, the same we felt in the vision?"

I'd been so distracted by the mist and the knife edges of the stone, I hadn't fully tuned into the low, almost imperceptible throb. A sense of deep dread accompanied it, which I'd assumed was just my own trepidation until Jasper pointed out the sky iron.

"Yeah," I said. "They're using it on Oberon, so that's where we need to head. Toward the sky iron."

I swallowed hard and took one last look at the cloud-strewn gray Irish sky. Thinking of Oliver and hoping to do right by him no matter what happened next, I plunged through the opening in the huge columns of the Giants' Causeway.

Chapter 15

MY PULSE SPED as I looked around wildly in the dark, trying to orient myself. The light from outside only penetrated the first few feet within the crevasse, and beyond, the darkness seemed nearly complete. The Tuatha must have installed some kind of magic shield that prevented the normal filtering of light into a space. I reached up for Mort and sent magic through my arm and into the blade. Violet flames of power cast a dull illumination around me. It wasn't much, but it was enough to see by.

"We can't do this blind," I muttered to Jasper by way of explanation.

We'd had a sort of unspoken agreement to not draw our weapons, but stumbling around in the dark shredding our clothes on the razor edges of stone lining the narrow walls wasn't going to give us any advantage. Plus, it just plain freaked me out to be so abruptly plunged into darkness.

He gave me a quick nod, his eyes scanning the tall, slender passage. "Not exactly welcoming, is it?"

Between the slice-and-dice walls, the thick darkness, the cold fog that chilled the passage to an uncomfortable temperature, and the dark pulse of sky iron, the message was pretty clear.

There was barely enough width in the crevasse for Jasper to walk through it without angling his shoulders. We'd be forced to walk single file.

"You were right about the army," I said. "We couldn't have gotten a bunch of soldiers in here anyway."

We both peered deeper into the columns, but the far edge of my magic's illumination only extended about ten or fifteen feet. Just enough to show that the path into the stone mountain jagged this way and that. Even with a brighter light, we wouldn't have been able to see much of what was ahead.

My insides twisted, and a swirling unsteadiness swept through me. I hardened my resolve, pushing back against the survival instincts that were hollering at me to not go deeper into such an enclosed space.

"I'll go first," Jasper said and angled to sidle past me.

Even with both of us turned sideways and sucking in, I heard the soft scrape of the back of his rock armor against the wall. When he moved ahead of me, the purplish light of my magic showed rips through his shirt, as if a large clawed animal had taken a swipe at him from behind.

I held Mort up higher to light the way for Jasper, who'd drawn his broadsword. To his credit, he didn't hesitate but took off at as quick a pace as he could probably manage in the confines of the narrow passage.

Inside the stone mountain, the sounds of our movements didn't echo as they would have in a normal cave. The razor edges lining the walls seemed to slice every noise out of existence, and a stern silence reigned.

I wasn't sure what I expected—monsters, lightning from the gods, or some other show of force—but the quiet and the claustrophobia were enough to make me almost wish for an attack. As we moved, the ugly pulse of iron grew stronger and stronger.

What I didn't expect was a door. But after about ten minutes of trekking through the crack in the rock mountain, the passage opened up into a cavern. The walls were still armed with protruding razor edges of stone, and the floor was very uneven. At the far end stood a set of giant double doors. They appeared to be made of stone, maybe carved from the basalt itself, decorated only with a simple lattice design made of metal strips. Iron rings as big as a pair of hula hoops appeared to be the only thing to grasp to pull the doors open.

Jasper and I stopped in the open space. The dull purplish light of my magic flaming around Mort didn't do much to dispel the dark of the pitch-black underground room. My eyes had adjusted somewhat, but gloom seemed to press in on us.

I gestured at the doors with Mort. "That metal. It's cold iron. I can sense it from here."

"Aye," he said.

Cold iron caused extreme pain to Fae if we came into contact with it. I could still feel the thumping pulse of the far deadlier sky iron beyond the doors.

There was a hypnotizing quality to the sense of nearby sky iron, an awful rhythm that carried a sickening dread, like that feeling you get in your stomach as a child when you're lying wide-awake in the dark, frozen with absolute certainty that something monstrous is lurking under your bed.

The two of us were walking slowly across the cavern, and my eyes were glued to the doors as I tried to work out a way to open them without burning the hell out of myself on the cold iron rings. I was so absorbed in the task, and when the ground dropped out from under me, it took me completely by surprise.

A couple of things happened at once: Jasper's hands clamped hard around my left arm, and my legs swung through empty air and then banged into the wall of the hidden crack in the floor. My right arm spasmed—either because of the annoying muscle tics or in reaction to my fall—and Mort fell from my grasp.

"Shit! No!" I screeched.

Hanging by one arm as Jasper fought to keep a hold of me, I tilted my gaze down for a split second, just in time to see the violet magic around my prized broadsword flicker out.

"Petra you're slipping! Give me your other hand!" Jasper commanded with a grunt.

I grabbed his wrist with my right hand as a shudder of pure distress wracked me.

From far below, I heard the clatter of metal against rock as Mort continued to fall into the impossibly deep crack in the floor.

In utter darkness, Jasper hauled me back up. I lay on my back, slapping my hand over my face in dismay as I caught my breath.

"My sword," I moaned.

I sat up, but in the darkness, I was afraid of accidentally stepping into the gap again, so I stayed where I was. Jasper was shifting around next to me.

"I'm sorry you lost Mort," he said with sincere sympathy. "But better the sword plunging down there than you."

I shook my head, refusing to accept that my spellblade was gone. "I can invoke the magic imbued in the blade. Mort will come to me if I spill enough blood."

"Aye, the trick is seared in my memory. But we don't have time for it, and we can't afford to let you bleed yourself dry."

A dim, greenish orb of magic lit into existence. Jasper had formed the golf-ball-sized swirl of power in his palm.

I leaned forward to look down into the crack in the cavern floor that had nearly claimed me. It wasn't wide—Jasper and I could jump over it with a few steps running start—but he was right. If I'd fallen, there'd have been no stopping my descent.

"We must press on, Petra," he said, gentle but firm.

I sighed heavily, tried to push down the sorrow that was welling up, and stood.

"This sort of magic is not my strength," he said, his eyes on the little green orb he'd created that bobbed in his palm. The illumination was already sputtering and weakening. "Can you light our way?"

I drew magic from within and directed it down my arm. Violet wisps danced off my fist, much fainter than when I used power to illuminate Mort, but still brighter than Jasper's magic.

Inside, I was fuming. How could I have let go of my weapon? So stupid.

I could sense Mort's presence, but it was very distant. Just a little tickle of the connection between me and the spellblade. It made me sick to my stomach to think about pressing on without it. Without Mort, the only weapons I had on me were a couple of karambit knives—claw-shaped blades that I could use with vicious efficiency in close combat. But the knives weren't imbued with my blood and magic like my shadowsteel broadsword.

I went to the edge of the drop-off and held my hand aloft to light Jasper's way. He backed up several feet and then ran forward with his elbows pumping. He cleared the fissure easily, displaying an admirable blend of power and grace for a man his size. I did the same, my heart skipping a beat as I passed over the dark chasm and felt Mort's presence.

We both faced the giant double doors that loomed ahead. The ring pulls were a good five feet off the ground, the scale obviously not meant for beings the size of me and Jasper.

Together, we approached slowly. When we'd covered about half the distance, a sudden metallic groaning rang through the cavern. Both of us froze, and I reflexively lifted my hand for Mort before I remembered.

I was just about to ask Jasper if he knew what the noise was when I realized the doors were moving. The groan was coming from the great hinges as the doors swung outward.

"Guess we don't have to worry about handling the cold iron," I muttered, squinting into the darkness beyond the doors.

My pulse and my thoughts raced as the thump of sky iron intensified. We shouldn't have come. The gods knew we were there. They weren't going to let us just skip out of the Giants' Causeway with Oberon. We were idiots. We were going to die under this mountain of rock.

Jasper was breathing hard beside me, perhaps thinking similar things. "You reckon we should go in?" he asked, his gaze glued to the dark space opening up beyond the doors.

I opened my mouth to say we might as well, seeing as how our hosts had opened the way for us. But I didn't get the chance. Cool mist began billowing out at us, and then there was a flash so blindingly sudden and bright I shouted in pain and slapped my hands over my eyes. Yet even with my eyelids squeezed closed and my palms pressed over them, the light still came in, burning me blind. It seemed to work its way into my brain. I tried to push back against it, but it seemed to short out my synapses, within seconds sending me into the oblivion of unconsciousness.

Some undeterminable time later, I jerked awake. I blinked, but my injured eyes sensed nothing. My heart jolted as I realized there was sky iron nearby. Very near.

And then the gods began to speak.

Chapter 16

I KNEW IT was the Tuatha speaking because the voices had the same quality as in the vision where Jasper and I had discovered the gods were holding Oberon. The words seemed to come from everywhere and reverberate around in my brain before fading. The gods had spoken to Oberon in the vision. They'd tortured him with sky iron.

And now the Tuatha had me and Jasper, too.

I blinked rapidly, hoping my shocked optic nerves would start to recover, but all I could see was a field of dark splotches against white. I shifted, expecting to feel the burn of iron shackles, but I wasn't restrained. My skin suffered no iron burns, but the low throb of sky iron was so intense I shrank against the wall at my back. The poison metal was very near, only a handful of feet away.

I inhaled sharply as I suddenly recognized that one of the voices in the conversation was Jasper's.

". . . but what you created has evolved into something too beautiful to destroy," he was saying. He spoke with such vehemence and commitment I nearly teared up. "It may not be what you envisioned, but that doesn't make it wrong. It's flawed, yet wonderful. There is only one Faerie, and in spite of the divide between Seelie and Unseelie, the pettiness and the fighting, we Fae love our realm with an ardor that runs through our very blood. Please, I beg you to see that your displeasure is unwarranted."

"You dare accuse the Tuatha of not seeing?" one of the god-voices boomed. "We created the lands you claim to love. We pulled existence into the dimension you call Faerie. We molded the first Fae realms. Do not tell us to see. *We see all.*"

My heart jumped into my throat. What was Jasper doing, trying to pick a fight with our immortal creators? I was torn between trying to shush him and wanting to hear him say more. I couldn't imagine speaking with so much fearless intensity to the Tuatha De Danann.

But what he was saying was clearly pissing them off. The echoes of the words seemed to continue to beat against my eardrums, as if the Tuatha's message was getting physically nailed into my mortal brain.

There was a moan from a different part of the room, the area where I could feel the awful pulse of sky iron most strongly.

"If you must blame someone, blame me." I recognized Oberon's voice, though the words were slurred. It came from the direction of the sky iron. He had to be in terrible pain. "Punish me, not mortal Fae for living under my rule. Take my life. Leave Faerie be, I beg you." Oberon's plea trailed off into a rising keen of pain, and I winced, my skin aching in sympathy of the torment he endured.

The High King was coming to Jasper's defense, asking to take his punishment. Begging the gods to spare Faerie even as he know it would bring more punishment.

"Silence yourself," a different god-voice commanded. "We shall convene to determine your fate."

Oberon didn't respond, and by his silence, I figured he'd probably passed out from the effort of speaking through the torture of sky iron.

The cool humidity that had permeated the room began to recede, and the presence of the gods left with it. I didn't fool myself that we had privacy, but in the physical sense at least, I knew that Jasper, Oberon, and I had been left alone.

I'd never felt a deep devotion to Oberon or his High Court. Loyalty, yes, as he was the highest Seelie ruler in Faerie, and I'd always thought he'd done a decent job of keeping the realm in the peace of summer. But I'd judged him a self-indulgent hothead who engaged in silly feuds with his Queen and other Old Ones. I had never seen Oberon as a noble ruler who would gladly volunteer to sacrifice himself to save us all.

We had to get him out.

I was blind, weaponless, and at the complete mercy of the gods, but I was determined to save the High King. Yeah, my decisions weren't always the most reasonable.

Using the wall for support, I stood.

"Jasper?"

"I'm here, Petra."

"Can you see?"

"No, can you?"

I waved my hand in front of my face. Nothing. "Nope." I licked my dry lips. "We have to get Oberon out of here."

"The gods aren't going to let us go," Jasper said.

"No. We're clearly not going to be able to sweet talk them. If I can get to the sky iron, I can spill enough blood to call Mort to me."

I wasn't completely sure it would work. My sense of my spellblade's presence was so faint I couldn't be certain I wasn't imagining it or calling it up from memory.

"And then what?" Jasper asked. "You'll swing your broadsword around blindly at the mists?"

In the legend, the Tuatha could take Fae-like form or dissolve themselves into mist. Jasper was right—swinging a blade through a room full of fog probably wouldn't help our cause all that much. And if I used the spellblade blood magic to call Mort to my hand, I'd probably be unconscious from the blood loss anyway.

"Yeah, okay," I said. "What are we going to do?"

"Petra Maguire, Champion of the Summer Court," Oberon said, the sudden sound of his deep voice making me jump.

"Uh, yes, your majesty." On reflex, I made an awkward curtsy and hoped I was doing it in the general direction of the High King.

"You were the last to wield Aurora?" the High King asked, naming the enchanted blade I'd used to defeat King Periclase's brother in a Battle of Champions. Oberon was supposed to attend that fight, but he'd disappeared not long before. I hadn't known at the time that he'd been coming here to plead with the gods to spare Faerie.

My eyes popped wide. He'd disappeared before my battle in the arena. How could Oberon have learned I was the champion? He must have gotten word before the Tuatha began his torment in this seaside mountain of basalt columns.

"Yes, your majesty," I said, finding my voice after a second or two of surprise.

"That is very good news, indeed."

I frowned in confusion, thinking maybe Oberon was delirious or perhaps the exposure to sky iron had finally begun to affect his mind.

"Your majesty?" Jasper asked, clearly trying not to be impolite but probably having similar doubts about the High King's soundness of mind.

"I can summon Aurora to appear in an instant," Oberon said, his voice hoarse but otherwise sounding lucid. "But only to the hand of the last sworn Champion of the Summer Court to wield the sword. I did catch wind of your victory, by the way. You are clearly a worthy champion."

My mouth went dry at the praise. On reflex, my head swiveled toward the direction of Jasper's voice, my eyes seeking to see his reaction to the news that Oberon could conjure Aurora.

"But in your condition, your majesty, using so much magic would surely be dangerous, even to an Old One," Jasper said, picking his words carefully, his tone heavy with concern.

Jasper was treading lightly. What he really meant was that such conjuring magic—pulling an object from its place to make it appear somewhere else—could just about kill an Old One who was in perfect health. But one who'd been tortured with sky iron for days on end? I was hard-pressed to imagine how Oberon could possibly summon enough power.

The High King muttered something about Unseelie, and my heart sank. Maybe he wasn't quite as coherent as I'd thought a moment ago.

"Pardon, your majesty?" I asked.

Oberon cleared his throat loudly, a noise that ended in a short groan. "Damn sky iron. I said, you're a good one for an Unseelie," he said. "I approve of you, bastard prince."

"Oh, I, uh . . ." Jasper stuttered. "Your compliment is met with gratitude, your majesty."

"Now, then, let's get on with it," Oberon said, nearly managing a crispness to his words.

"But I can't even see any—" I started to protest.

"No, you won't survive—" Jasper said at the same time.

But neither of us got the chance to make our case. A roar filled the room, drowning out both of us. I slammed my hands over my ears as the sound punched into my head with such force I thought my skull might crack open.

A few seconds into the torrent, I realized golden light was penetrating through my eyelids. I cracked them open to see a dizzying psychedelic churn of colors swirling around me—pale blue, warm yellows and oranges, delicate pinks—and somehow, I recognized the palette. These were the hues of the summer dawn, the colors captured in Aurora's blade.

In the space between breaths, the roaring died, my vision returned completely, and I stood with my hands against my sternum, clutching the handle of a sword. A few inches from my nose, Aurora glinted like the sunrise.

I tried to gasp, but my breath hitched in my throat, snagging on the sudden emotion welling up. I loved Mort like a best friend, but Aurora was a legend, an absolute glory to behold.

"Petra, the mist!" Jasper shouted, his vision apparently returned as well.

I had about a half second to register my surroundings—a dark rocky box of a room where the only things besides Jasper, me, and Oberon were the sky iron shackles restraining the High King. Only, he didn't need to be restrained because his body was completely limp.

And the cool mist was creeping through vertical cracks in the small cavern's walls. The gods were coming in. Aurora blazed like a thousand-watt bulb, lighting up the small space and making the mist glow.

On instinct, I began swinging the legendary sword. The mist burned away wherever the blade contacted it, but it quickly reformed just out of my reach. I arced Aurora through the air faster and faster until the blade whistled.

"How the hell do we get out?" I yelled at Jasper, who'd gone to Oberon and was trying to rouse him.

If I allowed the mist to coalesce, the gods would take shape and then we'd really be screwed.

"You have to break the shackles!" Jasper said, ignoring my question.

My stomach tightened as I crossed the small cavern, swinging the sword like a madwoman. The pulse of sky iron reverberated through me. I'd been near the stuff before, but it hadn't felt like this. The Tuatha's sky iron must have been the most pure in existence to create such a sensation.

I stayed a few feet away from Jasper and the High King, still fighting the mist. I was barely keeping ahead of it. I tried to take stock of Oberon's situation as I kept swinging Aurora. I couldn't pause in my battle against the fog for more than a second or two, or the Tuatha would have time to take their corporeal forms.

The High King of the Summer Court lay on a narrow table about three feet off the ground. Straps of sky iron encircled his bare chest, upper arms, wrists, and ankles. Where the poison metal touched him, his flesh was a gory, oozing mess. A dark pool of blood had collected under him and was still fed by the dripping from his wounds.

Oberon's eyes had rolled back in his head, and I couldn't detect any movement or rise or fall of his chest.

"Step aside," I warned Jasper.

Then I shuffled forward in a fencing move, took aim, lifted Aurora overhead, and brought the blade down across the sky iron caging Oberon's chest. My heart in my throat, I sent up a prayer that I hadn't swung so hard that I would slice the High King.

The blade made contact with the iron in an explosion of silver sparks and dark smoke. The smell of blood and metal filled my nostrils, and there was the heavy clink of metal impacting rock. When the smoke cleared, I saw the iron strap had fallen to the ground.

"Petra, the mist," Jasper said, gesturing wildly.

I whirled, already swinging, and sliced Aurora through the air as fast as I could to dispel the fog. Then I turned and swung at the sky iron around Oberon's arm.

Clink, clink.

Two more shackles broken.

Again, I swiveled to fight the billowing mist.

Break sky iron, burn the mist. Break more iron, battle more mist.

I alternated between the two until Oberon was free.

Sweat poured down my temples and dripped into my eyes. My heart pounded with adrenaline, and I panted with the effort of exertion.

Out of the corners of my eyes, I saw Jasper maneuvering Oberon, trying to get the huge king over his shoulder. The High King was over seven feet tall, and though he was slim, he was muscled and probably weighed three hundred pounds.

Gritting his teeth and groaning, Jasper rose with Oberon on his back.

"Where the hell is the exit?" I shrieked in frustration.

"Try the sword," Jasper grunted.

I went to one of the vertical slits in the wall, where the mist was still creeping through, stuck Aurora in, and tried to wedge the crack open. The stone didn't budge. I stepped back and swung the sword at the wall. The impact sent a jarring clang through me, and a few chips of the wall showered onto the floor. At that rate, we'd die before I hacked my way through the wall. For all I knew, it could be solid rock for miles.

With another strangled cry of frustration, I reached for my magic, letting it rush through me like a surge of adrenaline and guided it into my arms. I pushed power into my hands and the blade I held, as I'd done hundreds of times with Mort.

I had no real expectation it would work, but desperation drove my actions. Instead of igniting with violet flames of magic as my spellblade would have, Aurora flared with blindingly bright colors of the dawn sky.

For a split second I stood there stunned and frozen as the warm high of new magic surged through me. It was electrifying and calming all at once. On instinct, I stepped to the wall again, drew Aurora back, and then swung like a power hitter going for the fences. Twisting at the waist, I put all my strength into the move.

The blade crashed against rock, and I felt the wall give way. The light of the sword flared again, and when it died back enough to reveal the damage, I saw I'd punched a hole big enough to step through. Aurora still shone with the gentle colors of a summer morning sky, softly illuminating the dust swirling through the air.

"Jasper!" I hollered over my shoulder. "Let's go!"

Then I ducked and charged through the opening.

Chapter 17

I BARELY HAD time to register that we'd been trapped inside a room-within-a-room as I ran around the edge of what had been our prison just a moment ago.

Looking back to make sure Jasper was following me, I sent out a desperate prayer that I would come to an escape route. Holding Aurora aloft, I scrambled through an opening to find it dead-ended in a cavern.

When I spun around to retrace my steps, I nearly crashed into Jasper, who was almost bent double with Oberon slung across his shoulders. I couldn't imagine how Jasper managed to keep up with me. He stumbled and his back hit the wall, which saved him from falling.

"The mist!" he ground out, his jaw clenched with the effort of carrying the High King.

I realized the chill had started to surround us again. I shouldered past Jasper and Oberon and swung Aurora, fighting back the fog of the gods.

"See a way out?" I hollered, still swiping at the encroaching mist.

"I think so," he said, to my surprise.

I flipped a glance over my shoulder and saw he was already several feet away and heading to a different opening.

I maneuvered backward, still fending off the mist, as I approached the spot where he'd stopped.

"How do you know that's the exit?" I grunted, slashing at the air.

"I can smell the sea on the draft coming through this one."

I caught a faint whiff of that unmistakable blend of fish, salt, and decaying seaweed that signaled the ocean was nearby.

I flapped my hand hurriedly at him. "Go, I'm right behind you."

We plunged into a corridor like the one we'd come through when we'd first entered the basalt column mountain. Maybe it was the same one. I was fighting too furiously to notice.

The mist was still pursuing us, and it was accompanied by a whispering that rushed into my ears. I only caught a snippet of the words here and there as I slashed Aurora through the air in a tight criss-cross pattern. But the gods seemed to be trying to frighten us. The whispers conjured up nightmares in my mind—war, blood, death, and desolation.

As I fought, it occurred to me that the Tuatha might be describing a preview of what they planned to do to Faerie.

The corridor was so tight, Jasper had to shuffle sideways with Oberon across his back. I moved backward, facing the mist and with my back to Jasper. Aurora kept clipping the walls, sending razor-edged chips of stone plinking to the ground. But I was, somehow, holding off the gods.

I was so focused on the rhythm of the sword, I let out a strangled shout of surprise when I stumbled into the wide cavern, the place where I'd lost Mort.

Suddenly aware of my spellblade down in the crevasse somewhere, I hesitated in my fight. The gods took advantage, and the chilly white mist rushed around me.

My vision began to spot and fade. If the Tuatha took shape from the mist, Jasper and I would be blind. As the myths said, mortals were forbidden from laying eyes upon the gods.

I redoubled my efforts, pushing magic into Aurora and swinging the sword with blinding speed. The mist retreated, and my vision cleared.

"Petra, mind the crack!" Jasper shouted.

I looked over my shoulder and found he'd made it across the fissure with Oberon. I shook my head, trying to imagine how Jasper had managed such a feat.

I took one last huge swipe at the encroaching fog, then turned, got a few steps' running start, and hurdled the dark opening in the ground. Freedom wasn't far—the Tuatha couldn't follow us outside into the Earthly realm.

We crossed the cavern and squeezed into the corridor that would take us out of the mountain. Dismay arrowed through my heart as I realized I truly had to leave Mort behind.

But we made it, bursting out into the salty air with the gray sky opening up overhead. Tendrils of mist crept after us, but the Tuatha couldn't take their corporeal forms out here. They couldn't follow us.

We skidded down to a short plateau. Jasper fell heavily onto one knee and let Oberon sag from his back. Jasper's hair was darkened with sweat, beads of it pouring down the sides of his face. He was breathing too hard to speak. His head drooped, and he propped a fist on the ground, staying down on his knee as if in prayer.

I eyed the dark space between the columns, ready with Aurora even though I knew we were safe.

After a few minutes, Jasper looked up.

"Do you suppose I just hauled a three-hundred-pound corpse all that way?" he asked.

We both angled our gazes at Oberon's still form. I went and knelt next to the High King and pressed my fingers against the side of his neck. Holding my breath, I waited. There it was—the thump of life. Weak, but it was there. I waited a couple of seconds longer until I saw his chest move with breath.

"He's breathing and has a pulse," I said and rose. "I don't know how you carried him all that way, but he's alive. It was worth it."

Jasper heaved a deep sigh and gave me a faint smile.

We rested a few more minutes, and then I slid Aurora into Mort's scabbard on my back and positioned my hands under Oberon's shoulders. Jasper grasped the High King's legs behind the knees, and carrying Oberon together, we picked our way down the slope leading to the wide plateau that separated us from the doorway that would take us back into Faerie.

Oh, what I would have given for a trio of Great Ravens to take us the rest of the way.

For the next few minutes, the world seemed to narrow to two things: keeping my hands locked under Oberon's arms and trying to put one foot in front of the other without stumbling.

We were a few hundred yards from the doorway when Jasper's boots ground to an abrupt halt.

His eyes were cast back the way we'd come, and his face had gone pale. I followed his gaze.

Men on horseback were trickling out of the dark fissure from which we'd escaped. My blood froze. No, those weren't men.

"Oh, for the love of Faerie, no," I breathed, my mouth suddenly dry.

"The Dullahan." Jasper was already scrambling to heave Oberon back onto his shoulders. "You're going to have to fend them off."

Rumor was the Tuatha had raised the Dullahan—the terrifying Bone Warriors, believed to be only the stuff of scary stories until recently—to come back and help them raze the world and people they'd created. The Dullahan were no longer myth nor rumor.

I swallowed hard and drew Aurora from my back scabbard. The sword slid free with a soft metallic ping, glinting with the hues of dawn.

The Dullahan—the terrifying Bone Warriors—weren't myths as I'd always believed. Jasper had told me the Tuatha planned to send the Dullahan to do the dirty work of razing Faerie, but it was hard to reconcile that bit of intel with the stories from my childhood. Fae mothers and fathers used tales of the Dullahan to warn their children not to stray too far from home, and especially not to go into the Earthly realm alone. For the Bone Warriors were waiting out there to claim more victims to grow their army. And once you were claimed by the Dullahan, you were sentenced to ride forever with them.

The real kicker in the stories was the description of the skeletal horseback riders carrying their own heads under their arms as they rode into battle—or waited to pounce on an unsuspecting child. They used their decapitated heads for intimidation and as weapons. If you were touched by a Dullahan head, you were done for.

These thoughts flashed through my mind in a split second. Jasper had already taken off, stumbling as fast as he could toward the doorway. I shuffled in a sideways run after him, my eyes glued to the growing crowd of riders at the base of the cliff.

Why were they just milling around there? Perhaps they had some territorial restriction. My heart lifted a little at the idea. Maybe, like the Tuatha, they couldn't move beyond the basalt mountain.

The Dullahan were forming a neat row facing us. No. I was wrong about the restriction. It hit me a split second before the skeletal riders reached up in unison, removing their own heads.

With a bone-chilling shriek coming from every detached head, the line charged.

"Oh, shit!" I screeched.

I turned and ran for all I was worth. I had to slow down when I caught up with Jasper. If I flew past him, I'd leave him and Oberon defenseless.

"They're coming," I warned, my voice surprisingly steady. "But I've got you. Just focus on getting yourself and Oberon through that doorway. Go without me if you have to."

Turning my back to him, I gripped Aurora and faced the headless riders. I skip-jogged backward so I could watch their approach, careful not to accidentally run into Jasper.

The wailing was rapidly growing louder, punctuated by the drumbeat of hooves across the hard ground, and the sky was darkening to a bruised blue-black.

If we could sprint to the doorway, we could probably beat the Dullahan. But there was no sprinting under the weight of an unconscious Old One.

I took a slow breath, both to steady myself and to focus within where my magic resided. Drawing from my heart center, I let my power flow across my skin, forming stone armor and joining with Aurora. The colors of dawn flared from the blade. I pulled more deeply, trying to open the way for a river of magic. It was dangerous to try to max out how much I drew, but if ever there was a time to do it, it was now. I'd deal with the consequences later. If my heart didn't stop from the strain.

My head filled with the hoofbeats and shrieks, while headless skeleton riders filled my vision. It was a waking nightmare.

Lightning, seeming to come from nowhere, crackled low overhead.

"Run, Jasper!" I shouted over the noise. "I'm right behind you!"

"Don't let them block our way," he wheezed back at me.

"I won't," I said through gritted teeth, gripping Aurora in both hands and opening myself to the magic in my blood.

Magic flowed like lava in my veins, and it nearly stole my breath. I hadn't pulled so much of it since I was a child, first learning to guide my inborn power and accidentally opening the floodgates too far.

The lead Bone Warrior palmed his own skull, drew his arm back, and hurled the head at me. I thought he was still too far away to hit me, but the skull left his hand like an arrow from a bow, arcing low and straight at me. Damn, but the aim was true, perfectly anticipating my movement.

I raised Aurora and swung, shattering the skull. There was a nightmarish high-pitched keening, and then a burst of maroon fire surrounded the Dullahan who'd tried to nail me. After a moment, both he and his horse were consumed by the flames, leaving only a wisp of ash that was carried away by the stiff sea wind.

My power had flickered when the blade contacted the skull, sending an unpleasant shockwave into my heart and leaving me gasping and clutching my chest with one hand.

But there was no time for recovery.

Half a dozen more skulls were about to rain down on us. I eyed them, quickly calculating which ones would miss and which I'd have to defend against. With reflexes borne from years of drilling, I arced Aurora in a snaking pattern, battering three of the skulls to bits with one swing. The other three hit the ground harmlessly.

The victory was brief. Jasper and I were moving at a clumsy jog due to the load he carried and all of my sword swinging, and it wasn't fast enough.

The remaining Dullahan, two dozen or so, caught up to us and split into two groups that streamed around us.

"They're surrounding us," I hollered at Jasper. "Watch yourself!"

Up close, they were horrifying—skeletal figures with patches of leathery flesh clinging to the bones.

The riders caught us inside their circle. I spun, my heart trying to climb up my throat, and tried to anticipate their attack. But for a long moment, they only seemed to want to taunt us, surrounding us in the chaos of pounding horse hooves and earsplitting shrieks. The lightning was going nuts overhead.

"I'll look for an opening," I said to Jasper, not daring to take my eyes off the riders to meet his gaze. I sounded confident, but trying to cut a path through the riders probably wasn't going to end well.

My face firmed in determination as I mentally planned my attack. I just needed to give Jasper a chance to get Oberon to the doorway. In the name of my father's life, I had to give them a chance. If I was going to lose my life to the Dullahan, I had to make it mean something. Not for myself. For Oliver.

"Get ready to run," came a gravelly voice from behind me.

My eyes widened, and I whipped around to see that Oberon was awake. He lifted one shaking hand and extended his index finger to the sky. The black clouds above growled, the undersides of them sparking with pent-up energy. And then the sparks gathered, flowing like liquid and joining into a massive bolt that streaked downward.

I reflexively covered my head and ducked, as if the gesture would do anything to protect me from the lightning, and kept one eye open and tipped toward the sky.

The bolt broke into several forks, striking a handful of the Dullahan. Oberon's lightning didn't appear to kill the Bone Warriors, but it did freeze them in place.

"Go, go, go!" I screamed.

Jasper was already in motion. Oberon flopped across his back, passed out again.

I sprinted ahead of them. The doorway was only twenty feet away. Ten. Five.

Sliding to a sudden halt in front of the arch, I realized with a jolt that I didn't know the sigils to get us back to the doorway from which we'd come. We had to go back to the doorway in the pyre from here. Only one way in and out. That was why Jasper had been forced to give something up to the white-clad Lorelei to get us here. Gods, if anything had happened to Jasper, I'd have been stuck on the Giants' Causeway, forced to try to outrun the Dullahan until I located another doorway—or more likely, joined the Bone Warriors. I shoved that alarming thought away.

My hands moved like lightning as I sheathed Aurora in my back scabbard and grappled Oberon off of Jasper while he traced the sigils and said the words. He clutched my arm with one hand and linked his other arm under Oberon's shoulder. Together, we dragged the High King through.

The three of us fell into the void of the netherwhere.

Chapter 18

OBERON, JASPER, AND I landed in a heap on the sand at the foot of the Lorelei's pyre.

My brain was screaming at me to get up, to run. I had to assume the Dullahan could move through doorways, and if so, they were bound to pour through any second. But my entire body shook with fatigue, and the center of my chest felt cold and crampy after pulling too much magic. I tamped down on the alarm that tried to zip through me.

"The Lorelei won't let them through," Jasper panted. "We're safe here for the moment."

I let out a long breath and flopped back onto the damp sand, staring up at the dark sky. It was nighttime. The clouds high above drifted on the breeze, moving over the backdrop of the stars beyond, covering and then revealing the twinkling little points.

We rested for only a minute or so, just enough time to catch our breath. Jasper and I roused at almost exactly the same time, both of us going for Oberon.

"They let us get away," I said, grunting the words as I slung my arms under Oberon's and hefted his upper body. My knees creaked. I had to be lifting about two hundred pounds of dead weight.

Jasper faced away from me, positioning himself between Oberon's knees. He squatted and grabbed the High King's legs under the knees and rose in one smooth motion.

"I thought they seemed rather serious about killing us," Jasper said over his shoulder.

I didn't answer, too intent on keeping hold of Oberon while stepping through the squishy sand. We conveyed the High King in a two-person first-aid carry. I was bearing most of the weight, and even though Jasper faced away from me, I could see how exhausted he was by the way the cords of his neck stood out. His grip on Oberon's legs kept slipping, but Jasper didn't pause or remark on his exhaustion.

"Let's just get a bit of distance from the pyre," Jasper said.

It did seem wise to move away from the Lorelei, even though all I wanted to do was rest. "Good idea."

A few minutes of silence passed as we both focused on trying to move as quickly as possible.

"Even if they weren't going for kills, they probably wouldn't have minded nicking one of us as a prized addition to the Dullahan army," Jasper said darkly, obviously still thinking of the attack.

That sent a chill through me.

"You're probably right on that," I said. After a pause, I frowned. "So where are we going to take him, anyway? Certainly not back to the Duergar realm."

"Gods, no. Though can you imagine Periclase's face if we delivered the unconscious High King of the Summer Court to him?"

In spite of my fatigue, I snorted a laugh.

"So, you're just going to betray your king and the Unseelie by taking Oberon to safety?" I said it with a light tone, but my stomach tightened at the thought. If Periclase ever found out the Jasper had rescued Oberon and then set him free . . . Death wouldn't be a surprising punishment. Not with how things were currently going in Faerie.

"Getting Oberon back to the Summerlands is the only thing that's going to stop all of this madness," Jasper said, his tone suddenly angry. "Damn fool Unseelie rulers can't see past their hunger for power."

My former conviction about Jasper, that he was the key to saving Faerie, flooded back to me. Along with it came the certainty that my own involvement was irrevocable. Instead of the internal groan that would have been my usual response to such a thought, I focused on Jasper laboring a few feet ahead of me. Instead of resistance, I felt determination and, to my surprise, loyalty. He'd somehow known that Faerie needed me. I understood now that it was true, and that I had a responsibility to show up for my people. But there was something deeper than that, and it had everything to do with this Unseelie man, the son of a banished king who everyone thought was an average soldier.

Jasper stopped, and we gently set Oberon on the sand. I sat down heavily near the High King's head. Jasper sat, too.

"How will we get Oberon to the Summerlands, Jasper?" I asked, noticing how his name felt on the tip of my tongue, even through the fog of exhaustion. "Neither of us can deliver him there if we want to keep Periclase in the dark."

"I will have Drifte and his people do it."

I nodded, though Jasper couldn't see me. It was wise to choose someone who seemed more or less unaffiliated. And from what I'd witnessed, Drifte seemed the type of man who could take care of himself, even in the face of a raging battle for the High Court.

I bolted upright, my heart bumping hard in my chest, as I became acutely aware of having been absent from the Duergar palace for some time.

"I have to get back," I said, scrambling to my feet. I raked my hand through my tangled hair. "My father. I've been gone for much too long."

Jasper quickly stood, though even in the dark I could see by the way he pushed heavily on his knee to leverage himself up that he was exhausted and hurting.

I looked from him to Oberon's limp form and back to Jasper. The moonlight glowed in his eyes, the silvery light softened by the gold of his irises.

"We're back in Faerie," he said, reaching into a pouch on his belt. "I can call the Ravens to help me with Oberon."

I let out a whoosh of relieved breath. I didn't want to abandon him, but worry already circled around in my chest. Surely by now Periclase had noticed my absence.

Jasper had pulled out his whistle and blew a tone that seemed to send a little shockwave outward. Three dark winged creatures appeared around the rocky cliff half a minute later.

"Your Raven will take you straight to the Duergar palace," he said.

The birds descended at a sharp angle, landing with light hops on the sand a dozen feet away.

I stepped into Jasper, grabbing a handful of his shirt in my fist and pulling him to me in a rough-edged gesture.

"Someday soon, all of Faerie is going to know exactly who you truly are, Jasper Glasgow," I whispered.

"*We* saved the High King, Petra. I wouldn't have made it out with him if not for you and your sword."

I pressed my lips against his for a delicious second and then turned and ran to my bird. She was slightly smaller than the other two, and the feathers on the top of her head were permanently ruffled, sticking up a bit where most other Great Ravens' crowns were perfectly sleek. She was the one I'd ridden before.

"Take great care, Petra," Jasper called softly. "I'll send for you as soon as I return home."

I raised my hand in a wave as my Raven took flight. I wanted to think that Jasper and I would indeed meet when he returned to the Duergar palace. But in my gut, I knew I would not arrive back in Periclase's realm to business as usual.

My stomach twisted tighter with each beat of my Raven's wings. She took me through doorways in the sky that only she could see, plunging us into the void and out again, three times before we emerged over a forest. I could tell by the smell of the fir trees below, the dryness of the air, and the distinct silhouette of a distant mountain range that we'd arrived in the Duergar realm.

We circled, and I caught sight of the palace a couple of miles away, the outline of the turrets giving away the structure's identity.

I felt my expression go grim as I realized how well I'd come to know Periclase's realm. I'd spent entirely too much time here. That needed to change.

My Raven plunged us into the netherwhere once again, and a second later we popped out almost on top of the palace. She nearly bobbled me off as she dropped sharply for a rough landing on a balcony. I recognized it right away—I'd arrived at Jasper's quarters. There was a passage leading from there to my room, but damned if I remembered all the twists and turns to take in between.

I slid from the Raven's back, giving her glossy neck a quick pat.

"Off with you, now," I whispered. "Be careful to avoid the sentries."

I knew I didn't have to warn her but wanted her to know I cared about her safety.

With a powerful whoosh of wings and air, she was in flight.

"Gods, do you have to be so dramatic," drawled a bored-sounding voice.

I jumped straight off the floor, whirling in a crouch and drawing Aurora all in one motion.

"And so damn *loud*." Bryna pushed off the wall where she'd been leaning.

My heart pounding, I straightened.

"Did Jasper tell you to meet me?" I asked, my gaze darting around, still alert to danger.

"Duh," she said. She was tossing me her usual pissy attitude, but she was also clearly trying to be very quiet. "Why else would I be here? C'mon, I need to get you inside. And I'm tired, so I'd prefer to go as fast as you can move in those clompers, if you don't mind."

"Wait," I whispered. "What's going on in the palace? Does Periclase know I'm missing? Are the servitors gone? Is Nicole okay?"

"Lots of things, yes, yes, and yes." She moved toward the secret panel that would take us into a secret passage through the walls.

"*Wait*," I hissed, frustration and alarm spiking through me. "Where does Periclase think I went?"

She threw her arms out in an exaggerated shrug. "I don't know? He probably thinks you tried to run away? Let's *go*."

I sucked in a breath and pinched the bridge of my nose with my thumb and forefinger. Don't punch her, don't punch her, don't punch her.

"Bryna," I said with as much patience as I could muster. "This is really important. He has Oliver, the man who raised me. Periclase tortured him, gouged out . . ." My words faltered, and I paused to clear my throat. "He gouged out Oliver's eye. If he thinks I, well, if he thinks I did anything he doesn't want me doing, he'll punish my father for it."

Bryna pressed her lips together for a moment, the moonlight glinting off her long, pale hair. For a second, she looked a bit softer, a little less like a pain in my ass. "I'm sorry, I honestly don't know where the king thinks you've been. But you've been gone for a long time."

My heart seemed to tighten into a fist. "How long?"

"If you left sometime during the servitor attack, about six or seven hours."

I'd guessed it was less than a day and was relieved to find it was just a handful of hours. Still, it was a longer than I'd wanted to be away. Plenty of time for Periclase to take notice and exact his anger on Oliver. "Okay. So where are you going to take me? Not my quarters. That wouldn't help anything if I just appeared back in my room."

She let out a sigh. "Yeah, that's true. What about this. You let the guards find you and bring you in."

I brightened a little. "That might work."

"Oh!" She snapped her fingers. "Let them find you unconscious. Pretend to be disoriented."

I shook my head. "Eh, that might be taking it too far. I need a spot where I could have been trapped all this time. I went to fight the frost giants and got stuck somewhere. And finally, a passing guard heard my yells."

"Yeah," Bryna said, obviously getting into it. In her enjoyment of scheming, she even seemed to forget that she loathed me. "I can tip off one of the guards, say I heard a cry for help coming from, uh, from . . . I know! I've got just the place."

She beckoned at me to follow her and then disappeared into the secret passage. I stepped in after her, trailing her silently as we traced a winding path through the palace.

Bryna wasn't someone I'd normally trust—hell, she'd tried to kill me with a wraith once—but I knew Jasper wouldn't have sent her to help me if he thought for a second Bryna would put me in danger.

There wasn't much noise coming from the other side of the walls. Just the occasional low conversation or rustle of clothing as someone moved through an adjacent corridor. My senses became lulled by the dark, the muffled sounds, and the need to keep quiet. When Bryna stopped abruptly, I nearly plowed into her.

"What?" I whispered.

She responded by jabbing her elbow back at me. It poked me in the diaphragm, and I let out a soft *oof*. The only light we had came through pinholes poked in the walls at random, allowing only the tiniest bits of illumination through. Not enough to see her face, but I didn't need it—her alarm was clear in her body language.

She grabbed my head in both hands and yanked my ear to her lips.

"Go back the way we came," she whispered hurriedly. "*Now*."

Then she shoved me roughly away.

My heart pounding, I about-faced and began retracing our steps. I turned a corner just as light poured into the passage behind me. Voices—including Bryna's—floated after me.

Something had gone wrong. She'd gotten caught, or . . . I wasn't sure. But she seemed to be trying to stall whoever was back there so I could get away.

With my fingertips brushing the walls to keep me steady, I moved as quickly as I could. Bryna was right. My combat boots were shit for sneaking around in secret passages. I was making too much noise and had to slow down.

I came to a crossroads in the walls and stopped. Damn, which way had we come? I should have been paying more attention. I looked right and then left. Darkness either way. The smell of bread baking wafted past from the left. I remembered kitchen smells from before. I turned that way.

I made it about five steps when a large rectangle of wall to my right popped out and fell away. Two beefy guards loomed in the hole.

There was just enough time to suck in a breath of surprise before I got slammed by the electric kiss of a magi-zapper.

Already fatigued and magically drained, I didn't have a chance. My entire body stiffened, and then I was falling like a cut tree.

The world faded to black before I hit the floor.

When consciousness began to return, the first thing I noticed was that my arms were twitching violently of their own accord. I was sitting in a chair with my wrists secured behind me in shackles laced with cold iron, my muscles jerking hard enough to chafe the restraints painfully.

Those damn muscle twitches. Maybe they'd been made worse by the sting of the magi-zapper. I drew a bit of magic and directed it down my arms, bringing the small relief of a layer of stone armor around my burning wrists.

When I raised my head and the room came into focus, my stomach dropped to the floor and I forgot all about my spasming muscles.

Before me stood Periclase, Finvarra, and Eldon, the Fae sorcerer who'd held me frozen and nearly suffocated me. They stood in a semi-circle with a crumpled form at their feet. Through the caked blood, I recognized my father's close-cropped head, and my breath died.

Chapter 19

EVEN THOUGH I knew I was handcuffed, my first instinct was to reach for Mort. My spellblade wasn't there—Mort was still at the bottom of the fissure under the stone mountain in the Giants' Causeway. But when I shifted on my chair, I realized Aurora was still strapped to my back. That meant something. There was no way Periclase would have allowed me to keep my weapon, even while I sat there restrained.

I focused on my father, trying to discern whether there was new damage. My breath hitched in my chest when Oliver stirred and groaned. He didn't raise his head. At least he was still alive. Still, something broke within me. I'd left with Jasper, and just as I'd feared, I'd put my father at risk.

My arms locked behind me as a painful spasm gripped my muscles. I grimaced, hoping it looked as if I was struggling against my restraints rather than in the throes of uncontrollable convulsions. The cold iron burned into my skin. Warm blood was already drying on my palms and the backs of my hands. Better not to form stone armor, as my captors would likely see any use of magic as an attempt to move against them. The cold iron hurt, but I could bear it.

My gaze lifted to Periclase.

"What do you want?" I asked quietly.

A silent understanding passed between us. The Duergar king knew I would do whatever he asked.

"My stone warrior princess," Periclase said, and tsked. "You've misbehaved, haven't you? We'll get to that in a moment, but first let's have some introductions. After all, we're a civilized society here in the Duergar realm."

I stared at him, unblinking, letting him play out his lines. But Periclase's reference to civility wasn't lost on me. It was a subtle homage to Finvarra, crediting the man who'd modernized and united so many of the Unseelie realms. By that one small comment, Periclase had tipped his hand—Finvarra was the one in charge here.

And suddenly the frost giant attack made sense. Finvarra had sent the servitors into the palace as a threat, a show of strength. That he stood here with Periclase probably meant they'd reached some sort of agreement. The Duergar king was now aligned with Finvarra and whatever he had planned.

My stomach tightened as my eyes flicked over to the banished Unseelie High King. It was still difficult to reconcile that this cold man—aged, but still muscled and exuding power—was Jasper's blood father.

"King Finvarra and I have met before," I said evenly.

Periclase's brows twitched in the smallest show of surprise before he composed his expression, and a little ping of satisfaction zipped through me. It was quickly replaced by silent scolding. I wasn't in a position to be provoking the Duergar king's anger, no matter how satisfying it might feel to let him know he wasn't in on everything.

"But I haven't met this other man," I said quickly, trying to let Periclase save face. "Perhaps you could introduce us?"

His eyes tightened, and then he gestured with a lifted hand to the Fae sorcerer, who stood as always stock-still with his hands clasped in front of him.

"The legendary Eldon, whose magical prowess is surpassed by no Fae," Periclase said grandly. He gave me a little smile. "But you got a sample of that already, didn't you?"

I licked my dry lips.

"Meet Petra Maguire," the Duergar king continued. "Champion of former High King Oberon's Summer Court. And my daughter."

Eldon didn't even blink through the entire introduction, but I cringed at the reference to Oberon and his High Court. When Periclase mentioned Oberon, Finvarra's eyes darted to the area just above my right shoulder, where Aurora's handle protruded from Mort's scabbard. It happened so quickly I wasn't sure it had happened at all. Was that a flicker of unease in his stony eyes?

I gave the Fae sorcerer the tiniest of nods and hoped the hate in my eyes wasn't too obvious.

Inside, I was aching to beg for Oliver's life. To promise whatever these Unseelie rulers wanted, if only they would let my father go. But I bit down hard on the inside of my cheek and waited, trying not to focus on how painfully slowly this was all unfolding. Oliver was still breathing. That was the most important thing. Periclase enjoyed a certain style of pageantry, and I understood, after being in his presence many times, that it made him feel powerful. I needed to allow him that. Anything to keep him from punishing Oliver any further.

Periclase's expression turned somber, the stone part of his face accentuating his intimidating demeanor. He could be a windbag at times, but he was an imposing figure.

"Now then," he said. "I understand you left the palace during the attack of the frost giants."

I couldn't help a glance at Finvarra. He was controlling the servitor attacks. I remembered what Finvarra had said when Jasper and I had met with him in the kingdom of the Undine. He was weakening Faerie in preparation for the Tuatha De Danann's return. Finvarra didn't care about Periclase or the Duergar, even though this was an Unseelie realm. Finvarra wanted to see a new era of Unseelie power rise from the ashes. He intended to rule Faerie, and he wanted every Fae leader to understand exactly who would be wielding all the power.

But Periclase hadn't quite given up. He still believed he could ingratiate himself to Finvarra. Periclase seemed to think that Finvarra might decide to spare him if he played the politics correctly, but I sincerely doubted that would happen. Finvarra and the Tuatha were beyond diplomatic maneuverings. I couldn't blame Periclase for trying, though. After all, his life—and the lives of most of the Fae rulers—were defined by political strategy frameworks. They didn't know any other way.

"Uh, yes, your majesty, I did leave the palace when the frost giants attacked," I conceded, knowing that lies could turn around and bite me in the ass. Or get Oliver killed.

My arms spasmed again, hard enough to pull uncomfortably at my shoulder joints. I shifted in my chair, trying to mask the involuntary movement.

"Where did you go?" Periclase asked.

I licked my dry lips, trying to discern whether the men before me already knew I'd played a part in rescuing Oberon. There was a chance they didn't. Finvarra had crossed his muscular arms and stood in a wide stance, regarding me with mild interest. Periclase's eyes had tightened as he waited for my response. I had no idea what either of them knew.

But then my eyes flicked to Eldon. I hadn't been sure why he was there. I was well-restrained with cold iron rings around my wrists. I sensed more of the poison metal nearby. They could string me up with the stuff, if they wanted to. I was no threat.

Eldon was there to punish me if I decided to be difficult. My gaze once again dropped to my father.

"I went to an unknown realm," I said. I couldn't lie outright—Fae weren't capable of lying to each other, though we could refuse to respond—but I didn't have to offer up every detail, either.

"What was there?" Finvarra asked, his eyes flashing with menace. "Who did you speak to? Why were you there?"

He took a couple of steps toward me, his fists balled at his sides.

I hesitated, surprised he'd jumped in and that he seemed to be so irate. "A primitive settlement."

Periclase let out an exasperated breath. "*More*, Petra. This isn't a game." His words snapped like whip cracks.

Finvarra leaned in, all icy calm in contrast to Periclase's heated annoyance. "Do not screw with us. We know you were involved in taking Oberon from the Tuatha," Finvarra said, his tone flat, which was somehow worse than wrath.

Shit.

"There was a man, a raven shifter there," I said quickly. "And there were other people. The raven shifter helped me get information about where to find Oberon."

"You and whom?" Periclase asked, emphasizing the last word.

I swallowed, my throat suddenly dry. Damn it to Maeve. I had no choice. I was going to have to name Jasper. I took small comfort in the idea that they probably already knew of Jasper's involvement, anyway.

"Jasper Glasgow," I said. No surprise registered on any of the faces before me. At least I hadn't been the one to expose him. "Then we went to the Giants' Causeway, where the Tuatha were holding the High Ki—ah, Oberon." I silently admonished myself. This was the wrong audience to be calling Oberon the High King. "We got him out. Jasper took Oberon, and I came back here."

"You took Oberon from the Tuatha?" Periclase asked.

I nodded.

Finvarra's expression was an odd cross between cool testiness and apprehension. Periclase looked pissed, his face clouding over and his arms stiffening at his sides, but he also looked worried. They exchanged a brief look.

My thoughts bifurcated, half aching again for Oliver and the other half flying to Jasper. He couldn't come back here—not ever. He had friends in other places, though, so he'd be okay as long as he didn't unwittingly try to return to the Duergar realm. I wasn't exactly in a position to try to warn him.

It was grimly amusing, in a way: Jasper and I were both exiles of our sworn realms, with both of our sovereigns keen to see us dead.

I bit down on the tip of my tongue, forcing myself to hold Periclase's gaze and silently begging any powers that would listen to protect Oliver from more punishment.

Periclase composed himself, lifting his chin and looking down his nose at me. "You came to me, begging for asylum. I took you in and have protected you and your sister from Marisol, who would murder both of you given the opportunity. And then you go and do *this*. Your betrayal is not only disappointing, it's punishable by death."

The word hung in the air, and I swallowed with a dry click of my throat. Fear and adrenaline surged through me. I wasn't afraid for myself—I'd pay for my own actions, if it came to that—but it terrified me that they'd thought it necessary to bring my battered father to this little meeting.

And Periclase was right. To him, saving Oberon was a crime of the highest order. I'd undermined the Duergar king, disrespected him as an Unseelie ruler, humiliated him as his blood daughter, and taken advantage of his protection. Even sitting there shackled with cold iron and not knowing what the consequences would be, I knew that liberating Oberon had been the right thing to do. But I'd been caught, and that had been my biggest mistake.

Periclase's face, the part not masked in stone, had turned a deep reddish purple. His eyes flashed with rage, and the nauseating fear that he would kill Oliver to punish my actions rushed through me.

I sucked in a breath, ready to beg, to offer my life right there. But before I could utter a word, Periclase flipped his fingers at the Fae sorcerer.

Eldon's hands unclasped. He chanted rapid words under his breath, and glittering magic surrounded his hands. Filaments of it darted to me, and I was instantly encased in an invisible but immovable substance.

My face froze with my mouth partway open and my eyes wide. I'd inhaled just before Eldon attacked me with his magic, and I held that breath like a diver under water.

The magical substance that surrounded me began to shift. I felt the cold iron unlock from my wrists and then heard the clink of the poison metal falling to the floor. The Fae sorcerer's magic began manipulating me, moving my arms around to my sides, and then forcing me to stand. Like a puppet master, Eldon shifted my limbs, walking me forward a couple of steps as smoothly as if I were doing it under my own control.

My pulse thumped in my head as the air in my lungs began to expire.

Suddenly, the magic blocking my nose and mouth fell away. I sucked in a breath, and the magic chased it, filling up my airways. I tried to raise my hands to my face, desperate to dig at the magic I couldn't even see, when Eldon began to control me in a whole new way.

Pressure increased around my lungs. Magic tensed my vocal chords. Eldon's power tightened around my tongue and lips.

Then, he forced me to speak.

"I am ready to atone for my transgressions and obey your orders, Father." I felt myself pronounce the sentence and heard my voice saying the words, and new horror gripped me.

There was nothing stilted about the way I spoke. Eldon's control was so perfect, it sounded as if it was just me, naturally and voluntarily speaking.

Eldon moved his fingers through the air in quick patterns. In response, my arms fanned out at my sides, one ankle crossed behind the other, my knees bent, and my head and upper body bowed forward in a deep, graceful curtsy.

I wanted to vomit.

Then, as quickly as the magic had surrounded me, it was gone. I tipped, stumbling a little before catching my balance.

"See?" Periclase said with a dark smile at me and a little nod at Eldon. "That wasn't so hard, was it?"

I was panting, still recovering from having oxygen withheld and the awful sensation of being controlled by the Fae sorcerer.

"One last thing we want you to know before we take you back to your quarters," Periclase said. His mouth twisted into an unhappy line. "We are unable to confiscate the fabled sword you carry. Because we cannot take it away, we had to find a different means to disarm you, so to speak."

He took a swift step forward, swinging his leg back like a soccer player carrying out a penalty kick. Grunting with the force of it, he drove the toe of his boot into Oliver's ribs. My father was lying on his side, facing away from me, but his cry nearly ripped my heart in two.

I clenched my teeth, but a small, strangled noise escaped, and tears sprang to my eyes. To react that way to a kick, even a hard one, Oliver must have already suffered broken ribs and possibly serious internal injuries. I'd seen him get battered much worse with barely any reaction. When I was a kid, I wasn't even sure he could feel pain at all.

My lips had begun to tremble, so I pressed them together hard and inhaled sharply through my nose, trying my damnedest not to let tears fall.

"If you raise Aurora against anyone without my permission, you will get to watch this man die," Periclase said. "Understand?"

For a split second, all I could do was stare at him, frozen in fear and rage. Then I quickly nodded.

He turned to Finvarra. "I do believe she's ready to return to the stone fortress and carry out our coup."

I focused on my breath, on trying to quiet the shaking in my body and agony in my heart.

I would have to do whatever Periclase wanted me to do. Even if I were willing to sacrifice my father, Eldon could still use me like a puppet so smoothly that no one would know my actions weren't my own. I was screwed no matter what.

But as my armed escort arrived to take me back to my room, a strange calm of acceptance began to replace the terror I'd felt a moment ago. I was going to have to play along for the time being. As long as Periclase had me, I was his puppet. My only hope was to bide my time and look for a way to strike back.

Chapter 20

WHEN I WALKED into my quarters, Nicole sprang from her room with a little shriek and rushed to me. Dressed in a nightgown, she threw her arms around my neck, and I hugged her back, standing there for a long moment as I tried to collect myself.

I was the one to finally pull back, clearing my throat and focusing on my twin as a way to shake off the devastation of the past half hour.

"You survived the servitor attack in one piece, I see," I said.

She let out a heavy breath. "That almost seems like ages ago. You were gone so long, I thought you'd been caught for sure."

"I was," I said quietly.

"Oh, no," she whispered.

I lifted my scabbard over my head, bringing it with me to one of the sofas where I sat down heavily. I propped Aurora's handle against the wall next to me. Nicole did a double take at the few inches of the sword showing over the sheath, which was a bit too short for Aurora. The exposed metal gleamed like the morning sky.

"Where's your normal sword?" she asked.

"I lost Mort when Jasper and I went for Oberon."

She blinked a couple of times. "Oh, no."

I told her the whole story, not seeing any reason to withhold any of it. She listened quietly, her face clouding with anger when I got to the end.

"They're going to dance you into the stone fortress and force you to kill Marisol?" she asked incredulously. "It's just unbelievable."

I ran a hand over my hair, roughly pushing back the strands that had come loose from my ponytail. "They have very powerful magic."

"Eldon is part human and part Fae?" she asked.

I nodded.

"A halfling," she mused. "Like Bryna. It's very unusual for a halfling to rise to such a powerful position. They tend to be outcasts in Faerie."

My brows lifted.

"Something I learned in my homecoming studies," she said with a shrug.

Homecoming was the process by which changelings—Fae children who'd been raised on the Earthly side of the hedge without knowledge that they were descendants of Faerie—were indoctrinated into their true heritage. It involved learning to tap into their inborn magic as well as lessons about Faerie history, culture, and current events.

"Do you think Bryna could help you get a spell or something that could hold off Eldon's magic?" she asked.

"I doubt it," I said. "Magic that comes from someone else, whether a spell or charmed object or whatever, is never as powerful second-hand as it is when used by the one who made it. Eldon is an Old One. Someone like Bryna could never come close to matching his power."

I straightened and squinted at my twin. "But I know someone who might," I whispered.

Nicole leaned over, and I cupped my hands around her ear. "Melusine." I barely breathed the name. "Not that I'd know where to find her."

But I suddenly realized that we urgently needed to get word about Eldon to the High Court. Finvarra and his Unseelie supporters had a Fae sorcerer at their disposal. I'd heard that once upon a time, Melusine and Titania were BFFs. In usual Old One form, they'd had some sort of epic falling out, but if Titania could persuade her old friend to come out of hiding and help defend the Summerlands against Finvarra, Oberon might have a chance. And if Oberon managed to stay in power, we might have a shred of a hope at fighting the Tuatha and the Dullahan.

I pinched the bridge of my nose. So many things were blowing up at the moment, and so much was on the line. The worst part was being stuck in the Duergar palace, grounded like a naughty teenager. Except instead of my weekend plans being on the line, it was my father's life—and the future of Faerie—that hung in the balance.

"What are you thinking?" Nicole whispered.

"That there's so much to be done, and yet here I am, screwed to the wall," I said.

"I might be able to do something."

I lowered my fingers, which had moved over to rub my temple, and tilted my gaze at my twin.

"Periclase wants to puppet you back over to the stone fortress to take out Marisol, but he has different plans for me," she said. "He's still hot on the idea of getting me married off, and soon. I think he's working overtime to forge more alliances."

Her pretty rosebud mouth twisted with distaste.

"So you're probably going to get paraded around again soon," I said.

"Yeah, today for sure. I've already been informed that I'm to get all dolled up and let out of my cage. For all I know, old Dad's already made a selection, and he's ready to march me down the aisle."

She looked downright nauseous.

"Hopefully it won't get that far," I said. "But you're right. If you're going to get some time outside of this room, we need to take advantage of it." I swore under my breath. "If only we had some paper and a bit of generic sealing wax, I could make a magical seal on a note to Titania and you could probably slip it in a mail basket somewhere."

"I can do the seals," Nicole said with sudden confidence. "I learned it right before we had to leave the fortress. Tell me what to write, and

I'll take care of it."

I looked at her with surprise. "You know where to find stationery and wax, too?"

She waved a hand. "Leave it to me. I'll figure it out. This is my future on the line, too. If I'm forced to marry some random Fae ruler, well—" She shuddered. "I'm just *not* going to let that happen."

Her cheeks pinked as her words took a fierce edge. Ah, love. Such a powerful incentive to tap into hidden reserves of courage. My own thoughts flew to Jasper. I sent up a prayer that he'd made it with Oberon to Drifte and then found a safe place to go.

"Try to gather any news you can, too," I said. "If anyone's willing to tell you what's happening in the battle for the High Court."

She gave me a flat look. "Too bad I can't just hide in the walls and eavesdrop, as seems to be the fashion in this kingdom."

A soft metallic twang drew our attention to the area next to me. For a moment, I thought it was a slip-up of someone within the walls trying to listen in. But the few inches of Aurora's blade that showed above the scabbard were glowing as if reflecting the light of daybreak.

"It must be dawn," I said, and stifled a yawn against the back of my hand.

"Sleep," Nicole ordered, pointing toward my room. "You'll be useless if you're a sleep-deprived zombie. I'll wake you if anything happens. Promise."

My mind was spinning, and part of me desperately wanted to pace around the suite and try to think through the moves ahead, but she was right. I grasped my scabbard, slung the strap over my shoulder like a backpack, and trudged toward my bedroom. Without bothering to turn on the light, I laid the sword across the bed and then sprawled face-down next to it. I was asleep in seconds.

I woke to a full-body twitch so violent it threw me onto the floor.

"Oww." I rubbed my elbow, which had smacked the nightstand on the way down.

A silhouette filled the doorway.

"Petra?" The light flipped on, and my twin stood there. She frowned when she saw where I sat. "You okay?"

"Yeah, I just, uh, fell, apparently."

"Oh. Well, I was just about to come and tell you that my attendant is here. They want to take me out somewhere."

I scrambled to my feet and went to my sister, casting a glance at Damelle over Nicole's shoulder. The Duergar woman tapping her foot impatiently. We needed to take advantage of Nicole's time outside the confinement of our quarters, and I had an idea.

I pulled my twin into my room, out of Damelle's line of sight, and stepped close to Nicole. I cupped my hand around her ear.

"Write a note to Titania," I whispered. "Tell her Eldon is with Periclase and Finvarra, and it would help our cause if she could rouse Melusine."

Nicole nodded and started to turn. I grabbed her arm again.

"And if you have time, tell her about the situation with the Stone Order, and what Periclase plans to do with me," I said.

I knew how it was going to look, with me taking the Stone Order from Marisol. It would be helpful if Titania and Oberon knew I wasn't really on the side of the Unseelie. They'd likely already caught wind of my plea to Periclase for asylum. The rescue mission that brought Oberon home had to score me some big points with the Seelie High Court, but the less ambiguity, the better.

Nicole's eyes met mine. "If I don't see you again before they take you to the fortress, will you—" She cut off abruptly, her eyes brimming.

My brows rose at her sudden strong emotions. "I'll tell Maxen you're thinking of him and doing your damnedest to dodge Unseelie suitors," I said. "And that you send your love."

"Thank you," she breathed. "I mean—oh, crap."

I shook my head. "Don't worry, I won't demand any binding oaths. Just try not to say that phrase to anyone who might take advantage of it."

"Princess, we can't waste any more time," Damelle called briskly. "Please, come."

I watched Nicole go to her attendant, reflecting on her teary expression of a moment ago. When we'd first arrived in the Duergar palace, I'd been struck by the hunch that more had transpired between her and Maxen than I'd realized. That suspicion returned to me now.

Damelle spent the next couple of hours doing Nicole's hair and makeup and getting her dressed. The clothing was similar in style to the previous time my twin had been taken to meet potential husbands—ridiculously flouncy and frilly. That was a good thing. It meant Periclase was likely still showing her around and hadn't made any decisions yet regarding potential suitors.

I gave Nicole an encouraging smile as she left with her armed escort. She held her chin high, her shoulders squared, looking more confident than I'd seen her since she'd arrived in Faerie. I realized, belatedly, that I should have given her things to do before. There was nothing worse than feeling powerless, and Nicole had been nothing but a pawn since coming to this side of the hedge.

But I didn't have much time to ponder ways to give Nicole more responsibility. A few minutes after she departed, my own attendant arrived. She wasn't alone. Two manservants followed her into the suite.

"You can set that over there," Darla said, pointing a spindly finger at the wall next to a chair and ottoman.

Sweating with the effort of having carried a large chest, the two men put it down. They faced Darla, and she dismissed them with a nod.

My stomach tightened as she went to tip back the brass lid. She pulled out what I immediately recognized as part of a suit of armor in the Duergar style—heavy leather, made to go under formed metal plates that went over the chest, back, and upper arms. The leather part was designed as a short-sleeved top with a dropped hem that hit around mid-thigh. The male Duergar soldiers wore the same style, with fitted pants underneath. The skirted part was designed to deflect blows that might slice the femoral arteries while still allowing range of motion.

"I'm to help you dress for battle, Princess," Darla said. "Please strip down to your underdrawers."

So, I would be attacking the Stone Order before the next sunrise. Most likely sometime after darkness fell over Faerie. I dreaded following Periclase's orders, but there was some relief in knowing that the time was finally here.

I turned toward my room, where I pulled off my jacket and then began removing my clothes.

When Darla came at me with the leather dress, I stifled a withering sigh. I hated wearing armor. I didn't need it. I could form my own plates of rock armor that were more maneuverable, light, and strong than the type of protective gear that came in the trunk. But it was fruitless to argue. Periclase would insist that I wear his uniform—not for protection, but to make a statement.

Once I was fully geared up, Darla left. The door barely closed behind her before there was a sharp knock.

"Princess, your escort to the battle room," a deep male voice said through the door.

I settled my scabbard across my back and chest, tucked my helmet under my arm, and went to the men who were waiting in the hallway.

My eyes scanned for Jasper, but of course he wasn't there. It was better that he was far away, I reminded myself. But I couldn't help the forlorn tug in my chest. I was truly on my own.

Two of the half dozen soldiers who'd come for me walked to my right and left, and the rest marched behind. When we turned into increasingly larger corridors and I caught the excited murmurs, my face tightened.

Periclase was taking the opportunity to parade me around the palace in front of the Duergar people. I kept my eyes straight ahead, refusing to acknowledge the nobles and courtiers lining the grand hallways near the center of the main part of the palace.

The sword on my back was drawing attention, as I caught the name of the legendary blade on the lips of bystanders. It gave me some small satisfaction to be carrying the weapon of the Seelie Champion forced on display through the palace of my Unseelie blood father.

We took a roundabout route, obviously to maximize visibility. In one of the longer corridors, I glimpsed another small escort ahead, a group of soldiers taking some important person to the battle room, I assumed. I felt the slightest twinge of relief. At least this little parade wasn't solely for my benefit.

The doors leading into the battle room were grand—huge, heavy, and plated as if with armor. High above them was a beautifully painted mural depicting a battle with the Duergar palace in the background. Well, it was beautiful if you didn't mind the splashes of blood and graphic renderings of guts spilling from stomachs and heads rolling from spurting necks.

The soldiers who'd brought me peeled off to either side of the doors, where others were already lined up with ruler-straight precision. I continued on through the doorway alone.

The high-ceilinged battle room was decorated with all manner of weapons mounted on the walls—axes, knives, swords, bows, even a huge mace. At one end was an enormous modern monitor, darkened at the moment.

A long table was positioned in the middle of the room. At one end, seated in a ridiculously high-backed chair, was Periclase. To his right sat Finvarra, dressed in his own armor and leaning back with one elbow propped on the chair's arm as if he were lounging by the pool on vacation. His gray eyes watched keenly, though. At Periclase's left was the Spriggan King Sebastian. He looked scared shitless, his eyes wide and his forehead slicked with sweat. Everyone with their backs to the doors twisted to look at me. There were maybe a dozen others besides the three rulers, all men except for one muscular woman with her hair in two auburn braids, one resting over each shoulder.

There was only one seat left at the table. With all eyes on me, I went to it, set my scabbard next to my chair, sat down, and placed my helmet on the table as the others had done.

It wasn't until I glanced back at the large double doors, which were being dragged closed, that I spotted Eldon standing in the shadows. I squinted at him, realizing there was no shadow cast in his corner, yet he still stood in murky near-dark. The gloaming. It was part of his unique set of magic. He could pull the deep shadows of dusk to him at will.

I couldn't help recalling the last time I'd seen Eldon. Thoughts of my father brought a sharp ache to the center of my chest, but I couldn't afford to expend mental energy on worry or grief.

The doors clanged closed with a heavy sound of finality. King Periclase leaned forward, sweeping his eyes over everyone at the table. His gaze snagged on me, and his lips seemed to twitch with the hint of a suppressed smile.

He turned to the man sitting on Finvarra's other side. "General Stanchon, you may proceed with outlining the attack on the stone fortress."

I swallowed hard against the bitter bile that threatened to rise up my throat and reluctantly turned my attention to the General.

Chapter 21

I WAS FOCUSING on General Stanchon, Periclase's top commander and a bald hulk of a man with a grizzled goatee, but feeling a set of eyes still boring into me, I cast a quick look around the table. Everyone else was watching the General except for one man, Periclase's brother Darion. He sat between King Sebastian and another commander I didn't know, and if were possible for Darion to murder with a look, I'd have been dead already. Apparently, he was still a little pissed about me nearly killing him in the Battle of Champions.

I stared back, debating whether to give him a little wink or blow him a tiny kiss, when King Sebastian caught my attention. He was shifting around on his seat, his eyes glued on me. By the intensity of his face, I got the idea he wanted to speak to me, and urgently. But we weren't going to get the chance in the middle of this meeting. I tilted my head toward Stanchon, trying to indicate that we'd have to wait out the presentation.

" . . . our previous occupation of the stone fortress, we gained thorough knowledge of the layout, armaments, and defenses," Stanchon was saying. He was referencing the brief time Periclase had managed to take the fortress with the help of the Undine. That event had forced me to make the deal with Sebastian, who'd helped me push out the Duergar and the Undine. And now here we all sat together, with the exception of the Undine Queen Doineann. Funny thing, life. "No doubt the New

Gargoyles have tightened their security and tried to make any possible breach even more difficult. Lucky for us, we have someone who can gain access through the fortress's lesser-known doorways."

There was a small rustle as everyone shifted and stared at me. The sour feeling in my stomach returned.

"We've selected the doorway through which we'll enter, and our Duergar Princess will be the key that unlocks it," the General continued. Behind him, the large monitor lit up, white at first and then resolving into a diagram. I recognized the layout of the stone fortress immediately. A red dot appeared next to one of the interior doorways. "The New Gargs will likely be heavily stationed at all doorways, so we can expect a fight, though we might surprise them for a second or two."

My heart sank as I listened and watched the screen. I'd been so focused on the idea of being forced to kill Marisol and what would happen afterward when Sebastian called in the oath we'd made, I hadn't thought about what other casualties might occur. But the New Gargoyles would be looking for a fight, and my people never backed down. Trying to warn them wouldn't help. This was happening whether the Stone Order saw it coming or not.

"Wait," I cut in. Stanchon's head swiveled around. "If I can get the New Gargs to back off, will you spare them?"

His eyes narrowed, and he and Periclase exchanged a look. "They're not going to stand down on your order. They'll be following the orders of their own commanders."

"But isn't the whole point of acquiring the Stone Order to add a battalion of the best fighters in Faerie to your own forces?" I looked between Periclase and Stanchon, with Finvarra in my periphery. "Surely you don't want to mow down a bunch of your future top soldiers."

"You can try, Princess, but we can't make any promises," Periclase said to me. His tone made it obvious how he expected my efforts to be met. He gave an impatient flip of his fingers. "Carry on, General."

My stomach knotted as I sat there and listened to Stanchon outline the attack. I'd be among those leading the charge, but not at the very front. The goal, of course, was reaching Marisol. More specifically, getting *me* to Marisol.

"If Marisol Lothlorien has enough warning, we expect she will take cover in her bunker. We hope she does. That is far preferable to her disappearing through a doorway to another realm. If she does flee, however, we have a plan in place to force her to return."

I had an ugly feeling about what that plan would involve. Probably torture, with the most likely victim to be Maxen, if the Duergar forces managed to catch him. If not, then something equally terrible.

The general gestured at the screen. "If she does hole up in her bunker, we'll simply take measures to breach it."

I wondered how they planned to get to her if she was in her safe room. It'd protected her last time. I'd been in it before—it was basically impenetrable and also set up as a miniature living quarters so she could survive there for a long time if needed. My eyes slid to Eldon, and suddenly I was certain the "measures," if they needed to be taken, would come from him. In fact, he was the secret weapon of this entire operation. His magic was far more powerful than any regular Fae's, and he'd already demonstrated how completely he could control another person. He could probably win the whole fight single-handedly, once he was inside the fortress. But that wasn't Periclase's plan. He needed me to oust Marisol. For show. For politics. And most especially for what he planned to do immediately after.

I swallowed and looked at Sebastian. The Spriggan king was sweating bullets and gripping the arms of his chair as if it was the only thing keeping him alive. I felt bad for him. He'd overstepped, gotten greedy by backing me into a corner and forcing an oath that would allow him to take the Stone Order under his rule. His kingdom wasn't big enough to pull off such a feat, and his plan had been thoroughly appropriated by Periclase. Sebastian had to know he wasn't getting out of this alive.

It pained me more than I'd expected. Sebastian was a bit of a pompous ass, but he was more tolerable than many of the rulers in Faerie. He had the unfortunate position of ruling a small kingdom, and he'd overstepped what he could realistically expect to defend. Because of that, the Spriggan and New Gargs alike would pay the price for his miscalculation.

General Stanchon continued outlining the plan of attack, and it struck me that it wasn't strictly necessary to allow me to be there for the entire meeting—or any of it, for that matter. They could have kept me in my quarters until the moment of departure, and then let Eldon force me to do their bidding. That they were making me privy to all the details likely meant the Duergar would be watching me like hawks from now until the attack to ensure I didn't try to subvert their plans. Or maybe they were just that confident in their ability to control me.

Everyone was shifting around and rising. The meeting was over. Nightfall was almost upon us, and that would be the time of our attack—after the first and second dinner shifts, when everyone in the stone fortress would be slowing down for the day.

I slung my scabbard over my head and across my chest, and I picked up my helmet. A few of the Duergar officers were chatting with each other in low voices, and Finvarra had turned to speak to Periclase. Sebastian was trying to maneuver his way past the other two kings but then seemed to think better of it and changed direction to come around the other end of the table. I drifted that way, intending to meet him.

He turned his hand, and something silvery flashed in his fist. A small blade. Blood dripped down his clenched fingers. My eyes widened. Sebastian had a plan of some sort. I started toward him. I saw in his eyes that he meant no harm, and my pulse quickened as I began to guess what the blood was for—to dissolve the oath between us. But one of the soldiers near Sebastian saw the knife, too.

Thinking Sebastian was going to use the knife to attack someone, the soldier drew his broadsword and lunged at the Spriggan king. Sebastian didn't even attempt to defend himself against the much larger soldier. The sword scraped across Sebastian's chest plate and the soldier redirected his aim to Sebastian's neck. Suddenly, the room was in a whirl of chaos.

Periclase was bellowing at his man to stop. Others were exclaiming and hollering about protecting the king. Swords were drawn.

The soldier's blade edge sliced Sebastian just above the collar bone. Blood spurted from the gash. The Spriggan king's eyes went wide. He dropped the knife and grabbed his neck. Crimson spilled through his fingers.

"Help him!" Periclase commanded. "Don't let him die. We need him!"

As if appearing out of nowhere, Eldon was suddenly at Sebastian's side. Everyone else stumbled in their haste to get back from the Fae sorcerer.

I stood there with Aurora nearly forgotten in my hand, my lips parted as I held my breath and watched Eldon try to keep Sebastian from bleeding out. The gloaming surrounded them in swirling shadows, nearly obscuring them. Dark mist streamed into Sebastian's flared nostrils and open lips.

Periclase wanted Sebastian alive because of the oath between me and the Spriggan king. Periclase would force me to take the Stone Order regardless of what happened to Sebastian. But if I claimed the Order and then Sebastian invoked the oath—which essentially gave him the Stone Order—the New Gargs would become part of the Spriggan kingdom. Then Periclase could kill Sebastian and take the Spriggan kingdom, which would include the Stone Order. Periclase was primarily interested in taking control of the New Gargs but acquiring another kingdom in the process was obviously too tempting for the Duergar king.

Even through the gloaming, I could see Sebastian's wide, desperate eyes. They were locked on mine.

I inhaled a ragged breath. The blade in Sebastian's hand was a simple steak knife probably stolen from dinner service. He hadn't meant me or anyone else any harm. He'd intended to free me from the oath.

Damn it. I should have realized it faster, and I should have helped him. But instead he lay dying on the battle room floor. Periclase wouldn't allow him to die, though, not if there were any magic in Faerie that would keep him alive.

"Put away your sword, Princess," said an authoritative voice at my shoulder. It was Stanchon. Two of his largest commanders flanked him. "On the King's order."

I sheathed Aurora. They hustled me out of the battle room, through the corridors, and into a cell—one I recognized, actually. It was where I was briefly held during my first visit to the Duergar palace. The first time I met Jasper, when he had my magi-stunned, limp body slung easily over his broad shoulders. Maybe it wasn't the exact same interrogation room, but it was identical to the one I remembered, complete with iron chains and shackles pooled on the floor on either side of a simple straight-backed chair.

The soldiers unceremoniously dumped me inside and left me there. I let out an exasperated sigh and rattled the locked door but knew I was stuck there until someone decided to let me out.

To calm my irritation, I drew Aurora and performed a quick little figure-eight sequence I'd learned as a warm-up drill when I was a girl. The movements were so familiar, my arm seemed to trace the patterns of its own volition. I watched the orange, pink, yellow, and blue hues glimmer across the metal.

One of the most incredible weapons in Faerie, and I wasn't allowed to use it unless dear old blood-Dad gave me permission. My inner teenager groused, and my mouth pressed into a grimace.

Periclase was going to command me to kill Marisol with this sword. I knew I had to do it—she'd tried to have me murdered once and would do it again—but I hated that I was doing it on someone else's order. Especially that of the Duergar king. Oh, how it *grated*.

After about fifteen minutes, the door sprang open and a stocky, gruff-looking Duergar soldier with a scar that traced a line across one cheekbone appeared.

"Time to put toys away, Princess," he said, his voice as rough-edged as he looked. In spite of his condescending words, he eyed Aurora warily. "The battle is upon us."

Gritting my teeth as I imagined sticking him in the ribs with the tip of my blade, I sheathed the sword and then followed him out into the hallway.

"Did the Spriggan king survive?" I asked.

He ignored me.

"Asshole," I muttered. But my thoughts were already jumping ahead.

My stomach tightened. I'd soon be back in the stone fortress. My childhood home. The Faerie realm of my people. But this time, I'd be storming in as an enemy.

Chapter 22

THE SOLDIERS' FACES around me were grim, their eyes gleaming. The marching ranks were quiet as we made our way through the Duergar palace toward the doorway through which we would depart, but the air was thick with anticipation and the musk of aggression. Though I hadn't participated in many battles in Faerie in my life, I recognized the fever of battle coming over the fighters. I understood it. I was a born fighter, too, and people like us all had little parts of our souls that lived for these moments.

I couldn't help thinking of my father. Not the broken, bloodied man I'd seen recently, but the Oliver in my mind. The warrior in his prime, fearless and nearly untouchable.

My heart clenched, and I pulled my thoughts back to the present and funneled my fears into battle-ready focus, the way Oliver had taught me.

Periclase accompanied us to our departure point, but he wasn't fully suited up for battle. He wore only light armor with metal accents that were decorative rather than protective and ornate scroll work burned into the leather. Over it all hung one of his many regal capes. He would remain safely back until we'd reached Marisol.

Up ahead, alongside King Periclase, trudged Sebastian. Eldon had managed to heal the slice that had been inflicted on the Spriggan king, but not before substantial blood loss. Sebastian was still alive, but it was obvious even from the way he walked that he was weak. He was flanked by guards who appeared to be there equally to keep him on his feet as to ensure he didn't attempt anything else.

I was still cursing myself for not seeing what Sebastian had intended with the knife. But there was no helping it now. If only the Spriggan king would have realized earlier that our binding promise was so ill-fated.

General Stanchon, who would be orchestrating the attack, raised his fist at the head of the column of soldiers. "Halt!" he barked.

We'd reached an interior doorway in the Duergar palace, a twenty foot high four-poster ceremonial arch in a cavernous room with murals of several beautiful, bare-breasted women, a couple of nearly-naked men with chiseled abs, and sparkling gems and treasure chests drifting among the clouds. Portal jewels, incredibly valuable marble-like objects that could open a doorway anywhere, appeared to rain down into a pond that was full of them. The setup was cathedral-like and at a glance seemed more like a place where marriage oaths would be exchanged than a jumping-off point for a battle charge. Then I realized that right behind the arch was a painting of the sun breaking through clouds. The stylized rays of light were a commonly-used symbol of victory and dominance in Faerie. The nudes and treasures were meant to inspire soldiers going off to war. Clever.

The battalion stopped neatly, and after not-so-gentle prodding of my assigned babysitter, I began weaving my way through the soldiers to the front, where Periclase, Stanchon, Sebastian, and Eldon waited.

I stood under the arch and slid a sidelong glance at the Spriggan king, who was to my left. He looked like he'd aged two decades in the past couple of hours. He stared at me with haunted eyes. His stooped posture was one of defeat, but I thought I saw a flicker of determination when his eyes met mine.

"Princess," Periclase said, drawing my attention his way. He strode over to me and looked down into my eyes with what was probably supposed to be fatherly pride. "We are honored to have you fighting for the Duergar on this historic day."

I glared up at him. I didn't give a shit about niceties at that point. I would do what he wanted, but I didn't have to smile about it.

My blood father loomed over me, bending down slowly until we were almost eye to eye.

"And remember, Petra," he whispered. "We will not hesitate to use whatever *motivation* necessary to ensure your cooperation."

He gazed at me, the stern father waiting for the wayward child to acknowledge the consequences of misbehavior.

"I understand," I ground out.

I pushed past him, raised my forefinger, and began tracing sigils in the air as I whispered the magic words that would take us through the doorway to the stone fortress. Eldon stepped close and grasped my shoulder, his long fingers curling in a tight grip that sent a small shiver through me.

Normally, everyone needing to pass through the doorway would have to be in physical contact with me, which would have meant many trips through the void to transport all of the Duergar soldiers to the fortress. But in the battle briefing, I'd learned Eldon had magic that would hold the portal open to allow the soldiers to stream through. That scared me. I hadn't known such magic existed. The doorway system was sacred in Faerie. Forcing a doorway to remain passable felt like a violation of nature.

With the Fae sorcerer clutching my shoulder firmly, the two of us stepped through the arch and into the chill of the void.

I felt the pull of the world, but our reemergence seemed delayed, as if the void had become sticky enough to hold us there. I'd passed through doorways hundreds of times in my life, and this didn't feel right. When we emerged back into the world, it was in a cloud of bluish-brown fog so thick I couldn't see my own feet when I looked down. Bodies shoved me from behind—the soldiers crowding through the arch behind me.

The dark fog puffed and billowed. I'd known Eldon would help to mask our arrival, but I didn't realize we would be standing in the middle of his gloaming magic. A hard shiver passed through me. The fog on my skin left vaguely aching trails wherever the thickest parts of it touched me.

Suddenly, Stanchon was next to me. There was jostling and the sound of movement as more soldiers poured through, but the Duergar remined mostly quiet. The New Gargs we'd surprised, however, were shouting in alarm and calling for backup.

As expected, Marisol had people posted at the doorway—and probably at every other doorway in the fortress. By the shouts, the New Gargoyles were having a hard time seeing us through the gloaming. I could see through it just fine from my vantage point, though my eyes kept wanting to lose focus.

A soldier roughly took my upper arm and dragged me forward but allowed many others to stream around us. He must have been the one assigned to keep me in the proper position within the charge.

The first clangs of weapons and grunts of the people wielding them rang out. The battle had begun.

A yell went up among the Duergar forces, and soldiers began charging in earnest. I was swept along with the others, and after about ten yards of stumbling through the gloaming with my babysitter's hand clamped around my arm, we broke through to the edge of the shadowy fog.

We'd come through a doorway that was under one of the towers in the practice yard, the area where New Garg soldiers and students trained in hand to hand combat and weapons. It was always closed by this time of night, with the lights shut off. There was only moonlight and the weak light from the windows of the fortress to illuminate the yard.

I could clearly see the New Gargs, but by their squinting and confused looks, Eldon's gloaming magic was making things difficult for them.

Then with painful swiftness, the area flooded with harsh light from above. Someone had flipped on the spotlights mounted on the towers.

It didn't seem to do much to dispel the gloaming, but I felt incredibly exposed. Any second, someone would recognize that I was part of the attack. As if speeding that moment along, the soldier gripping my arm began moving forward faster, forcing me to keep up with him.

"Draw your sword," he commanded, his lips at my ear.

I nearly elbowed him in the bridge of his nose. I needed to reach a New Garg commander and beg them to stop fighting. With Eldon on the side of the Duergar and the massive number of soldiers Periclase had sent, the New Gargs weren't going to win this battle. I had to try to prevent needless casualties.

"Do it now," the Duergar said with what he probably thought was a menacing squeeze of his meaty paw.

I rolled my eyes, drew Aurora, and pulled magic to form stone armor, forcing him to loosen his grip. Squeeze *that*, asshole.

Eldon was focused on his gloaming magic and holding the doorway open, giving me a little opportunity. I half turned toward the Duergar soldier and swiftly rammed my rock-plated knee under the skirt of his leather armor and into his groin. In that moment, my petite stature paid off, giving me just the right angle, and I hit my target square on.

He exhaled and doubled over like he'd been punched in the gut.

With Aurora still in my hand, I sprinted forward, searching for a New Garg in charge.

I spotted Shane, one of the youngest officers in the New Garg ranks.

Angling toward him, I raised Aurora to try to get his attention. "Shane! Back down!" I yelled. "They're going to get Marisol no matter what you do!"

He spotted me, his eyes widening with shock and then narrowing in anger. I wasn't sure if he heard what I said. The cacophony of battle had increased to a near-deafening level. My plea might not have done any good, anyway. It wasn't in our blood to shy away from a fight, especially when our small piece of Faerie was threatened.

My attention swiveled. I probably had only a few seconds before Eldon or one of the Duergar reached me. Sapphire blue eyes locked on mine. Maxen. He'd been close enough to hear what I'd yelled at Shane. The world seemed to freeze for a split second.

Maxen had paused in his battle with a Duergar. The soldier charged, and Maxen snapped back to the fight and ran the man through with his sword. I stumbled in his direction, dodging blows and bodies. The battle was getting bloody. There were already still forms on the ground.

I dodged weapons and bodies and moved closer the son of the Stone Order's monarch. My childhood friend. The man in love with my twin.

"Maxen, you have to pull back," I yelled. "You're not going to win. They have the Fae sorcerer. He's going to force me to kill Mar—"

My words dissolved into a screech as my spine arched in pain. Eldon. The pain receded. That had been only to get my attention. The familiar feeling of his magic slipped into me and around me.

Then I lost control of my body. Eldon's magic moved my limbs, marching me forward. Some of the Duergar soldiers angled my way, probably on some signal from Stanchon. They were going to escort me to Marisol.

More soldiers joined my guard. We moved within a cloud of the gloaming, and it was painfully obvious the New Gargs were struggling to make out their targets when they tried to attack us. Eldon's magic was too much. The Duergar could see the New Gargs coming, and Periclase's people mowed down their ranks with horrible blows aimed at New Garg faces—one of the few areas that weren't protected by our stone armor. Bile rose up my throat as I watched a Duergar sword partially decapitate a New Garg woman. Her blonde ponytail fanned out as her body and nearly-detached head jerked backward. Gertie was her name. I'd trained with her when I was a kid. Another New Garg, a man around

Oliver's age with a son a couple years older than me, caught a short sword in the eye.

We continued to cut a bloody path through the practice yard. None of the violence was by my sword, but I felt a horrible stab of responsibility for each maiming slash, and a deeper wound in my heart for every death.

Eldon forced me through the corridors of the stone fortress. We were headed toward Marisol's bunker. Periclase and Finvarra must have determined she hadn't fled. I was almost grateful. At least once Marisol was gone, the fighting would end.

Maxen's blue eyes flashed through my mind. Would they compel me to kill him, too, to secure leadership of the Stone Order? The thought made me ache with revulsion. Marisol had tried to murder me, but I didn't believe Maxen had known she was going to do it. I believed he would have stopped her if he could have.

When we neared a plain door that I recognized—it was the outer seal of Marisol's shelter—Periclase was waiting. The door was inconspicuous from this side but made of steel a foot thick. No soldiers guarded it. The fortification of the safe room itself was better protection than any Fae. Next to Periclase stood Finvarra on one side and King Sebastian on the other. The Spriggan king looked pale, his shoulders stooped and his breath coming fast through his parted lips. His gaze landed on me and sharpened.

Eldon brought me to a halt before the Duergar king. The Fae sorcerer was behind us somewhere, but not far. I could feel his presence as the source of the magic that threaded through me, as if it pointed back to him like a compass needle.

"Princess," Periclase greeted me. "Are you ready to fulfill your destiny?"

I looked up at him, and hate surged within me. But I forced it back, allowing a deadly calm to take over.

Eldon released his hold on my vocal chords, allowing me to answer under my own power.

"I'm ready," I said.

I knew what was going to happen next, and I understood that it was inevitable. But later, I would kill Periclase. *That* was my destiny. I tightened my grip on Aurora and faced the door.

Chapter 23

ELDON STEPPED UP to the door of Marisol's hideout. I could feel his magic swirling around us like a restless breeze, though it didn't actually stir the air. He'd used his power on me a few times at that point, and it seemed that each time I was more attuned to his movements and the changes in his magic. When he placed his palms on the door and bowed his head as if in prayer, his hold on me shifted. Before, he'd seemed to control me with an iron grip. But now, it eased to a light touch. I eyed the Fae sorcerer as he chanted softly, his long white hair hanging in a curtain that obscured his face from my view.

I licked my dry lips. I had an opportunity to move under my own control. What could I do?

I didn't have time to formulate a plan or act. Within a few seconds, the door began to give way under Eldon's touch. I sensed human magic—mostly fire. How did he manage to channel so much of it here in Faerie? The solid door turned crystalline, glass-like, and then melted like ice. A grayish puddle formed in the doorway, and my mouth fell open.

The Fae sorcerer had just melted a solid foot of steel door. The entrance gaped open, revealing a small anteroom. And New Garg guards. The acrid smell of hot metal invaded my nostrils.

Eldon's power snapped back around me like a vice, and then seeped through my skin. He propelled me forward behind four Duergar soldiers but let me control Aurora. A second later, I understood why.

The New Garg guards came at us, mowing down one of the Duergar right away. By reflex, I lifted Aurora to fend off their attack. My moves were primarily defensive as I focused on keeping my head connected to my shoulders while not inflicting any more harm than necessary.

I recognized all the New Gargs. They were men and women who'd been part of Marisol's elite guard since I was a teenager. They were people I'd admired. And they were bent on killing me.

But Eldon wouldn't let that happen, even if I did lower my defenses. Dark clouds of the gloaming puffed around us, pieces of it breaking off and smashing into the eyes of the New Garg soldiers. They shook their heads and made fast swipes across their faces, but the gloaming clung to them where Eldon had hurled it.

I took the opportunity, knocking out one New Garg with a hilt swing to the head and shoving aside another with the heel of my boot. The Duergar had killed the third New Garg and maimed the fourth.

We pressed on through the anteroom toward the door beyond. This one was magically sealed, opening only to those Marisol chose.

I felt Eldon's power flare behind me, and a beachball-sized orb of bright-yellow light shot through with green tendrils hurled past me, carrying with it a strong wind that whipped my hair across my cheeks. Some part of my brain registered that he'd used an enormous amount of human air magic mixed with earth just as the whole mess blasted its target.

Marisol's door exploded inward. New Gargs poured through toward us.

I stiffened for a split second when I saw Jaquard. The master swordsman had taught me when I was younger and advanced past the skills of the New Garg battle school's teachers. He'd been one of Marisol's advisors and protectors for years, almost as long as my father. He'd been the one she'd sent to murder me and Nicole. And instead of following through, he'd let me escape.

The gloaming parted for a moment, and we locked eyes.

"Pull back!" I yelled at him. "Let us have Marisol!"

As with Shane before, I couldn't be sure Jaquard had heard what I said. His sword whipped through the air at the nearest Duergar soldier. If Jaquard had heard me, he clearly wasn't interested in getting the New Gargs to yield. I lost him in the crowd.

Adrenaline surged, and I pushed magic into Aurora. Light flared around the sword. I couldn't afford to be careful anymore. I jumped into the fray full-force, swinging Aurora with all the skill I possessed. The din of battle rose in my ears and then faded as I entered the flow state of fighting.

But my dread and heartache didn't completely give way to my instincts. It was a nightmare fighting my own people. At one point I tried to pull back, but Eldon forced me forward into the thickest part of the fight, keeping careful control of my position while allowing me to use my sword under my own power. And so, I wielded Aurora against the New Gargoyles of the stone fortress with Periclase's soldiers fighting beside me.

Soldiers fell around me, New Garg and Duergar alike.

As I fought, I yelled at the New Gargs to surrender. In a hellish dance, I begged them to back off even as I cut through their ranks with Aurora. I didn't blame them for not listening. I wouldn't have. The stone fortress was all the New Gargs had. If it fell, my people had no place in Faerie. If it fell, it would mean subjugation to another ruler. Sweat ran into my eyes, and I relished the pain of the sting.

A roar behind us made me turn. More New Gargs had come to help, and battle was raging out in the hallway beyond the entrance to Marisol's hideout. But the critical fight was in here, at her door. And the Duergar and I were winning.

Eldon's magic darted through my legs in sharp little icy-hot points, and he propelled me forward through a clearing in the fight. Another door exploded, and Eldon forced me through the doorway. I burst into Marisol's quarters, my chest heaving and my eyes leaking. I didn't know if it was sweat, the gloaming, or sorrow that made tears stream down my cheeks. Maybe all three.

Marisol was there. She stood not far from where I'd sat with her and Maxen for tea only weeks ago, after we'd defeated the Duergar and the Undine.

Her sapphire-blue eyes flashed, and she reached behind her and produced a dagger. I knew she knew how to use it. But we both understood she was no match for me. She was a queen, a diplomat. I was the Champion of the Summer Court, wielder of Aurora.

The Duergar soldiers at my sides hung back. Eldon drove me forward. Marisol brandished the dagger.

My arms were shaking. Vibrating. At first, I thought it was an effect of the Fae sorcerer's magic, but the stinging points of Eldon's power had weakened.

I gripped Aurora and faced my sovereign. Anger surged as I remembered Jaquard locking his arm around my neck and the realization hitting me that Marisol had ordered me executed. But something else crept in as I watched Marisol's expression turn fierce. I felt sadness for her. All she'd ever wanted was to lift our people up in Faerie, to secure our position and increase our ranks. It wasn't going to happen. Not while she was in charge, anyway. Her dream was shattering.

"Here we are," I said quietly. "Nicole and I live, and your prophecy is dead."

"You are a traitor, Petra Maguire." She spat the words. "You betrayed your people. You've destroyed their future. Treason is far worse than anything I've ever done."

Oliver flashed into my mind and, along with the thought of my father, an agonizing stab of failure. He would have died before letting someone else wield his sword. He would endure torture, but he was no one's puppet.

Eldon had come up next to me, moving his hands in furious gestures, and I suddenly realized the sensation of his power had completely disappeared from my body. I flicked a glance over at him and inhaled sharply. Something was wrong. I could see through him. I blinked and looked back at Marisol. The room was suddenly silent, the clangs and screams of battle gone. The room itself was shifting, fading.

The vibrations in my arms had spread, taking over until my entire body trembled. Cold wind stirred my hair.

I was no longer standing in the stone fortress. Instead, Marisol and I were outside, atop a grassy rise in a field marked with more bumps like the one we stood on. The ground under my boots began to rumble.

I looked down. "What the—" But the words came out wrong, in some other language.

The woman across from me had Marisol's sapphire-blue eyes, but that was the only resemblance. She had cherry-red hair and was dressed in strange, old-fashioned battle gear. By her stance, ferocity, and muscled arms, I knew she was a warrior.

Hollering words I didn't understand, she raised the dagger in her hand and sprang at me. I gripped Aurora in both hands and swung the broadsword in an upward diagonal motion. The blade struck the woman's wrist gauntlet and sparks burst from the impact. She somehow kept hold of her knife. Gripping it in both hands, she screamed and swung it through the air toward my neck.

I dodged and drove Aurora into her diaphragm and up into her chest. The edge of her dagger sliced my cheekbone. Her mouth dropped open, and her blue eyes widened as she hung there on the blade for a moment. With a sound somewhere between a groan and a slow exhalation, she sagged and fell off the sword.

I blinked, and I was back in the stone fortress. Marisol lay crumpled on the floor with her hands pressed into her abdomen, her head turned up. Blood spilled between her fingers.

Eldon's magic surged into me, taking complete control. He forced a two-handed grip on Aurora. The sword rose as high as I could reach. I realized what he was forcing me to do and had time only to mutter a plea.

"Oberon, no," I breathed.

Eldon brought my arms down with brutal power, the blade heading straight for the side of Marisol's neck.

He could force me to do this, but he couldn't make me watch it. I squeezed my eyes closed just before my sword hit its mark.

Shaking, I opened my eyes but kept my gaze lifted, refusing to look down. My arms fell limply to my sides, my hand still gripping Aurora.

In a daze, I turned to find Periclase sweeping into the shelter, followed by Sebastian and Finvarra.

The horror of this day wasn't over yet.

Chapter 24

MARISOL LOTHLORIEN WAS dead. She'd died by my hand, except . . . not exactly. The weeks of muscle twitches had somehow culminated into a full-body rumble and done something that should have been impossible—taken me into someone else's body, in a different place and time, complete with words spoken in an unknown tongue. I'd been there, but it hadn't truly been *me* who'd wielded the sword that killed her. And it hadn't exactly been *her* I'd stabbed.

It was possible I'd succumbed to a seizure or mental break. Perhaps Eldon's magic had fried my brain. I could almost believe that, but I'd felt myself inhabiting the body of that woman warrior, and I'd also felt Eldon's magic depart and then return. His control had been usurped by something else. Something more powerful.

No, it was no hallucination. I'd been there, in that other place, and I'd fought in a body that wasn't mine. And it all led back to the violent muscle spasms I'd had for weeks. I didn't have answers, and it wasn't the time to try to sort it out.

Periclase had moved forward to where Marisol had fallen and was standing over her body. I still refused to look down at her. She'd tried to have me killed, but she'd been my sovereign my entire life. I'd never loved her, but there'd been a time—much of my life, if I were honest—when I'd respected her. I wasn't happy to see her dead, even if it had to be done.

Having regained control of me, Eldon drifted off to the side to take his usual inconspicuous hands-clasped stance in the shadows that seemed to gather to the wall where he stood.

I'd expected King Periclase to immediately force the rest of his plan in motion, but he was very still, towering over Marisol's body. His cape was wide enough to block all but her feet to his left, which were clad in lovely lace-up brown leather boots, and a swath of her hair played out on the floor to his right.

He was mumbling something. I crept forward a step.

". . . shouldn't have refused me, my dear," I thought I heard him murmur. "We could have ruled all of Faerie."

My lips parted with surprise. Partly at his words, but more at his tone. He sounded genuinely sad, tender almost, and most shocking of all, affectionate. I gave a slight shake of my head as I tried to make sense of what I seemed to have heard. Something significant had most definitely transpired between Periclase and Marisol in the past.

Marisol's prophecy came back to me. What would happen now that she was dead and Nicole and I lived? Did it mean there was no chance for the New Gargs to remain independent? I couldn't accept that. There had to be another way. Prophecies usually showed *one* potential path to an end, but not every possible way to get there. And perhaps that had been Marisol's biggest mistake—sticking too rigidly to the vision she'd had, without allowing for other possibilities.

Or . . . I stiffened as a new thought occurred to me.

Maybe Marisol had seen another way, but it was one that led to her death. It made sense. She couldn't accept the idea of a New Garg kingdom that didn't have her at the helm, so she'd chosen the path that required me and Nicole to die.

When Periclase whirled around, his cape shifted and gave me a brief view of Marisol's face. I looked away, but not before her expression seared into my mind. Her jewel-blue eyes were slightly widened, but not with pain or anger. Her face was frozen with focus, capturing the determination and drive that had defined her entire life. I had a sudden stab of certainty that the events that had led to this moment had begun long before I was born.

King Periclase stood over me, his face glowering as usual, as if he'd never spoken the soft words I'd overheard.

"You've done well, daughter," he said with a magnanimous boom to his voice to make sure everyone nearby heard. The outer corners of his eyes crinkled with approval. "I commend you for your strength and loyalty to your blood family."

"It wasn't loyalty. I had no choice." I spat the words through clenched teeth, and his satisfied leer faltered for a split second.

He cut a look at Eldon. Magic prickled across my mouth, and my lips sealed together against my will. Defiant anger heated my insides. Using his magic, Eldon moved my hands over my head, sheathing Aurora across my back and then letting my arms fall to my sides.

Periclase's focus sharpened on something behind me, and he swept past me with quick strides and swishes of his cape. Eldon allowed me to turn to see who'd caught the Duergar king's attention. Stepping through the bodies scattered through the anteroom and into the shelter was General Stanchon. A slash of drying blood blotched his face from one temple to his chin. His sleeve was soaked with crimson, a deep gash across his forearm peeking through a hole in the fabric. He didn't seem to notice the wound.

"The fortress is ninety-five percent secured, with nearly all the New Gargoyles subdued, Your Majesty," Stanchon reported.

The Duergar soldiers nearby let out guttural, victorious hollers. My stomach dropped. How many of my people had fallen?

"Good, good," Periclase said. He was clearly trying to play it cool, but pleased anticipation leaked through in his tone. "You deserve great accolades for your victory today, General. We will celebrate with a feast after we return to the palace."

Stanchon's expression didn't change. He was clearly still focused on the aftermath of battle. The ninety-five percent containment likely meant that his forces were still disarming the remaining New Garg soldiers. I hoped it meant only taking their weapons, rather than killing them.

"How long until our soon-to-be subjects will be gathered?" Periclase asked.

"Give us twenty minutes, your majesty."

"Excellent." Periclase nodded, and Stanchon turned smartly on his heel and went back the way he'd come.

If it weren't for Eldon and his magic, I was positive Periclase wouldn't have won. I slid a look at the Fae sorcerer out of the corners of my eyes, my hands involuntarily trying to clench as I added him to the list of people I planned to kill. My heart bumped when I caught him staring at me. I recognized the lingering confusion in his eyes before he managed to harden his expression. Losing control of me had rattled him. I'd vaguely registered it before but had been too absorbed in Marisol's death to give it much thought.

I peered at Eldon, trying to decode anything at all in the stillness of his face. Where had I gone in that moment when the fortress dissolved away and I'd stood on a hilltop facing a blue-eyed warrior? Who had I become there? Remembering the strange words I'd spoken, I swallowed drily. I tried to lift my hand to my neck, as if to confirm that my vocal chords still felt like mine. Eldon could control my voice if he chose, but what had happened on that hill had nothing to do with the Fae sorcerer. And by the startled look in his eyes, he had no idea what it was, either.

Eldon was revealing nothing, so I turned my gaze to the kings and men in charge. Finvarra had been silent, allowing Periclase to do all the talking. But I had the distinct impression the banished Unseelie High King was there to remind Periclase that there was a higher authority present. A pecking order of kings, with Sebastian being crushed at the bottom and Periclase pinched in between Finvarra and the Spriggan king. Periclase seemed too busy relishing his victory to show much concern about Finvarra. It occurred to me again that Periclase was overestimating the strength of his alliance with Finvarra. The two of them exchanged a few words I couldn't hear.

Periclase turned on me once more. "You understand what comes next, Princess?" he asked.

Eldon's magic hold on my lips dissipated. I was suddenly acutely aware of King Sebastian, swaying on his feet and looking more haggard by the minute.

"I understand what you have in mind," I said grudgingly. "You intend to make a show of this, I suppose?"

Sebastian swayed, and I couldn't help glancing at him. His skin had taken on a gray pallor, and he looked like he might pass out or vomit. Maybe both.

Periclase gave me a mildly disapproving look. "Not a show, daughter. Just the level of ceremony it deserves. This is a terribly historic day. Let's proceed to the auditorium, shall we?"

He wasn't really asking me, so I didn't bother answering.

He lifted his chin at the soldiers nearby, clearly indicating it was time for us to vacate Marisol's bunker. As the soldiers shifted around to form a procession, there was a *thunk* followed by a groan. I turned to see that Sebastian had collapsed a few feet from Marisol's boots.

"Get him up," Periclase said irritably.

There was some shuffling as two of the Duergar pulled Sebastian up by his armpits. The man looked half-dead, but when his eyes met mine, a little glint of intensity returned. A flicker of metal, so quick I almost might have imagined it, disappeared within the folds of his loose sleeve. But I recognized it. He'd picked up Marisol's dagger. Apparently he wanted to make one more attempt to dissolve the oath.

I clenched my jaw in frustration. If only I could get a moment alone with Sebastian, if I could get him out of here, we might be able to come up with a way to work together against Periclase. Sebastian and I had the same goal—avoid being taken into the Duergar kingdom. We could do *something* to improve our situation, I was sure of it. We could use the oath between us in a way that would help us. If only we had an opportunity.

As all of us trooped through the corridors toward the auditorium, Stanchon and Periclase chatted about how well the attack had gone. I gave a derisive snort. As if the victory had really had much to do with the Duergary military. Eldon had won it for them. I kept as close as I could, listening for Maxen's name. Had they allowed him to live? In Marisol's shelter, I'd dreaded turning around and seeing Maxen's face and the knowledge in it that I'd assassinated his mother. Thank Oberon he hadn't been there.

My attention shifted away from the Duergar king and his general. Sebastian, who was slightly ahead to the right, was fiddling with something. I couldn't see from this angle, but knowing he had a knife concealed in his sleeve, I tensed. What was he going to try?

A second or two later, I had my answer. Sebastian halted abruptly, curled forward, and let out a pained bellow. Then he pitched over like a felled tree to land face down on the floor. I reflexively tried to dart ahead to help him, but Eldon's magic froze me in place.

Periclase, Stanchon, and Finvarra had continued on a few steps before the commotion and a shout from a soldier made them turn.

"What is this?" Periclase demanded, marching back and staring angrily down at King Sebastian's prone form. A trickle of blood began to creep out from under the Spriggan king's torso. Periclase whipped his gaze to Eldon. "Don't let him die!"

One of the soldiers grabbed Sebastian's shoulder and hauled him over onto his back. The handle of Marisol's dagger protruded from his chest.

Dark blood soaked the front of his shirt. Eldon swiftly knelt next to Sebastian and began to chant. Puffs of the gloaming streamed from the Fae sorcerer's fingers into Sebastian's nostrils and open mouth.

Sebastian was fading but wasn't dead yet, and his eyes locked on mine. His lips moved as he struggled to say something. I held my breath, watching him.

I couldn't hear the words, but I read his lips. "I'm sorry."

Then the Spriggan king's eyes lost focus and the lids drooped. Eldon's back stiffened, and he stopped chanting.

"Damn you, do not let him die!" Periclase roared and then began to curse a blue streak.

A cold shiver poured over me, and the air between me and Sebastian sparkled for the briefest of moments. The oath between us had been severed. Periclase could no longer use me as a means to take the Spriggan kingdom.

Eldon turned his head to slowly look up at the Duergar king. The Fae sorcerer didn't say anything, but his expression, a mix of surprise and indignation, spoke volumes. He was clearly not accustomed to being screamed and cursed at, and he didn't enjoy it. He rose and faced Periclase, and somehow Eldon seemed to tower menacingly even though he only had an inch or two on the Duergar king.

Again, I tried to imagine why Eldon would have aligned himself with Finvarra and Periclase.

Periclase puffed his chest, but apprehension clouded in his eyes. He knew he'd crossed a line.

"Death does not yield to demands, even those of kings. It cannot be held at bay forever," Eldon said evenly, his voice smooth and edged with a Scottish brogue. "He is dead, and no magic can save him."

Eldon's tone held no overt threat, but Periclase blinked and drew back a bit. Silence hung heavy in the hallway as everyone stood frozen, waiting.

The Duergar king's nostrils flared. "Remove the body."

Periclase didn't wait for his order to be carried out but turned on his heel and strode away.

I stared down at Sebastian's slack face. It was too late for the Stone Order, but he'd managed to save his people from Periclase's rule. If Periclase truly wanted the Spriggan kingdom, he wouldn't be able to use the oath between me and Sebastian to get it. Periclase would have to use his military and take the Spriggan realm by force. But I knew he wouldn't. The Spriggan kingdom had just been an alluring bonus on top of the Stone Order, an easy grab while he took the New Gargs.

Only time would tell whether the Spriggan would see their dead king as a fool for getting into this situation in the first place or a martyr for his sacrifice.

Eldon's magic pricked at my muscles and propelled me forward along with the rest of the party, minus King Sebastian and the Duergar soldiers who stayed behind to deal with the corpse. Ahead, Periclase's cape rustled as he moved with agitated, quick strides. I stared at the back of his head. The Duergar had taken the fortress by force, and Marisol was dead as a result. Periclase would easily be able to make a case to the High Court to take the Stone Order.

Unless Oberon rejected it. Such a move would be unprecedented in Faerie's modern history. The High Court didn't make rulings when it came to one realm absorbing another—it simply recognized the legitimacy of the change and made it official. Kingdoms had fought and fallen throughout Faerie history. It was just the way of things here.

I pulled in my bottom lip and bit down. But I'd helped save Oberon's life. Perhaps I had some sway with him. I needed to make an appeal to the High King. Maybe I could do something for my people. Assuming, of course, that Oberon was conscious, in his right mind, and still in control of the Summerlands.

I let out a long breath. First things first. I couldn't do much of anything at the moment, and there were people up ahead. A line of Duergar guards shifted, forcing the crowd off to the side to give us a pathway through the people beyond. New Gargoyles were gathered, weaponless and faces pale and stricken. Word of Marisol's death had already spread. Their silent, accusing eyes followed me.

"Traitor," someone hissed, a female New Garg around my dad's age who was dressed in full battle gear. "Sovereign killer."

A Duergar soldier stepped out of line, twisted, and drove his short sword into her throat. I gasped, a sharp inhalation through my nose. The woman collapsed to the floor, gurgling as she clutched at her neck. The Duergar soldier left her there. He had moved so quickly, he only had to jog a couple of steps to catch up with our procession and resume his position.

My breath came raggedly as I made my way through a sea of accusing, hating stares. I silently begged them to remain silent. I couldn't stand to see another one killed for speaking out against me.

I saw people I recognized. Emmaline's solemn, troubled lavender eyes. Vera, the stylist who'd readied me for my first visit to the Duergar kingdom. Soldiers I'd sparred with since childhood. And Maxen. At first, my heart leapt with the knowledge that he'd been spared. But oh, gods, his sapphire eyes locked on mine and my knees lost strength. He looked haunted, grief-stricken, and hollow. If not for Eldon's magic holding me up, I would have stumbled, and I might not have been able to rise under my own power.

I gave a slight shake of my head and pleaded with my eyes for his forgiveness. He knew his mother had tried to murder me and my sister—his lover. But Marisol was his mother, his only family. Even if they'd been at odds, even if he hated her for trying to kill the woman he loved . . . she was still his mother, and I'd killed her.

When we finally reached a backstage entrance to the auditorium, my shoulders drooped as strength seemed to drain out of me. Did my people truly believe I was aligned with Periclase? Was there really any reason for them to believe otherwise?

I swallowed hard, trying to pull myself together as our procession gathered backstage. Off to the side, I recognized the podium that Marisol had often stood behind when she addressed the Order from the stage. I turned my back on it. I'd just about regained my composure when a couple of Duergar marched in, flanking Maxen. My heart sank like a stone at first, but then rocketed upward as my alarm surged. Why was Maxen here?

I whipped around to Periclase. "What are you doing with him?" I demanded, fear clear in my voice.

He frowned at me. "Do you see me as some sort of monster who would perform a sacrifice on stage? You should know me well enough by now to realize I'd never do anything so uncivilized."

My gaze cut over to Maxen. I shook my head. "I'm sorry," I said. "So sorry. I didn't have a—"

Eldon's magic cut off my words before I could finish.

Maxen's expression went from hollow to grim. His gaze flicked to Eldon and then back to me. Maxen's eyes narrowed. I thought he might have understood, or at least begun to suspect, that I wasn't fully in control of myself, and my heart lifted just a bit.

General Stanchon appeared through a curtained doorway that led to the seating area of the auditorium. "They're ready, and the room is secured, your majesty."

The flesh side of Periclase's face stretched into a pleased smile. When he turned it on me, I wanted to vomit.

"It's time, daughter," he said.

Eldon's magic took control of my legs and forced me to follow the Duergar king up a short staircase and through a velvet curtain to the stage.

Chapter 25

THE STAGE LIGHTS glared in my eyes, so bright it was impossible to make out the faces in the audience. I could see the armed Duergar soldiers lining the aisles, though. It was surreal, seeing the whole population of the fortress sitting there by force.

Periclase and Finvarra walked to the center of the stage. A soft murmur swept through the audience, and I heard Finvarra's name uttered several times.

I expected Periclase to speak, but instead, Finvarra stepped forward.

"This has been a difficult day, a shocking day for you," the Unseelie legend said. "Your ruler is dead, you've lost comrades and loved ones, and your Order is now under the Unseelie rule of King Periclase."

Indignation and hot wrath seemed to spread through the auditorium in palpable waves.

"I don't blame you for your anger," Finvarra said. "This is not what your former leader envisioned for you, and not what you envisioned for yourselves. You do not understand it now, but someday, hindsight will show this was for the best."

"We will never call you king, you Unseelie bastard!" someone shouted in the audience.

A roar of agreement went up through the crowd.

I cringed internally as half a dozen Duergar soldiers swiftly moved in to yank the offender out of his seat. They wrestled the man into the aisle and toward the stage. They threw him to the floor beneath the stage and began to beat the shit out of him—kicking him brutally and jabbing at his limbs with their swords. Stabs that were meant to injure and torment, not kill. Finvarra let it go on for what seemed like an eternity.

Finally, he raised his hand. "Enough."

The soldiers backed off. The New Garg man had gone still after a vicious kick to the head. I watched his still form until I saw a twitch of one bleeding arm that indicated he wasn't dead.

"The fact is," Finvarra continued as if the disruption had not happened. "It doesn't matter who you do or do not want to call king. This is your new reality. Part of that reality is that the Summerlands will fall to Unseelie forces. It's a new day in Faerie, and the sooner you accept it, the sooner you will begin to see how you fit into this new world. Not all kingdoms will have such a chance. You might, if you're smart and very lucky. Consider what you really want—to see your people have an opportunity to survive and possibly one day thrive, or to bash yourselves to death needlessly against the inevitable turning tide? Would Marisol Lothlorien have wanted to see the New Gargoyles die out within a generation of her passing? Is that really why you've fought so hard?"

I peered at him, wondering how a man who could speak with such placid logic had ever united the wild and animalistic Unseelie tribes. But I had to give him credit. He was striking the right chords in his words, whether or not the New Gargs were truly ready to hear them.

He paused, letting a few seconds of silence stretch out, swiveling his head slowly to scan the crowd.

"Again, I will say that you have an opportunity," Finvarra said. "If you are wise, you won't waste it."

He turned, raised a palm to Periclase, and then stepped back to allow the Duergar king to take center stage.

"King Finvarra knows of what he speaks," Periclase said, striding forward with a regal swish of his cape. "You will see the wisdom of his words in the coming days. In the meantime, we will begin the mighty task of absorbing the Stone Order into the Duergar realm."

His head turned slightly, and suddenly my legs were carrying me toward him. My stomach twisted nauseatingly in anticipation of whatever he had planned for me. Eldon brought me to a halt next to Periclase.

The Duergar king looked over at me with approval before returning his attention to the audience. "Your Champion and my blood daughter, the Duergar princess Petra Maguire, has already joined forces with me and played an important role in bringing this day to fruition. She represents the bridge between the former Stone Order and the Duergar kingdom and will continue to serve all of us in the days ahead."

Like hell I would.

My lips parted, and Eldon's magic forced out words. "I will devote myself fully to this worthy task, your majesty," I felt and heard myself say.

The sound of my own voice made me physically ill. Tears of frustration sprang to my eyes.

Periclase spouted more platitudes about the future while I tried not to vomit.

Finally, we all trooped off stage.

A Duergar soldier approached me with something in his hand. He unceremoniously jabbed a magi-zapper against my ribs and activated it. Every muscle in my body jumped and then stiffened. My teeth ground together as I fought for consciousness. Just before I blacked out, I glimpsed Maxen getting the same treatment.

I awoke to darkness, sprawled with my arm twisted awkwardly behind me and my cheek pressed against a cold floor. Keeping perfectly still, I tried to assess where I was and whether anyone else was there with me. By my position, I guessed I'd been dumped where I was without ceremony shortly after the Duergar soldier zapped me into oblivion. The room was quiet, but not completely silent. Dark, but not pitch black. A pencil-thin strip of light along the floor not far from where I lay indicated a door. No sounds of breath or movement. If I had company, it was either dead or unconscious.

I pushed slowly up to one hip, propping myself on my hand. My head screamed at me, thumping pain radiating from the right side of my forehead. Probably where I'd landed when I was dropped here. I frowned. My New Garg blood normally brought quick healing, but I didn't feel the familiar tingle of it as my head continued to throb. Something wasn't right.

A faint clang of a heavy door beyond the room I was in set a couple of puzzle pieces sliding together in my mind. I was in the fortress jail. Not in one of the cells I'd seen before—those had windows in the doors—but deeper in, where the most dangerous offenders were kept. I'd never seen or felt it before, but I'd heard about it. A cell warded with magic so strong, it was neutralizing the Fae magic that flowed through my blood. No wonder the pain in my head wasn't subsiding.

I stood, tuning into the odd numbness of absent magic. I was just about to go to the door to see if I could hear anything useful when there was a soft scraping in the ceiling.

My pulse jumped, and I automatically reached for Mort. My hand hit the handle end of a sword, and I remembered—Mort was gone. I had Aurora now. I drew it, but it felt wrong. Dead in my hands. Still, it was a weapon.

Dancing silently over to the wall, I gripped the sword in both hands. I couldn't see a damn thing above, but it sounded like something was trying to claw its way through. I lifted Aurora as a high-pitched metallic screech scraped my eardrums.

"Shit," someone muttered.

My eyes popped wide. That voice was familiar. I stared up at the opening—really just a slightly darker square in the rectangle of darkness that was the ceiling. But my eyes were starting to adjust, and I saw movement.

"Maxen?" I whispered. "Is that you?"

Legs appeared through the opening. Then a figure dropped down with a soft slap of shoes on the floor.

"Yeah, it's me."

I looked up at the ceiling again and shook my head. "How . . .?"

He scoffed softly. "My mother designed this place. I know more of its secrets than anyone alive."

My chest cramped at the reference to Marisol, and I lowered Aurora. "Maxen, I'm so, so sorry. I can't express how terrible I feel. I know that's horribly inadequate, and I don't expect you to forgive—"

"Stop," he cut me off so sharply, I blinked in surprise. "We don't have time for heartfelt talks. And I sure as shit don't want to hear about your emotional trials and tribulations right now."

I nodded in the dark. Maxen rarely swore, and twice within the span of a couple minutes? I let out a tiny, sad sigh. I couldn't expect him to be the same person I'd known my whole life. Not after what had happened today.

"Is Nicole okay?" he asked.

"She was safe last time I saw her. And I don't believe Periclase would harm her."

I barely heard his relieved exhale.

"She sends her love," I said gently. My eyes were starting to adjust. I couldn't make out his features, but his posture was stooped, tense.

He ran his hand through his hair, seeming to struggle for a moment to pull himself together.

"Maxen, I need to contact Oberon," I said. "Jasper and I broke him out of the Tuatha's stronghold. I think he'll help us."

"I've sent word already. But things are grave in the Summerlands. Oberon has bigger problems than the fate of the Stone Order, and chances are slim that he'll drop everything to help us." His words were clipped, almost harsh.

"What's your plan?" I knew he had one. Otherwise he wouldn't be standing there, as he clearly felt no love for me at the moment.

"To jailbreak you," he said. "You must go to the Summerlands. Persuade Oberon to block the Duergar absorption of the Stone Order. Find Jasper Glasgow. He must kill his father."

"Periclase?"

"No, his blood father."

My brows shot up. "You know about . . . ?"

"Finvarra, yes."

That answered that. I wasn't sure how he could have discovered this fact, but apparently his information networks were much more extensive than I'd ever imagined.

"This is our only chance," Maxen said. "Oberon must regain control of the High Court before the Tuatha De Danann come."

I opened my mouth to respond but then stopped.

Oliver.

Periclase still had my father. If I left, Periclase would threaten his life. If I didn't come back, Oliver would likely die.

Maxen read my silence as hesitation.

"Petra, look at where you are. Periclase will keep you imprisoned and then when he needs you, he'll dance you out and do what he wants with you. There are several hundred New Gargoyles who would happily see you dead right now. The fortress is far more dangerous for you than it is for me. You need to go."

"Periclase has Oliver," I whispered. "If I disappear . . ."

"If you don't go, Faerie will fall first to the Unseelie and then the Tuatha will destroy all of us who resisted Finvarra."

I pulled in my lips and bit down for a moment. I'd never heard Maxen so hardened.

"You're right. I must go."

He moved under the hole in the ceiling and squatted. "I'll boost you up." He laced his fingers together.

I sheathed Aurora, went to Maxen, and placed a hand on his shoulder to steady myself. I planted the bottom of my boot on his hands and pushed off the floor, springing up with his assistance. My fingers clamped onto the edges of the opening in the ceiling, and I kicked up and rolled over. Leaning through the hole, I reached an arm down. Maxen crouched and then jumped up. His hand locked around my wrist, and I heaved back until he was able to prop himself up by the elbows.

"Are they going to know you did this? That you got me out?" I whispered.

"Not your problem."

He pushed the trapdoor over the opening, plunging us into darkness. His hand bumped my arm and slid down to my hand. He moved my fingers over the floor until they hit a ridge.

"Follow this as far as it goes," he said. "You'll find a hatch in the wall that drops out into the southwest courtyard. There's a doorway there."

"I swear I will succeed," I said softly.

He let go of my hand, and I started to move away. Magic was returning to me like feeling coming back into a numb limb. It zinged through my blood, and the throbbing in my head subsided. I pushed magic onto the skin of my forearms, just a bit to test that my stone armor still worked. Satisfied, I released it.

"Maxen, wait."

The sound of his movements paused.

"Is Nicole pregnant?"

He didn't answer for a long moment. "Yes," he said finally.

A smile touched my lips as unexpected, tender warmth flooded my chest. "Congratulations."

"Thanks."

I wanted to say "I'm sorry" again but held back. He didn't want to hear apologies, and if I said it, it would be more for me than for him. So instead, I turned and began crawling away, my hand trailing the ridge that would take me to escape.

True to Maxen's word, I made it to an outer wall with a panel. I inched it aside and peered through the opening. It was dusk, and the evening air seemed a few degrees cooler than typical. To the right about a hundred yards away, some arborvitae were trimmed in spiral patterns. Two of them joined at the tops to form an arch—my way out. Unfortunately, the arch was obvious enough that the Duergar had noticed it and stationed a couple of guards in front of it.

My right hand curled into a loose fist as I anticipated reaching back for Aurora. I hesitated. Periclase had told me that if I raised the sword against anyone without his permission, Oliver would die. But I was leaving Periclase's custody, all but ensuring my father's death anyway.

If Oliver were there, I knew what he would tell me to do. Without hesitation, without fear or regret, he would command me to go.

I squeezed my eyes closed and dropped my chin to my chest, my throat suddenly too tight to draw air. My chest hardened with sharp sorrow as I wished for one last chance to speak to my father, to thank him for raising me as if I were his, for teaching me that my size wasn't a disadvantage, for showing me how to be fierce. I would apologize for getting so angry when I'd discovered he'd kept secrets from me.

I had to wait for a moment until I could breathe again.

"I promise I will kill the ones who hurt you," I whispered.

I pushed the panel aside, sprang from the opening, and landed on the ground with Aurora already gleaming in my hand. With a strong push of magic across my skin came my stone armor.

There was no way to hide my approach, so I ran full throttle across the courtyard at the doorway and the Duergar guards. I held Aurora aloft in my right hand while already running through my mind the sigils I would trace that would open the door to the netherwhere.

The soldiers jumped in surprise and then charged me, their short swords drawn. The shorter of the two stopped short.

"No blades, man! It's the princess!" he shouted the warning to the larger fellow, who was in the lead.

The big guy let out a strangled noise as he tried to halt his attack mid-swing. I ducked around him while he tripped over his own feet. The other guard was fumbling with his belt, trying to palm his magi-zapper, which appeared to be snagged on his shirt. If he used the zapper on me, I'd be toast.

Instead of going for a mortal wound, I swung Aurora like a baseball bat. The blade connected with the guard's wrist, slicing off the hand. Appendage and magi-zapper fell to the soft grass.

I sped past the screaming man, my sights on the doorway. Behind me, I heard a zapper's crackling flare. I reflexively jagged to the right. The electrified magic zipped past me and lit up one of the spiral-cut arborvitae.

I started chanting the magic words and jumped, diving at the doorway. Just as I reached it, I traced the sigils in the air.

The nothingness of the netherwhere opened to me, taking me into its chilly embrace.

A moment later, I tumbled ass over teakettle on the hard ground, Aurora flying from my grip.

Completing my awkward somersault flat out on my back and with the wind knocked out of me, I stared up at the deep-blue evening sky of the Cait Sidhe kingdom—a realm I knew well enough, but not a place Periclase would likely think to look for me.

I'd made it. Now I just had to make good on my promise to Maxen. I had to succeed so Oliver's death wouldn't be in vain.

Once I could breathe again, I sat up and looked around for my sword. I'd landed in a remote spot my best friend Lochlyn, who'd grown up in this kingdom, had shown me. It was in a lightly wooded area just beyond the edge of her native village, a location of a well that had dried up long ago. The well itself was still there, and nearby were two aspen trees bent together marking the doorway I'd just come through.

I gave my head a shake and scrambled to my feet. I didn't have any time to waste. I had Aurora in my hand, just about to stow the sword in my back scabbard, when there was a rustling in the bushes fifty yards off.

I froze and firmed my grip on my sword. There were soft voices, at least two people approaching. I whipped my gaze around, looking for a place to hide. The last thing I needed was to be seen. But the thickest aspen tree was no bigger than my thigh. There was nowhere to conceal myself, and if I ran, they'd hear me.

Damn, I'd have to go back through the doorway and come out somewhere else. I scooted over there and raised my hand to draw the sigils.

"Petra!" a familiar voice called.

I was halfway through the chant but stopped mid-sentence and twisted around, my eyes wide with disbelief.

Two figures were emerging into the clearing—willowy, beautiful Lochlyn, and Bryna, my conniving half-sister.

Chapter 26

I BLINKED HARD, for a second wondering if I'd smacked my head on the way out of the stone fortress and was hallucinating the two figures hurrying toward me.

"Oh, thank Oberon," Lochlyn breathed, rushing over and folding me into an embrace.

Bryna stopped a few feet away and let out an exasperated sigh. "We don't have time for this, Lochlyn."

I glared at my half-sister around my best friend's arm but pulled back from Lochlyn.

"Nice to see you too, Bryna," I said wryly and then looked back and forth between the two of them. "What in the name of Maeve are you two *doing* here?"

"Retrieving you, of course," Bryna said with a roll of her eyes. "Escorting you around seems to have become my part-time job, somehow. The pay really stinks, in case you're wondering."

"She's a real charmer," Lochlyn said, one corner of her mouth twisting into a half-grimace. "But she's right. Jasper sent her to find you. She came to me for a best guess about where you'd show up after you got out of the fortress." Lochlyn threw up her hands with a flourish. "And I was right!" she crowed.

I shook my head. "How did you know I was escaping the fortress? How did Jasper know?"

"Maxen Lothlorien," Bryna said. She turned and beckoned to us with an impatient rolling motion of her arm. "Come *on*. More walk, less talk."

Lochlyn and I began following Bryna.

"Maxen got a message to Jasper?" I asked.

"Yes," Lochlyn said. "Maxen knew you'd need help getting to the Summerlands, and he wanted you and Jasper to go together, apparently."

Right. I hadn't thought ahead that far yet, obviously, but I had no idea how to get into the realm of the Summerlands on my own. I should have known Maxen was so on top of things.

Lochlyn shot me a curious look out of the corners of her eyes. I knew she was dying to ask about what had transpired between me and Jasper since the last time she and I had talked. I sure as hell wasn't going to say anything in front of Bryna, though. Not because I was modest, but because Bryna still believed Jasper was Periclase's son—which would mean Jasper and I were . . . yeah, half-siblings. Except we weren't. The world just didn't know it.

"Where are we going? And how do I get into the Summerlands?" I asked.

"To Jasper. And that's his problem," Bryna said shortly.

Full of useful info, as usual.

The Summerlands was an invite-only kind of place, which raised the question of how Finvarra had managed to attack it. He'd briefly gained power in the Summerlands, back when he'd first united the Unseelie, so he probably knew secret ways in. That was my guess, anyway.

Lochlyn made a face at Bryna's back, and then turned to me.

"So," Lochlyn said. "What in the name of the gods has happened?"

Bryna turned her head slightly. I could almost imagine I saw her ears pricking in curiosity.

I shook my head and blew out a long breath. "So much. Too much to tell you all of it now."

"Marisol Lothlorien's dead?" Bryna asked over her shoulder.

I blinked a couple of times.

"Word has spread," Lochlyn said. "Are you . . . okay?"

By the way she said it, it was obvious that the rumor of Marisol's death carried my name along with it.

"I can't afford to look back," I said, my voice low. "There's too much to do."

She nodded solemnly and peered at me again.

"Bet you're in good with Daddy now," Bryna said with a harsh edge of sarcasm. She was a subject of the Duergar realm and Periclase's blood daughter, but he refused to claim her as his because she was a halfling—part human. It wasn't something Bryna advertised. I'd only guessed she was a halfling after I witnessed her using human-magicked charms, which full-blooded Fae couldn't do. Her bitterness made a lot more sense after I discovered what she really was. Halflings were a source of shame in Faerie.

"Maybe for a moment I was," I said. "But now that I've flown the coop, I suspect there will be no forgiveness. I wouldn't be surprised if he disowns me." I tried to push the image of Oliver from my mind.

"Aw, we could have a club," Bryna said with false sweetness. "The banished daughters of Periclase."

She was being a little dramatic. Periclase never banished her, only refused to claim her. She was still one of his subjects.

My brows drew together as I thought of Oliver again. Before my thoughts could go too far, I hardened myself against the emotions threatening to swell up my throat and flood my eyes.

"What is it?" Lochlyn whispered.

I shook my head, and she didn't press. I sensed her worry as she walked beside me, but I couldn't let myself focus on it.

We'd been tramping through the woods, but the trees thinned and then cleared up ahead next to a road. Instead of taking us to the road, Bryna kept us parallel to it but still in the partial cover of the aspens.

"We're going to circle around to a farm on the far side of town," Lochlyn said. "It's owned by a relative of mine. That's where Jasper is waiting."

Bryna smirked back at me. "So, did the two of you decide incest is no big thing, or what?"

Irritation flared hotly through my veins, and I had to resist the urge to grab a fistful of Bryna's long white hair and rope it around her neck until she cried uncle.

"I mean, he's stupid hot, don't get me wrong," Bryna continued in a conversational tone. "But the brother-sister thing would cross a line even for me."

I was drained by recent events, frustrated by how thoroughly Periclase had manipulated me, and heartsick over Oliver. And Bryna had been a first-class asshole since she appeared in the clearing. It all added up to a shortage of patience and self-control on my part.

Lochlyn tried to grab my arm, but I was too quick. I hopped a long step forward on my left leg and swept my right across Bryna's ankles. She went down hard on one hip and elbow. When she twisted around to glare at me, her cheeks were bright red with anger.

I stood over her with my fists clenched at my sides. "It's not—" I started to growl through gritted teeth, but cut myself off.

Her face was screwed up, and she looked on the verge of letting loose with a torrent of four-letter words. But then her expression released the tension of anger, and her mouth formed a little O as her brows arched. I'd hoped she'd glazed past what I'd so nearly spilled, but I could already see by the gleam in her eyes that she hadn't missed a thing.

"Really," she drawled up at me with an almost predatory interest. "This is juicy. Verrry juicy indeed."

Shit. *Shit.* I shouldn't have lost my temper. I definitely shouldn't have said what I said.

"Just get up," I said.

She gave a little trilling giggle, hopped to her feet, and then continued at a slightly faster pace than before. Humming a soft little tune that made me want to punch her, she led the way to the edge of a fallow field. We took a dirt lane that ran in between the empty plot and a field of fragrant alfalfa toward a barn.

I peered around, paranoid that someone would spot me, but saw no one nearby. Perhaps Lochlyn had asked her relatives to stay out of sight for a time. I hoped so. It was in their best interest to not ever know I was there.

Inside the barn, the air was cooler and pleasantly weighty with the smell of straw, sawdust, and a hint of horse manure. A figure pushed away from the wall in the shadows of a corner. The faint light from lofted windows played across Jasper's face, highlighting the angles of his cheekbones and accentuating the squareness of his jaw. He strode toward us, his golden irises like twin candle flames within the shadows of his deep-set eyes were trained on me. He moved with even more graceful strength than I remembered, and my heart bumped in my chest.

Relief and warmth flooded his face, but he schooled his expression and stopped several feet away—a respectful distance for two acquaintances.

I gave him a tiny smile, and one side of his mouth quirked up.

"Oh, for the love of Oberon, stop your stupid charade," Bryna moaned. "Petra spoiled this episode of Incestuous Passion on the way over here."

Jasper frowned and squinted at her.

I stepped forward and rubbed the back of my neck with one hand. "Uh, I may have accidentally mentioned something about the fact that we aren't really siblings," I said.

His face stilled, and for a moment I thought he was going to be angry. But then his lids lowered partway, and he gave me a slow-burning grin as he crossed the distance between us.

"Well, in that case," he started.

I blinked, waiting for the rest of the sentence. But instead of speaking, he came to me, wrapped one arm around my lower back, and pulled me against him with enough force that the gesture was just this side of deliciously rough. His lips lowered to mine and he kissed me, the fingers of his other hand coming up to weave into the hair at the nape of my neck. He used that hand to press us deeper in to the kiss.

By the time he released me, I was breathless, and my pulse was galloping.

"I missed you," Jasper said, his voice rough-edged.

"I missed you, too." I let my eyes close as our foreheads touched, and I relished the still-lingering feeling of the seconds his lips had been pressed to mine and all of my sorrows and fears had momentarily faded to the background.

"I feel like I should applaud," Lochlyn said.

My eyes popped open, and everything came rushing back. I turned to see Lochlyn fanning herself with one hand and grinning at us.

Bryna stood with her arms folded, one hip jutted out, and her brows slightly arched. I expected her to say something cutting, but to my surprise, she didn't utter a word. Her expression was watchful, almost thoughtful. I'd noticed before that she seemed to behave herself somewhat better in Jasper's presence. I was dying to know what he had over her that kept her doing favors for him. It had to be something good, considering how sour she was every time she and I crossed paths. Or maybe her attitude had a tiny something to do with that time I knocked her out, took her to the stone fortress, and tossed her in jail. Heh.

I started to turn back to Jasper when something hit me. I cut a swift look at Bryna.

"You're not siblings, either," I said, looking at her and tipping my head toward Jasper.

She shrugged and slanted her gaze off to the side, but I thought I caught something unexpected in her eyes before she turned away. Was she wounded by this discovery?

"We'd best get on to the Summerlands," Jasper said. He faced Lochlyn and Bryna. "Both of you have my deepest gratitude for aiding me. I feel extremely fortunate that Petra has a friend who knows her mind so well she knew which doorway she'd come through. I was waiting here on pins and needles, expecting you to come back empty-handed and wondering what in Oberon's name we'd do if we couldn't locate her. Your swiftness in getting her to me may save Faerie."

Bryna was looking off to the side. He faced her and waited a beat until she reluctantly turned her head to meet his gaze.

He gave her a sly look. "And you. What would I do without you?" My mouth dropped open. He said it with clear, unabashed affection, and it surprised the hell out of me. His face softened into something I could only describe as true warmth.

Bryna's mouth twitched as if she held back a smile.

Lochlyn stepped over and embraced me. I wrapped my arms around her, emotion tugging at my heart. I wasn't ready to say goodbye to her again so soon. We'd hardly seen each other in recent months, and I missed her more than I wanted to think about.

"If there's any way I can help, don't hesitate to message me," she whispered in my ear. "I'm staying with a friend in another village of this realm, but if you can get a note to Aunt Anna, she will make sure it gets to me."

Her aunt had helped me and Nicole not long before, when we'd narrowly escaped the assassins Marisol had sent after us.

"I will," I said. "Please be careful."

"I'll be fine," she said, pulling back. Her eyes were misty, but she managed a smile. "You're the one who needs to take care."

I snorted a laugh. "Aw, you know me. Careful is my middle name."

She gave me a mock look of disapproval.

"We must be off," Jasper said. His voice was low, and his golden eyes unusually tight and serious.

"Is there a doorway nearby to take us into the Summerlands?" I asked.

He shook his head. "We won't be traveling by any of the standard doorways."

"Great Ravens?" I guessed.

"Not this time." He reached into a pouch on his belt, carefully, as if the object inside were very fragile.

I watched curiously as he opened his fist. A bright, rosy light flared in his palm and then faded. He held a perfectly round stone, the size of a small marble. I sucked in a breath when I realized what I was looking at.

"How did you get a portal jewel?" I asked. I'd never seen one in person.

"Oberon," he said.

The rosy light had retreated to the interior of the stone, where it spiraled and gyrated as if it were alive.

Jasper reached out his other hand to me, and I grasped it. Then he took a breath and tossed the jewel into the air about five feet over our heads. Its light burst forth again, so intense I had to squeeze my eyes closed. I heard him chanting under his breath, and then I lost all sense of the physical world as we passed into the netherwhere.

Chapter 27

THE PLACE WHERE we popped back into the world felt unfamiliar. Not totally foreign—I sensed by the sweetness of the air and the way my magic ran through my blood that I was still in Faerie—but some place I'd never been.

Jasper and I stood at the base of a small, grassy hill that appeared to be part of a larger green space. A nine or ten story wall stood about half a mile away. Beyond, rolling hilltops were just visible. The dusky sky of late evening was beginning to reveal the first faint stars overhead.

I could imagine this would be a very pleasant place if not for the din of battle that carried over the wall.

"This way," Jasper said, pointing to one side of the hill.

I was just about to ask him where exactly we'd landed in the Summerlands when there was an explosion that rocked the ground under my boots. Neon-yellow spitfire—weaponized magic combined with explosives—burst up into the sky from the other side of the wall. Spitfire was a specialty weapon of the Duergar. A chunk of red-hot rock hit the grass less than a dozen feet away and rolled to a stop right next to me. I grimaced. Even here, I couldn't escape King Periclase's reach. Spitfire was nasty stuff, the Fae magic equivalent of napalm in its destructive power.

Jasper clutched my wrist and towed me away from the smoldering chunk. We ran hard through what appeared to be a park, complete with ponds, burbling fountains, cobbled paths, flowered borders, and groves of trees. It was eerily deserted. When we passed a series of blackened craters each the size of a bus, I started to understand why no one was around.

Ahead, there was a grouping of white stone buildings, all of them fashioned like big, smooth sand castles with turrets, towers, battlements, watchtowers, and high walkways connecting many of the structures. There were enough of them to give the impression of a small city. The grandest structure stood in the middle, its turrets soaring over the smaller buildings around it. The tiles on the rooftops gleamed with subtle rainbow reflections, as if the roofs were constructed using shards of mother-of-pearl. It was breathtaking. Or it would have been, if not for half a dozen charred, smoking holes in roofs and walls.

Jasper let go of my hand when we approached a wall that was nothing near the scale of the one we'd run from but still tall and well-fortified. A moat ran along the base of it, and there was a drawbridge sealed up tight. A face appeared in a watchtower to the right of the drawbridge. Jasper raised his fist, and the man in the tower disappeared. A few seconds later, mechanisms began to groan, and the bridge tipped open at the top. It lowered like a giant's mouth slowly falling open. As soon as the end of it hit the flagstone-surfaced area where we stood, Jasper and I darted across.

At the mid-point of the bridge, something invisible but viscous slapped me in the face and slid over me.

"Keep moving," Jasper said. "It's a Fae-cast ward."

I blinked hard as I passed through some sort of magic shield that was several feet thick. I hadn't even sensed it until I physically ran into it. The thickness of it, and that it had been undetectable, meant it was made of unusually strong magic. Wards and shields weren't normally the stuff of Fae magic. Powerful human magic casters could draw upon the earthly elements to make such things, but Fae magic came from our own blood rather than from our surroundings. That meant our magic was always with us and easily accessible, but overall it was less powerful than human magic. Fae didn't have the power to make such a massive structure as the one I'd just passed through.

We made it through the shield, and a ruggedly handsome man stood there waiting for us. It took me a second to place him. The wolf face on the emblem of the leather vest he wore over his loose, long-sleeved top jogged my memory.

I skidded to a halt.

"Your majesty," I said, dropping into a curtsy—awkward when you're wearing skin-tight cargo pants and have no skirt to fan out. Jasper bent in a masculine yet graceful bow beside me.

"Rise, rise," the man said. His voice had a slight raspy edge to it, as if he'd strained it a bit from yelling—or maybe from howling. He was, after all, the king of the Dobhar Sidhe, the realm of the dog, most of whose subjects were canine shifters. I peeked up to see his keen green eyes on me. "If anything, I should be bowing to you, Champion."

I straightened and blew out a breath. "I couldn't allow it, your majesty. Please, call me Petra." My brows drew low over my eyes as relief at arriving safely in the castle mixed with the heaviness of just how dire things had become.

King Moreau Maclean was giving me a wolfish grin. "Of course, Champion Petra."

I snorted, and his eyes sparkled. He seemed pleased to have drawn an almost-laugh from me.

I knew of this man but had never seen him in person. His kingdom was affiliated with Oberon and the Seelie, but the Dobhar tended to keep to themselves. Their social structure was based on that of a canine pack, where the alpha couple took the throne and others could challenge for the position. The challenges usually ended with a death. Moreau Maclean and his mate, Idara, had held the throne for many years, since they'd first mated when they were not much past twenty years old. I estimated him to be in his mid-thirties.

"King Moreau, I did not expect someone of your importance to personally greet us," Jasper said.

The Dobhar king raised a dark brown brow at us. "You are too modest, Glasgow. Oberon and the rest have been awaiting you and the Champion of the Stone Order, the Summer Court, and wielder of Aurora with bated breath."

He slid a sly look at me, and I realized he was teasing me with the titles, and probably would continue to do so as long as he understood that it made me squirmy to be addressed that way. I made a little rolling flourish with my hand and inclined my head, humoring him.

Pride glowed in Jasper's golden eyes. "You make light, Petra, but you deserve every bit of it. You've already shown yourself to be a champion for the ages. And you've not yet tapped into even a small fraction of your potential."

My cheeks heated, and I gave my head a little shake. "Too much."

"Not even close," Jasper said.

Wanting to shift attention away from myself, I turned back to the Dobhar king. "Please, lead the way."

King Moreau appeared to be in an easy mood considering the Summerlands was under attack, but I wasn't fooled. He had a dark side, too. I'd heard tales of how frighteningly ruthless he was when threatened. There was a reason he and Idara held the Dobhar Sidhe alpha position for so long.

He sobered as he took us into the bailey of Oberon and Titania's castle. There were many signs of damage from attacks.

"The shield we passed through, your majesty," I said. "Isn't it strong enough to repel the assaults?"

"Aye, it is," King Moreau said, a bit of Irish accent. "But it was erected only earlier today. The stronghold of the Summerlands sustained much damage before then."

Workers were cleaning up rubble in some areas, and repairs were in progress here and there. We passed into the interior of the castle and away from visible evidence of the attacks. Servants roamed the corridors as if it were any other day.

"How does it feel to be the only Unseelie who's welcome in the Summerlands, Glasgow?" King Moreau peered at Jasper with in inquisitive upward shift of his brows.

"I believe I'm right where I belong, your majesty," Jasper said with a firm nod.

"The rest of us believe that as well."

King Moreau steered us around a right turn into a hallway that dead-ended at an oak door with a single woman standing guard. She wore armor and the colors of the Summerlands—orange, red, and touches of green the shade of tender new grass. With sharp, practiced movements, she stepped to one side, turned ninety degrees, grasped the polished brass knob, and opened the door for us.

Inside was an expansive office outfitted with masculine touches—heavy leather furniture, a huge cherrywood desk, matching conference table, and paintings of hunting scenes. The scale of everything was large, much larger than was comfortable for someone of my smallish stature.

There were several people gathered near the cold hearth. The tallest and most powerful-looking of them turned.

I drew a breath when Oberon's eyes fell on me, and I stopped and curtsied. Moreau and Jasper bowed.

"So glad you've safely arrived," the Seelie High King's voice boomed across the room at us.

"As are we, your majesty," I said. "And I am thrilled to see you in such strong form."

Relief prickled at the backs of my eyes. Last time I'd seen Oberon, I'd feared he'd never fully recover from his ordeal with the Tuatha's sky iron. He wore a long-sleeved top, but I caught glimpses of the bandages around his wrists. His wounds might never completely heal. He was in much better shape than I'd dared hope, though.

The others grouped behind Oberon had shifted around to get a view of us. There was Titania, looking breathtakingly radiant with her long waves of strawberry-blonde hair that seemed to flow around her as if on the gentle current of a summer breeze. Also present was Corrain, queen of the Baen Sidhe—the banshee kingdom—her curvy form outfitted in a snug violet velvet gown with a plunging neckline. Standing a bit apart was a man who looked so like the recently departed Spriggan King Sebastian, I drew back a little. He could only be Trey, Sebastian's son, already stepping in to take his father's place. Trey peered at me with hollow eyes that were completely devoid of warmth.

Also gathered were the stocky and barefoot king of Gnomes, the feather-lashed Sylph queen, and the long-legged, tall king of the water horse shifter Kelpie realm.

Then a black-haired, regal woman stepped out from the back. When her orange eyes met mine, my lips parted in surprise.

"Melusine," I said.

She inclined her head. "Petra Maguire."

Nicole's note must have reached Titania, and the High Queen had obviously acted quickly. I was frankly astonished that Melusine had come at all, let alone so soon. The Old Ones like Melusine, Oberon, and Titania loved to hold onto their epic grudges. Rumor was that Titania and Melusine had once been very close friends but had parted ways over some disagreement generations ago. For them to overcome their differences so swiftly meant that things were truly dire here in the Summerlands.

It gave me a lift to find Melusine there, and not just because of the powerful magic she could wield. When Jasper and I had visited her for the blood divining that revealed our true parentages, she'd been difficult and sulky, but beneath her moods I'd sensed a deep loneliness. Perhaps being here would help her find a bit belonging.

"I'm glad to see you here," I said to Melusine.

"I can't say I feel the same," she said and then gave a belabored sigh. "You've all made a terrible mess of things."

Okay, maybe she wasn't *quite* ready to be happy yet.

Oberon shot Melusine a withering look, but she was examining her black-painted fingernails and didn't see it.

"We have Melusine to thank for our defenses," he explained to me and Jasper. "So, we're forced to tolerate her delightful personality as part of the package."

My eyes widened, and I cut a look at Melusine to see how she took the insult. She stuck her tongue out at the High King, which he ignored. I thought I caught a pleased little quirk of her lips, though. Perhaps she liked the attention after all.

The shield around the inner wall of the Summerlands Castle made sense, since I knew it was the work of Melusine. She, like Eldon, was an Old One and a halfling—part Fae and part human. But she and Eldon were rarities in that they possessed the ability to wield very strong Fae magic and Earthly magic with equal power. Most halflings couldn't—they were generally weak in magic or had no ability at all. I suddenly felt slightly more optimistic about our chances against Finvarra, Periclase, Eldon, and the other Unseelie.

Oberon strode to the wide desk that stood under a cathedral-like window and crooked a forefinger at me, drawing me away from the others. My pulse bumped as I went over to stand across from the High King of the Summer Court.

In body, Oberon appeared to be in his prime—muscular, fit, moving easily and walking with a confident, long stride. But his eyes and the thousand-yard stare he occasionally adopted hinted at his age. His gaze intensified on me for a long moment, and tension pulled my insides tight as I stood under his silent scrutiny.

"I have a question for you, Petra Maguire," he said, his voice soft so that only I would hear.

My mouth went dry. "Yes, your majesty?"

"You left Faerie when you were young. You stayed away for many years. Now you're back. My question is, where do your commitment and your heart now lie—here in Faerie or across the hedge in the Earthly realm?"

I moistened my dry lips and drew myself up to my full height. "My heart, my soul and my sword belong wholly to my homeland," I said without hesitation.

A ghost of a smile passed over his lips.

"Now," he said crisply, looking first down at a stack of papers on his desk and then up at me. "We need to resolve a piece of business involving you and your Stone Order."

He held up a piece of paper in one hand.

"This is Marisol Lothlorien's original petition for kingdomhood," he said, projecting his words so everyone could hear.

My gaze cut from his face to the document he held and then back again. I swallowed hard. What was he doing?

Oberon lifted another piece of paper from the desk. "This is the certificate with which I've granted the request, signed by me last night."

My mouth fell open, and I stared dumbly at the words on the page. I was so shocked, I couldn't focus enough to read them.

"This decision supersedes the Duergar takeover of the stone fortress," Oberon continued. He pressed his lips together and then made a soft tsking noise out the side of his mouth. "Won't Periclase be disappointed when he hears the news?"

I blinked a few times. Oberon was saving us.

His eyes locked on mine. "The New Gargoyles were heretofore be known as the Carraig Sidhe, and the kingdom of the Carraig Sidhe will enjoy its rightful status as an independent kingdom within Faerie by the order of the High Court. As a condition of this decision, you, Petra Maguire, are the matriarch of this newly-formed kingdom. I just need your signature here." He jabbed his index finger at one of the signature lines at the bottom of the document.

What, *what*?

I began shaking my head, but it took a second or two to find words. "No, your majesty. I'm no queen. Maxen Lothlorien is the one you want. He knows how to lead. He's a lifelong diplomat. He's the rightful heir to this throne. Besides, most of the Stone Order—uh, Carraig Sidhe, I mean, they believe I'm a traitor. They'd like to string me up for killing Marisol. I'm pretty sure I couldn't even return to the fortress and expect to live. Not now. Maybe ever. I certainly can't expect the New Gar—Carraig Sidhe, I mean, to accept me as their leader. Which I don't want to be, anyway. I'm very grateful for your decision, though, please don't think I'm not. But you must choose someone else. With all, uh, due respect your majesty."

I was babbling, and my words had finally petered out. Oberon placed his palms on the desk and leaned forward until our noses were only about a foot apart.

I swallowed hard with a soft click of my dry throat.

"Listen well, Petra Maguire. I didn't make this decision as a favor to you, Marisol Lothlorien, or the New Gargoyle race," he said, his words a bare whisper, meant only for my ears. "I've seen kingdoms come and go, even witnessed races rise and fall, and I can count on one hand the number of times I interfered. I certainly never mourned the losses. It was not my place. I've granted Marisol's petition because only hours ago, my oracle informed me that if the New Gargoyles fell to the Unseelie, Faerie would likely follow. Do you understand?"

I gaped and then snapped my trap shut and nodded several times. Oh *gods*. Marisol's death must have set off a new prophecy.

"And I'm putting you on the throne because I believe Jasper Glasgow is right." Oberon's eyes flicked back to where Jasper stood and then settled again on me. "We will not prevail by continuing with business as usual. We need new ways. New blood. While Maxen Lothlorien is a fine politician and by all accounts quite a decent man, he is not what Faerie needs right now. Besides all that, when you and Glasgow came for me in the Giants' Causeway, I saw into the nature of your soul, Petra Maguire. You are a warrior. We need warriors." He straightened and peered at me. "Just don't let all of this go to your head."

He winked at me, and my brows shot up in surprise.

I worked some air back into my lungs so I could speak. "Your majesty? May I ask you something?"

"You may."

"How could I take the throne when my people want to murder me?"

He folded his sculpted arms. "I could issue a decree insisting that your people fall in line and send Summerlands guards to protect you at all times. But I won't. The Carraig Sidhe need to come to their loyalty to you through genuine means, not by some order from on high." If that didn't sound like an echo of things Jasper had said to me in the past, I didn't know what did. "I will advise you this: don't try to do it alone. Maxen Lothlorien can help you. He has many skills you lack. There are some in the fortress who are not shedding tears at Marisol's death. Find them. Your past actions and reputation are of enormous benefit, if you use them correctly. You risked your life for your people before, and you need to remind them of that. You are the Champion of the Carraig Sidhe and the Summer Court. You carry Aurora on your back. Do what you're best at and gather others around you who can compensate for your deficiencies. But know this. I'm not giving you an option in this matter. You are the ruler of the Carraig Sidhe kingdom, or there is no Carraig Sidhe kingdom."

"But I don't want this," I whispered before I could stop myself.

He snorted. "History has witnessed many great rulers utter those same words. Now, sign." He flicked the signature line that had my name printed under it.

I picked up the old-fashioned pen that lay next to the document, dipped the metal tip in a nearby inkwell, and signed my name. The air rippled with magic that emanated outward, like a stone tossed into a pond. My scalp tingled, and my blood seemed to liven in my veins.

Oberon inclined his head at me in a tiny bow. "Your majesty."

I swallowed hard. It was unreal.

"One more thing, King Oberon?"

"Yes?"

"Will we be aided in expelling Periclase from the fortress?"

"I can't spare any of my forces from the fight here. Even if I could, it wouldn't be proper to send soldiers of the Summerlands to aid one of the kingdoms in that way. That's a can of worms I can't afford to open."

Well, shit.

"I understand," I said.

"Now, we have other business to attend to. Let's rejoin the others, Queen Petra," he said loudly enough for the others to hear, coming around the desk and heading back toward the rulers still grouped near the fireplace.

Dazed and reeling, I turned. There was a smattering of applause from Jasper, King Maclean, and some of the other rulers. But not from Sebastian's son Trey. He just gave me an icy stare from under lowered brows.

I went to stand next to Jasper. "What the hell just happened?" I breathed.

His eyes shone. "Destiny gave you a little shove in the ass."

"Little? You call what Oberon just did *little*?"

"Shh, your majesty." He touched the side of his index finger to his lips. "The High King is speaking."

"Don't call me—ugh, never mind."

After a moment I felt Jasper's eyes on me.

"See? I said there was greatness in your destiny, and I was right," Jasper whispered. "You are the most remarkable woman I've ever met."

I was still spinning internally—I wasn't sure the sensation would ever fully disappear—but I did my best to try to focus on Oberon. Jasper and I were standing at the back of the group. He reached over and clasped my hand, squeezing it firmly for a second before letting go.

"My oracle has told me that Finvarra can only be defeated by one of his own blood," Oberon was saying. My attention perked, and I glanced over at Jasper. He was intent on the High King. Oberon lifted his gaze to where we stood. "Fortunately, we have such a man in our presence."

There were several gasps as everyone turned to stare at Jasper. He seemed unintimidated by the attention, simply nodding in acknowledgement.

"How do we know this man is of Finvarra's blood?" the Sylph Queen Vida asked.

Melusine stepped forward and turned to the group. "Because I have confirmed it."

"Is Jasper Glasgow indeed a blood descendant of Finvarra?" King Moreau asked Melusine, looking directly into her eyes. The question might have sounded oddly redundant or awkward to non-Fae, but Moreau was simply formally confirming the truth of Melusine's claim. Fae couldn't lie. Not directly, anyway. We could be evasive with words or refuse to respond, but we couldn't straight-up lie to each other.

"Jasper Glasgow is indeed a blood descendant of Finvarra, as confirmed by my own divining of Jasper's blood," Melusine said. She understood what Moreau was doing, too, and was unoffended by the direct question.

The other rulers murmured in surprise, and Oberon allowed a moment for the news to sink in.

"So," he said. "We have our blood descendant. And it's very fortunate for us that he is a worthy man who desires the best possible future for Faerie. He's a rare breed who sees past the Seelie-Unseelie divide to the greater good. We are lucky indeed to have him."

My chest tightened as my heart swelled with pride for Jasper.

Oberon gestured to the plush-looking leather sofas ringing the fireplace. "And now, why don't we all sit down? We still have many things to discuss tonight."

Titania knelt, graceful folds of her dress pooling around her feet, and lit the logs in the fireplace while everyone found places to sit. I perched on an oversized ottoman instead of one of the large sofas, where I would have been sitting there like a child with my feet dangling. I was the smallest person in the room by several inches. Jasper landed on the end of the sofa nearest me, just behind my left shoulder. Fire crackled softly as it spread over the dry wood. The sight of the flames and smell of woodsmoke were comforting, almost as much as Jasper's confident presence nearby.

"There is another concern," Oberon continued. "We've learned that Finvarra possesses the Stone of Fal. If you're not familiar with this magical object, it allows him to almost effortlessly persuade people to follow him."

My heart plummeted a few inches. Damn, *that* was bad news.

"Reports so far tell us that he hasn't utilized it yet. But it's only a matter of time, if he hasn't employed it already. The fact that he hasn't used it is, in some ways, more worrisome than if he had. If we wait too late, Finvarra will have so many followers and allies, he'll be untouchable. Jasper won't be able to get to him, let alone kill him. We must move quickly."

Titania went to stand next to her husband. "As Queen Petra no doubt knows, Finvarra has been keeping company with Periclase of late, presumably to oversee the takeover of the stone fortress as well as other interests." She looked at me. "Apparently, we aren't the only ones who sense the importance of the Carraig Sidhe race in the fate of Faerie."

I still couldn't grasp the reality of being addressed as "Queen." There was something absurd about the whole notion. Each time someone said it, my skin felt hot and tight, and I struggled to not cringe. And we weren't the New Gargoyles anymore. We had a proper Faerie title.

Oberon nodded. "We'll use Petra's return to the fortress, where we expect Periclase will attempt to oppose my declaration of kingdomhood, as our opportunity to take out Finvarra."

We talked long into the night, and I learned that there were several other Seelie kingdoms standing with us against Finvarra, but who hadn't been able to send their leaders to the meeting. Someone brought up the Tuatha, but Oberon cut that discussion short, saying we needed to first focus on pushing back the forces trying to take the Summerlands.

By the time the meeting broke up, the sky outside Oberon's office was just beginning to lighten with the first signs of dawn. A servant came to show me to my quarters. I nearly sent her away, intending to accompany Jasper to his rooms, but then remembered I wasn't just Petra Maguire anymore.

I was Queen of the Carraig Sidhe, and everyone would be watching and judging my actions.

I squared my shoulders, already feeling the phantom weight of the crown. There was so much to do. I needed to contact Maxen. We had to force Periclase out of the fortress as soon as possible. And somehow, I had to figure out how to rescue Nicole, yet again, from our blood father's clutches. My poor twin was still back in the Duergar palace, defenseless. My heart wrenched when I thought of Oliver. It wasn't right to even hope he was still alive, but I couldn't help myself.

Alone in my quarters, I went out to the east-facing balcony. The sun was on the verge of breaking over the horizon, and my view was unmarred by signs of battle. I drew a deep breath of fragrant Faerie air that was only a bit soured by the scents of spitfire and war, and I felt fortified by the scents of summer. Winter may have come to some remote regions, but it hadn't truly taken root yet. Oberon still held the Summerlands. We had a chance.

I drew Aurora, releasing the legendary blade from my back scabbard with the soft whisper of metal sliding over leather. Lifting the sword so I could watch the hues of sunrise play across the rosy-golden metal, I vowed to see my father avenged, my people free, and the dark forces of winter and chaos defeated.

**Look for *Reign of the Stone Queen* by Jayne Faith,
the next book in the Stone Blood Series!**

About the Author

Jayne Faith writes fantasy set in the real world. She's a meditator, dog lover, TV addict, clean eater, homebody, sun baby, and Sagittarius. Her superpower is her laugh. She owns way too many colored pens and pairs of jeans. Visit her website at www.jaynefaith.com, where you can sign up for her VIP list and get free books.

Also by Jayne Faith

Ella Grey Series

Demon patrol officer Ella Grey beat death after an accident on the job, but something followed her back from the grave. Will it eat her soul or become her greatest ally?

Stone Cold Magic (#1)
Dark Harvest Magic (#2)
Demon Born Magic (#3)
Blood Storm Magic (#4)

Tara Knightley Series

Between paying off a debt to a Fae mob boss, working as a professional thief, and keeping up with her busy three-generation household, Tara Knightley barely has time to eat and sleep. But now she's going to have to choose: her family, love, or her freedom.

Oath of Blood (prequel)
Edge of Magic (#1)
Echo of Bone (#2)
Trace of Fate (#3)
more to come

Stone Blood Series

When vampire hunter Petra Maguire discovers she has a secret twin who's been kidnapped, she's determined to rescue her. But it could spark a magical war.

Blood of Stone (#1)
Stone Blood Legacy (#2)
Rise of the Stone Court (#3)
Reign of the Stone Queen (#4)
War of the Fae Gods (#5)
The Oldest Changeling in Faerie (#6)

Sapient Salvation Series

An innocent young woman fighting to survive in a foreign land. A powerful overlord longing to leave his dark past behind. The moment they meet, worlds clash as forbidden love ignites.

The Selection (#1)
The Awakening (#2)
The Divining (#3)
The Claiming (#4)